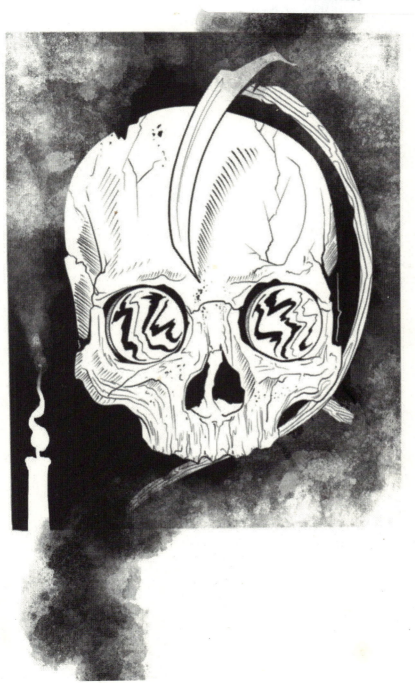

Copyright: 2020 by Chad Dingler

All rights reserved, including the right to reproduce this book or portions thereof, in any form whatsoever.

COINS FOR THE SKULL

A Black Magic Tattoo Novel

CHAD DINGLER

TABLE OF CONTENTS

Chapter 1 1

Chapter 2 6

Chapter 3 15

Chapter 4 22

Chapter 5 30

Chapter 6 38

Chapter 7 45

Chapter 8 53

Chapter 9 64

Chapter 10 73

Chapter 11 86

Chapter 12 97

Chapter 13 107

Chapter 14 127

Chapter 15 139

Chapter 16 153

Chapter 17 162

Chapter 18 177

Chapter 19 185

Chapter 20 193

Chapter 21 201

Chapter 22 208

Chapter 23 217

Chapter 24 224

Chapter 25 231

Chapter 26 237

Chapter 27 244

Chapter 27 252

Chapter 28 258

Prologue..264

Chapter 1

Tokyo, Japan 10:30pm

Kyle leaned back in his old computer chair and yawned. Working a double was always a hard shift for him; not only the long hours, but keeping his mind operating at its peak efficiency, as well. The lab he worked at kept strange hours, keeping the staff working at all hours of the day and night, never allowing for one to guess when they might be asked to work next. Apparently the company wasn't too worried about what the needs of the employees were, just the product.

NeuralGen carried out a wide range of job tasks, from working on cutting edge medicines for Dementia and Alzheimer's, all the way to tattoo inks for the body art industry. Apparently, they were also revolutionizing the way that people were learning about how the brain worked and all of its unknown functions. The Japanese were far exceeding in the research for this new and exciting field, so of course, NeuralGen's main headquarters was located in Japan; a country leading the way in many technological divisions.

Kyle was a foreign exchange student from America. He had worked hard his whole high school career to attain this honor, pushing himself harder and harder to reach his goals. After keeping a 4.0 through his entire four years of high school and scoring exceedingly well on the

SAT's, he was chosen out of many students for the internship. Japan was always a fascinating place for him, strong with history and allure, so it seemed only natural that he had fought to be the one chosen.

But, after all of that hard work, here he was sitting in the basement of a lab that he really didn't know much about. He knew about the different work on a superficial level that they employed in the company, though the science behind it all escaped him. "Only one more hour, then this twelve hour shift is finally over." Kyle said with an exhausted tone, his voice showing how he felt, coming out as a cracked and bitter whisper.

His job at this point was relatively simple, almost mundane in how little of a challenge it presented to him. Working an over glorified assembly line system had seemed below him, at first, but most work he had encountered had been designed to not need so many human workers. Companies had become scarily efficient, much more automated. The need for a human was not there, as much, anymore.

But, they still needed a human to hit the red button at his console, in order to start the machine's tasks at the appropriate time. Even though he had been a straight a student for so long, he was still only a high school graduate. So, being a button presser was all that the illustrious company trusted him to do.

While sitting at the console, he faced a large machine system. It consisted of two belt conveyor systems, one above the other. The bottom conveyor belt moved ever so slowly, mind numbingly slow, Kyle thought. With a line of small four ounce bottles spread six inches apart, each bottle would stop for ten seconds for a hose to dispense ink to fill it to the exact amount needed. Every time Kyle hit the red button, the belt moved six inches for another bottle to be filled. He hit the button every thirty seconds, observing that ink was in the bottle and that none had spilled. This was the majority of his job, the only task he had been entrusted with doing. It made him wonder what he was supposed to be learning, over here, in Japan.

The only time that his job got interesting was if some ink spilled out of a bottle. If that happened, things really could get lively. *Lively?* That was putting it mildly. Kyle was expected to then walk into the machine room and clean the area thoroughly, before going back to his seat and pressing the button to get the belt moving again. This happened, occasionally, but it broke up the tedium and kept him awake. It was about as exciting as his day got.

Such a mundane job only added more tedium to an extremely long twelve hour shift. Kyle could literally have done this in his sleep, which he thought he might have, once or twice. The thought of being able to do his work in his sleep made him chuckle, but this was easy, and muscle memory was a real thing. Sitting in front of the console, he happened to glance up at the belt system above him.

The belt carried vials of a clear substance spaced roughly two inches between it and the next. Every time the button for that line was pressed, a small arm came down and capped the vial to seal it. When Kyle hit the button every thirty seconds, the same thing happened for the following vial and so on and so forth.

Kyle knew that the bottom belt carried ink that was used for the tattoo industry. Inks for body art were priced high and NeuralGen was naturally cashing in on that trend. He had heard some rumors that the company was using some special chemicals to help bring out different and elaborate color schemes, creating a wide variety of tattoo inks, some that even glowed in the dark. He was not sure what the top belt system carried in the vials, though. The vial appeared to be used in the medical field. That was all he could gather from looking at it. They had no descriptive label as the tattoo ink bottles below possessed.

After eleven hours into his shift, with only an hour left, Kyle was very tired. He pressed the button, moving both belts to the next bottle and vial. But, instead of waiting the required thirty seconds and checking to make sure both tasks were complete, Kyle hit the button after only five seconds. The belts began to move, taking away the chance for the machine to cap the vial on the top belt, while the bottom belt was leaking all over the conveyor surface.

He jumped up out of his seat, heart pounding in his chest, knowing he had just made a mistake. All sense of fatigue was washed away, immediately, like water rushing across the beach, the results being quickly apparent. He was instantly alert, realizing the huge mistake he had just made. "DAMN!!" he yelled, fearful that he was going to get into trouble. He had to get it cleaned quickly.

Running from around the console, Kyle went into the machine room, stopping for a moment to view the horrific mess. He could only hope that his supervisor, Mr. Kusama, didn't take this moment to wander in for a surprise inspection. The man moved like a ghost. Kyle started to clean up the belt of spilled ink, wiping it furiously. It made such a mess he thought. It created a near complete stain on whatever it touched.

"This stuff is not coming off," he moaned, in a panic, "Hopefully no one notices." Which no one probably would have, due to the generally dirty conditions of the belt, until what happened next.

After scrubbing an area, Kyle lifted his head up too fast, in his hurry to get finished. While doing so, it slammed on the bottom of the top belt knocking five or six vials over and sending two falling off of the belt, completely.

He watched, almost in slow motion, as they spun in the air. The one closest to him, smacked him in the forehead, the clear liquid spreading all over his face. As it seeped into his eyes, Kyle yelled out loud, expecting a white hot agony to spread. He naturally began wiping frantically to get the liquid free of his eyes. It did not burn, but this was a natural reflex, for when a strange liquid got into one's eyes.

"Ahhhhhh...." he groaned. "Dammit.

This is not my day."

Using the bottom of his shirt, he got the rest off of him. Looking down, Kyle realized that the other vial had landed almost perfectly upside down on the tattoo ink bottle below it. Very little of the liquid was on the belt, although it was completely inverted. He realized that the clear liquid must have emptied inside the ink bottle. "Oh, well," he thought. "At least it's not another mess for me to clean up.

He put the contaminated bottle back in its spot, next in line, on the conveyor belt. He went back to his seat on the control console and pressed the red button. Ink filled the bottle and moved on down the belt. Kyle then continued to do his job.....every thirty seconds at a time. By the end of his shift, he had forgotten that it had even happened.

Chapter 2

New Orleans

Jessica Shaw was beaming with anticipation, as she was walking down the sidewalk, on her way to her first day of an apprenticeship. Growing up with a pencil in her hand, art was all that she had ever wanted to do with her life. In this modern day, tattooing had turned into a viable option; a serious career path. Her parents were slightly on the fence about Jessica being a tattoo artist, but they were willing to support her and her dream.

Her parents had never let her get a tattoo, no matter how much she had begged. She usually had been able to charm her father into getting whatever she wanted. But, for this one, he hadn't relented. So, it was with a lot of surprise, that she had been allowed to pursue this particular career. It was good that she had been, because she was hooked.

The weather was perfect, not too cold, and not too hot. It was a great day to walk anywhere in the New Orleans area.

The tattoo studio that had decided to give her a shot was located upon the infamous Bourbon Street. It wasn't a very far distance from her stomping grounds of the French quarter.

As she walked down the sidewalk, she took her time looking into every window that she passed of the shops and bars on the strip. It always felt like another little world here, to her. No one seemed to be concerned with their responsibilities or from being too proper. Everyone seemed to be more interested in having a great time or living vicariously. With the exception of some of the locals of course, they were constantly in a bad mood, not enjoying the constant flow of tourists. Jessica loved it all, though. She felt privileged that so many people wanted to see where she had spent her whole life.

Slowing her pace, Papa Midnight Tattoo came into view, partway down the street. It was in a perfect location, set directly in the center of Bourbon Street. Having such a location must cost a fortune she thought, which only just made Jessica want to be a part of it even more. She was thrilled to be here.

Reaching out, and grabbing the door handle, she opened it and stepped into the studio, with a feeling of exhilaration. Her new journey was about to begin. The owner was, to her surprise, extremely pleasant and very welcoming of her to begin an apprenticeship. He told her most apprentice applicants didn't have many drawings to show at all. But, she had been different. The reason he had picked her, was that she had had eight fully finished sketch books to present. This showed a lot of promise in the tattooing field, the owner had said

"Jessica.... great to see you!" Damion the shop owner called to her, from the other side of the shop. He strode forward, across the room, with a beaming smile on his face.

"Thanks, I'm excited to be here," Jessica all but chortled. Jessica still glowed with a deep and powerful happiness, so strong that it caused her to radiate a brightness about her, nearly like the rising sun. She was so happy to be here and it showed in every element and fiber of her being.

"Take a seat in the waiting room for a few minutes, while I finish these clients' paperwork for their tattoo," spoke Damion. "Ryan is in his booth in the back, about to work on them." Jessica simply smiled and nodded, before heading towards the specified area.

The studio consisted of five different booths for each artist to work on customers. The waiting room was set in front of a large set of front windows, so, if waiting, you could watch all the commotion that was happening on Bourbon Street. Decorations were everywhere, set to match the feel and ambiance of old New Orleans. Bird skulls, voodoo trinkets, spooky paintings, as well as tattoo art were everywhere. Jessica loved it, always being comforted by the fact of having had these things around her growing up in the city.

Damion was a tall, slender man that always seemed to talk and work with the clients with an infectious confidence. Being in his mid40s, though, Jessica thought his outfit was sort of funny, since he looked like a punk rocker from a 90's music video. He wore Van shoes, skinny jeans, and a blink 182 t-shirt with holes in it, but he did make it work. He walked over to Jessica and took a seat in front of her, in the opposite wingback chair from hers.

"So, welcome again to my humble abode," he spoke with a wry grin. "We are going to go over some art stuff today. We will then get into tattooing principles the next time you come to the shop. He handed her an empty, brand new, sketchbook. Then he sat a skull on the table in front them.

"We will use this as your object for today's still life drawing. To start I want you to draw this skull for me. I don't want a super detailed drawing, only a twenty minute sketch. I will watch you and how you go about it, then will evaluate once you finish. Does that sound good?"

Damion was so friendly and personable with his speech, that it made it hard not to like him, on the spot. Jessica was excited to be given any type of art task that she would have been willing to draw for hours, if asked.

"Of course," Jessica replied, instantly.

"Do you want me to start now?" She was hoping he would say yes. She could feel herself virtually tingling with anticipation. She wanted to start getting her hands dirty!

"Yes mam. I will stop you in twenty.

Have fun and no stress. Just enjoy yourself." Damion stepped away, back to the front counter and began to work on his computer.

Jessica eased back in her seat a little more to get comfortable, her mind already a blur with thoughts and ideas. She began to draw right away, looking up at the skull every so often for clarity. That had never gotten to draw a skull in her school's still life work. This was already a fun change and she instantly felt like a part of the industry, because of it. After all, she was on a drawing assignment for a shop owner of one of the best Tattoo shops in New Orleans!

As she worked, every so often, she would erase a little bit and carefully sketch some more. She would alter a line here, shade a bit more there. The skull was starting to take shape. The bottom jaw was all that was left.

After about twenty minutes of work, she began thinking. A slight amount of stress started to creep into her mind, clouding her thoughts.

He had told her to relax, but it was so hard. All she wanted to do was impress everyone. She knew she was a good artist; she needed everyone else to feel the same way, as well. She couldn't let any sort of self-doubt ruin this chance.

Looking up, she saw Damion glance at his watch. This was all it took to hurry her along, knowing that she didn't have much time left. Speeding up her work, she finished a minute or two later and then just began to knit pick at certain things; erase here and there, then redraw little tidbits.

That was when Damion walked back over to her. "And time, Jessica," he said, with some authority. "Pencils down. Please hand me your sketchbook."

Jessica handed the book over to him to examine. She felt more than a mild bit of trepidation and anxiety. This was it, the biggest moment of her artistic career. What would happen next, would probably make or break this internship. Normally her teachers would take a second glance at her drawings and give her a quick review of them.

Damion sat there for what felt to her like an eternity, just looking at it. In all actuality it had probably only been about five minutes. He was clearly breaking down and absorbing every move she had made with her pencils. Jessica felt ready to burst, seeing how he was critically analyzing everything. Jessica felt the doubt come in stronger.

Finally, he lowered the drawing, while looking at Jessica and smiling. It was as if a dam had burst in Jessica, from that one friendly and compassionate gesture, the smile. She felt her body surge with emotion, nearly at tears from relief, when she realized how this was going. 'Don't cry,' she willed herself.

"You did a great job. I can tell you have been drawing for quite a while," He said. "You are very talented. I especially like how you navigated to the eye socket area. Great depth there. You got in a hurry with the bottom jaw of course, but there was no harm done."

He smiled and continued. "This is supposed to be a critique, so let's go over some things. If you keep up with art, as you get older, you will constantly grow and improve; never more so than doing it for a living. After all, you will be completing one to three pieces of art a day, five days a week. That adds up quickly and provides for a lot of practice that builds into art knowledge in your mind. You won't even realize you had been accumulating so much, when you look back."

"To someone who doesn't do art for a living, this skull would look amazing to them. They are only looking to see if they can recognize what it is." He pointed theatrically at the picture, as if to say, it would be a winner to a client. "So, if it is easy to see what the image is, they will automatically love it. Does that make sense?

"I think so," Jessica said. "I guess I had never thought of it that way."

"Neither had I," Damion continued.

"Until a famous artist brought it to my attention. It is so true. When you ask a full time artist to look at the same picture, though, a whole different critique comes from the discussion. An artist will look at proportionality, depth, contrast, line weight, believability, style, and the list will continue over many, many other things. When I take a hard look at your skull drawing, it tells me a few different things about you as an artist and what point of artistic skill you are at."

"Your drawing is very timid, almost worried. It conveys that the artist tried very hard to get this sketch on paper. The multiple erase marks show you were not confident in your final strokes, when establishing your contour lines. Some of the shading does not make it great, since I cannot tell exactly where the light source is coming from. I can't tell how the light is supposed to make the shading happen on the skull. You are a great artist, but you are still young in your journey."

Jessica wasn't sure how to take the critique. She had always been told she was an amazing artist. She had definitely taken that to heart, believing it with all of her being. She figured her art was as good as it needed to be; that it couldn't get any better. He had delivered this news in a friendly manner though, so Jessica wasn't angry, only confused at first.

"You see Jessica," Damion spoke gently, "The majority of young artists love every piece they have ever finished. Just because they did it. But, if you talk to a veteran artist, they hate almost everything they do, even though it may look absolutely amazing. The first major roadblock in your art career is accepting that your art needs improvement and to learn from every piece and be ok with that. Some pick this up in a week, some take years to start furthering their development through this understanding.

"I understand," said Jessica. "What is a tip you can give me now, to start, that I can start using in my drawing to improve."

"I'm so glad you have asked," Damion replied with a truly genuine smile. "I was going to tell you a couple things anyway, to get you started. But your eagerness and the mass amount of drawings you already possess, is why I wanted you as an apprentice. The first thing I want you to keep in your mind when beginning a drawing is to stay loose and fluid.

Forget that your eraser even exists."

Jessica's head turned in puzzlement. 'No eraser?' she thought. 'That's crazy!'

"That's right, no eraser for now. It is just a piece of paper and we are having fun right? You start with what is called a pre sketch. You want to ever so lightly sketch the bones or major forms of the drawing first, to the point where you can hardly see the lines. So emphasis on soft, it helps exponentially to hold the rear of the pencil very lightly while pre sketching."

"Doing this will help not to focus too much on details. And the lines will not seem so forced. Also, try not to lift the pencil from the paper, while doing this. That will help you realize it is ok to make marks that will not be used later. This pre sketch phase should last for five to ten minutes.

I am going to leave you at this step for today. It is the most important part of a drawing and if not executed well, no matter how much detail a drawing has, it will never look pleasing to the eye. So, I will leave you now. I want you to do a ten minute pre sketch. Then, I will come back and see how you have done. Remember no erasing and no dark lines!"

She was nervous, very, very nervous. She had never had anyone tell her to draw like this. It didn't make sense to her. But, she was here to learn. She would play along and see what it brought her.

"Sounds great", she replied, without showing any of the nervousness that was welling up inside of her to the bursting point. Damion walked away and Jessica began sketching, desperately trying to be light with her pencil. It was an awkward feeling for sure. She felt like she had no control at all.

She was accustomed to holding the pencil close down by the lead so she could make precise marks. Remembering what he said, Jessica focused on being fluid and loose with her movements. Since she was not picking up the pencil after a mark, many unneeded lines were beginning to accumulate.

She felt her stress rising again, not feeling like she was in control. For someone who prided herself on her level of control, this was hard, almost painful.

'This is such a mess,' she thought. Her page consisted of a mess of scribbled lines. They were light and hard to see. At least that part she had pulled off, successfully, she realized, with frustration.

Damion stood behind her while she drew. "Looking great!" he whispered, softly. "Keep it up. Another tip is to try squinting at the object and only take the base shapes from it. Then loosely and lightly sketch these base shapes. No detail, just a light base shape sketching of the object.

"Ok," Jessica said, trying hard to concentrate, to focus on what he was saying and apply it to the paper. "I think I have it."

Damion walked away slowly, moving around the waiting room and looking at one of the oil paintings that hung on the wall. Jessica noticed him staring at it, like he had never seen it before this moment. 'He must really love art,' she thought wonderingly.

Chapter 3

Tokyo Japan

NeuralGen had a large dormitory built into the basement of its massive sky rise. On the first floor was a small university, in which the employees were a handful of professors and teachers. Kyle had lived in the dorm room for about six months now, while taking college level courses in the same building.

All the while, he had been working an entry level position in the company on the 11th floor. Upon arrival, he had marveled at how the Japanese were so efficient with their space. Nothing was left to be unused. Now, however.....It was amazing how six months of time sitting at that conveyor belt had changed his disposition.

Beep, beep, beep....

His alarm chirped at a horrible decibel, a level of noise that drove ice picks into his brain, bringing him from a sound sleep, instantly. Kyle sprang up with a start from the loud alarm. His short blonde hair was a mess from just waking up perfectly mirroring his disposition. He was still very tired from the long shift and very little sleep. Stumbling into the bathroom, he looked at himself in the mirror.

"Well here's to another fine day," he muttered, while still shaking off the grogginess. He could see that he looked about as good as he felt. Besides, he had been deep into an excellent dream involving that beautiful Swedish exchange student, Svetlana. Just the thought of the lovely girl brought an involuntary shiver to him, bringing him fully to wakefulness.

After brushing his teeth and combing the bed head, he threw back on the same clothes he had worn the day prior. Mom wasn't here, no reason to be overtly clean, he thought. Walking out of his dorm room, he pulled the door closed behind him with a thud that rocked the thin walls. With a smirk, he realized that that had made him feel a little bit better, though there was probably no one in their room, at this hour. He made his way down to the elevator at the end of the hall and hit the button a few times, in an agitated way. Standing there waiting for the infernally slow elevator, another student walked up behind him.

"What's up Kyle," the student said, "I heard you had a little accident in the lab last night?"

"Ummmm, maybe a small one," replied Kyle, hesitantly, "But, it was nothing serious. How did you know about that?"

"Everyone was talking about it at breakfast," came the reply. "If you ever got up early enough to eat, you would know. I think you're in deep shit. Mr. Kusama is going to be calling you to his office, later today, is what I heard."

"Are you serious?" Kyle's eyes got wide at the name. Mr. Kusama could deliver some serious damage to his time here, in Japan.

"Yup!" Tommy Lang almost seemed to enjoy the fear in Kyle's eyes. Tommy lived a couple doors down the hallway. He grew up in

Coins for the Skull

Japan with his parents and didn't love the idea of having Americans on the campus.

The elevator door opened and they both got in, the large metal doors slowly grinding to a close. Tommy had an evil grin on his face, staring at the back of Kyle's head. Kyle's face still carried a worried look. Tommy hit the number one button for the campus level, while Kyle hit the six for the offices.

"You aren't going to class?" Tommy asked, a look of confusion on his face.

"Not yet," answered Kyle. "I'm going to go see Mr. Kusama and learn what kind of trouble I'm in for last night." Kyle wasn't eager to be doing this, but he did believe in what his parents had tried to teach him. If there was a problem, you should deal with it. If you did something wrong, you should fess up and fix it. Still, he didn't want to be doing this.

"Good luck, Kyle," Tommy answered with an evil grin, "Wouldn't want to be you."

A few minutes later…..

Kyle walked slower than usual, after he had gotten out of the elevator on the sixth floor. He moved down the long hallway of offices like he was walking to his execution. Everything was so clean and dreadfully white, he thought. This level carried the offices of all the big shots. It was one of the few levels, of this nature, that students were allowed to venture to.

Towards the end of the hall, he came to a door with a sign on it, etched with the name Mr. Kusama. He knocked delicately on the door, almost afraid of the answer he would receive.

"Come in," a gruff voice called from inside the room, making Kyle's heart speed up further than it already was. Kyle opened the door and entered. The room was a total transformation from the hall just outside of this secluded space. Darkly painted and decorated with early Japanese artifacts, the room had an Indiana Jones meets Samurai sort of a feel. Mr Kusama's desk had a skull of what looked to be a bird on it, in a glass case. A collection of samurai swords had a light shining on them in the corner, where they were displayed in gleaming wood racks. Warrior masks hung on the wall underneath the swords. Mr Kusama was not a teacher at the campus. He was a coordinator that worked directly for NeuralGen Corp.

Mr. Kusama was sitting down in a large Executive leather office chair, placed right behind his desk, a wooden antique piece that looked bigger than Kyle's dorm bedroom. It was all set up to deliver power and intimidation. Kyle felt both, as he sat where he was directed, in front of the desk. Kyle

realized, with a start, that his seat was lower. In order to talk to Mr. Kusama, he would have to be looking up at him. The metaphor of power is complete, Kyle thought.

"Soooo, Kyle," began Mr. Kusama. Kyle always hated when someone dragged their words out like that. It grated on his nerves.

"Last night, an alert was sent to my email of a contamination on your work shift." He looked at Kyle in a manner that suggested he was waiting for a reasonable answer, but knew that there wasn't going to be any.

"Well," began Kyle, trying to squash the anxiety he felt from the situation, as well as what this room and his position did to his emotions. "I accidentally hit the button too quickly and there was a small spill of ink. A vial or two from the top belt line also fell over."

"You did not report this? He questioned Kyle, "Why?" Those eyes bore deeply into Kyle, intimidating him deeply. It was as if the inscrutable man could read his mind, peer into his soul, and see the terror that he felt over this situation.

"I didn't think it was that serious of an accident," Kyle spoke, with a forced sense of calm, that he did not anywhere feel in his body.

"The chemicals our company deals with are some of the most volatile in the world. You were given specific instructions to report any accidents whatsoever." His English was perfect, but still carried a heavy Japanese undertone, which to Kyle was very cool sounding. It was interesting, but it still scared him badly, as he wondered where this conversation was heading.

"Well I........" Kyle was quickly interrupted.

"I'm sorry, but we cannot have incidents like this," Mr. Kusama spoke with firmness. "You are going to be let go and sent back home to America. I know this may seem harsh, but it will serve as a lesson to the other students. Hopefully, it will also teach you a lesson for your future. Even the smallest mistakes can carry the largest of consequences."

Kyle just looked at him in disbelief, absolutely and completely shocked. However he had envisioned this meeting to go, this was not the end result. He was going to be sent home. He had worked so hard for years to attain this. All his friends had stayed out partying and sneaking out of the house, but not Kyle. No, he stayed focused throughout all the nonsense that peer pressure flung his way. Now some wannabe ninja, middle-aged man, was sending him home, because he pressed a button one too many times? No, life was not seeming very fair right now to Kyle.

Before he could stop himself, his anger got the better of him, and he began to speak, ready to tell this token beaurocrat what he could do with this decision. Just as he was about to speak, Mr. Kusama interrupted him with a slapped palm on his desk, the resulting boom sounding across the room like a gunshot.

"No!" he barked. "You don't get to say anything. You've done enough. Go back to your dormitory and begin packing up your things. There is no need to report to class. I have already withdrawn you from all of them."

Kyle slowly stood there, his anger quickly fading. He was just reeling from shock, now that the reality was sinking into him. He just dropped his eyes, his head cowering. He felt ashamed, and angry, as well as a bit of regret. All he had had to do was report this incident and he would not have been sent home. He allowed himself to be led to the door and out of it.

Stepping out of the office, Mr. Kusama just shut the door behind him, already dismissing him. Kyle only stood in the hall and didn't move. Still in shock, his mind raced with how his future had just changed.

Later....

Kyle entered his dormitory and sat on the edge of the bed. A headache had suddenly tore into his head, stabbing into his brain like a lightning bolt. Feeling dizzy, he sat down quickly to ensure he didn't have a fall that would injure him. The headache grew with intensity, magnifying like overlapping waves of rolling thunder.

He could almost feel it growing by the second. He laid back and slowly massaged his temples in hope of gaining some relief. His vision was beginning to blur and he was now seeing white spots everywhere. His forehead felt like he was sticking his head into a live and burning furnace.

"What is happening to me? Kyle groaned. He felt on the verge of tears, it hurt so badly. A sinking worry crept into his mind; a feeling that death was upon him. Never had he felt anything like this. Suddenly, his vision was gone, darkness all that he could see. The burning in his forehead felt as if a torch was burning into his skull. His body started to convulse with a dangerous thrash from side to side. While as quickly as the convulsion started, it then suddenly stopped. Kyle was unconscious, his chest slowly rising and falling.

Chapter 4

New Orleans

April walked up to Jessica's front door. She was always a slight bit jealous of how beautiful a house her friend had grown up in over the past several decades. She knew Jessica's father was in the export business, but she had no idea what exactly he exported. Hitting the door twice, it opened almost immediately. Jessica's mom, Karen, was always Johnny on the spot.

"Hello April," Karen responded, warmly. "Jess is upstairs. Go on up." "Ok, thanks Mrs. Shaw" April replied. She proceeded to a staircase that was made of beautiful wrought iron and wood, with ornate decorations throughout, bringing a true masterpiece together. She ran her fingers along the railing, as she ascended the steps. Such craftsmanship, she breathed, in her mind.

Jessica's parents had bought their historic home in the French quarter, when Jessica was only a baby. April often wondered what kind of things happened in such an old house in the past. It reminded her of something right out of an Anne Rice novel. She always had a feeling the vampire Lestat would come from around a corner at any second and latch on to her neck. It gave her a delicious giggle that she barely suppressed. A vampiric Brad Pitt, or even Tom Cruise, could bite her neck anytime!

Jessica's door was wide open at the top, allowing April to walk in unannounced. Jessica had on headphones, while sitting at her desk and drawing. Jessica was the opposite of April. Jessica was grounded, focused, and hardworking, while April was the life of the party and was always trying to keep the attention on herself. Both girls envied each other, but neither was the wiser. They only knew they had been friends since kindergarten and considered each other sisters and family. That was more than enough for each.

Sneaking up behind Jessica, April snatched the noise canceling headphones off her head. "You little asshole," Jessica hissed, "You about gave me a heart attack." "Oh, hush," April replied. "Don't be so crabby. Your drawing isn't going anywhere. Why are you in here drawing anyway? It is a beautiful day and you were supposed to meet me at the coffee shop."

"I'm practicing a sketching technique that the tattoo shop owner showed me yesterday. I just started my apprenticeship." "Oh, wow," replied April. "You go, girl. You know you draw like a beast. You have that shit in the bag. I wanna get a tat from you."

"Well, it will be a while," Jessica answered, truthfully. "We are working on the basics at the moment. I haven't even touched a tattoo machine yet, but Damion said it wouldn't be long.

"Girl, there is like a stack of drawings there. How long have you been up here?"

A few hours later....

"Screw that," Interrupted April. She had been watching Jessica draw, with mixed levels of fascination, for a long time and she was about done. April grabbed Jessica's arm and pulled her from the chair. "Get on your shoes and meet me in the kitchen. We are going to the coffee shop. I got a muffin with my name on it up there."

"Ok. Ok. Ok...," Jessica answered. "I guess I can sketch more tonight." Truthfully, Jessica was a bit tired and was ready for a change.

"You sure can lame ass," April said in a joking tone. The two came down the stairs laughing and chatting. Passing the kitchen they saw Jessica's mom Karen cooking in the kitchen. She looked up, when they passed.

"Where are you girls going?" she asked. "To the coffee shop mom," replied Jessica, barely breaking her stride. "We'll be back later."

"Okay, dinner will be ready in about an hour. Don't be late."

"We won't," Jessica said, as the front door slammed shut behind them.

April also loved coming to see Jessica, because her house was in a perfect location. It was only a five to seven minute walk to upscale shops and dining. It was not like the places on her side of town, which were a bit grimy and sketchy to say the least. Walking down the street, they gossiped the whole way, laughing and picking on one another. They passed historic Victorian architecture, one house at a ti me, each more amazing then the last. They had become complacent to the magical surroundings, after years of being there, and walking the same sidewalk a few hundred times.

"You should get decaffeinated today, April," said Jessica. "I couldn't get you to shut up after the two espressos you had last time. It tastes the same and you won't turn into a lunatic."

"Maybe I like being a lunatic," April said, while grinning and pulling the door to the coffee shop open for the both of them.

They were pleasantly surprised to see that the shop was not packed. Actually, there was no line at all, with only a few people sitting at the tables. They both put in their orders, while the barista, Becky, wrote their name on the cups. They were such regulars there, she already knew who they were.

After ordering, they sat at the table they always went to in the shop. It was the one nearest the front of the shop, in front of a large window, so they could watch people and make jokes, if the mood made them. Both of them seemed to be inhaling the smell of the shop. It was such an additive scent to the both of them.

Anyone passing them by could easily tell they were in their element.

"Jess and April", the Barista called. Both of the girls looked up, seeing the worker holding up two cups of delicious brew. Their drinks were ready. April popped up with excitement and then rushed over and grabbed the coffee, before heading back to their table.

Handing Jessica hers, April said, "Here's your coffee girl."

"Thanks….." Jessica said, with a sarcastic smile.

They drank their coffee and watched tourists walking down the street in front of them. It was always a hoot and a half, when thinking that most of the people around this part of the city were usually drunk.

Suddenly, they both stopped their drinking and stared in shock. A tall man had come walking by, wearing only his white underwear and carrying a guitar. He wore a cowboy hat and had hair that bounced as he walked. He was singing and strumming the guitar. They both looked at each other and started laughing.

"Isn't that the singing cowboy from New York?" Jessica asked with a laugh. In fact, she was laughing so hard that she was nearly starting to cry.

"No way," replied April. "It has to be a copycat. Why would he be here? Dude needs to put some pants on and quick." She was also laughing. "There are kids everywhere and besides, he doesn't have the figure for it." She had stopped laughing and started being more serious. "So, do you like the tattoo shop you are working at?"

"For sure," Jessica answered. "The owner has been super nice to me. I haven't talked with any of the other artists, but they seem to be ok. The shop is in a happening area of town, so I know there will be people wanting tattoos all the time. You would love the decor there, it has a real spooky vibe to it."

"Wow, I need to come see it. I turn eighteen real soon, so I will be there anyway to get me some ink."

"I'm glad you are wanting to have it professionally done and not letting your exboyfriend do it in his kitchen, with the equipment he bought at Walmart," Jessica said, with a laugh. "Come on."

"Ya, I almost let him," April said, also laughing. "Then I started to think the same thing. April laughed, while playfully pushing Jessica.

The bell jingled, alerting them to the door opening up on the other end of the store. Both looked over to see a man walking in, and they both froze. They stared at him, both feeling the ominous vibe, the frightening aura surrounded him. A black man, dressed all in black, wearing a leather trench coat that had a dingy and very worn look to it. His dreadlocks flowed far down his back, but were accented by the traditional top hat that he wore. April and Jessica watched him as he walked up to the counter to order his drink.

"Do you know who that is?" April whispered, as she stared fitfully at the new arrival. He stood straight and powerfully in front of the counter. She couldn't take her eyes off of him. The power that seemed to be all around him was breathtaking in its scope.

"No?" answered Jessica, seriously. She thought the man was interesting, but not nearly as much to cause the response that April was showing. "Why?"

"He runs the Voodoo shop down the street," April said, with a knowing look. Being longtime residents of New Orleans, they were both well acquainted with the allure that Voodoo, and sometimes Obeah, held over the community. It was an area steeped in myth and legends.

"How do you know that?" Jessica questioned, starting to become seriously disturbed by the way this conversation was going.

April didn't speak for nearly a minute, seemingly contemplating how to respond. She knew full well how Jessica would react to

'how, she knew.' Finally, she just said it in a burst, trying to get it out, quickly. "I've been in there before...."

"April!!" Jessica nearly screamed, barely keeping it in, but then only because they were in a public place. "Why would you go in there?" Jessica was surprised at April. "That could be a dangerous place."

"Well, look at you," chuckled April. "Somebody is a scaredy-cat. All that stuff is fake obviously. Voodoo, witches, magic....it's all a bunch of stories and movie BS."

"I don't know about that April," answered Jessica, very seriously. "We live in New Orleans, one of the most famous cities in the world for paranormal happenings and stories of the Occult. You should be more careful, that's all I'm saying."

"Ya whatever, did you see this dude's top hat? Who does he think he is?" She chuckled in a mean way. "Nobody wears shit like that. Walking in here looking like the black Jack the Ripper."

"April shut up!" Jessica hissed. "He probably heard you!"

Becky the Barista had finished taking the man's order and went to start preparing it. Instead of walking away, the man just stayed at the counter. Little did April know, but he had heard everything she had said. He tapped his index finger gently on the countertop, as he waited, while humming a melody quietly to himself.

Then, without warning, he quickly turned his head and stared directly at April. April froze in her seat, her heart must have dropped into her stomach. He kept his gaze on her for what felt like an eternity, then slowly he brought his head back to the counter, and the Barista, and began humming his soundless tune, again, as if nothing had happened.

"Who's the scaredy cat now?" Jessica said. She looked at April's face, which had seemed to go white with fear.

"Let's get the hell out of here," April finally whispered. "That dude just scared the piss outta me."

April got up and made her way to the door and then went outside, quicker than

Jessica could even stand from her seat. Jessica stared at the man at the counter, looking at him with puzzlement. April had thought he was a freak, but Jessica thought he was pleasantly original, standing out in his own way, which was refreshing to her. She walked up to him and nudged him on the shoulder.

Don't let Becky talk you into a double shot of espresso; I think they put Crack in it," Jessica said to him, with a slight giggle. The man smiled and tipped his hat to her, as she walked out to go meet her friend in front of the shop.

"Did you just talk to him?" April asked, once Jessica had made it out of the building.

"I didn't really talk," Jessica answered back, "I just made a joke. He smiled. It was fine."

"Well that was a little crazy," April scolded. "He might be a murderer or something."

"For someone that doesn't believe in ghosts, or magic, or anything like that, you sure seem to be worried about a lot."

April thought about this for a minute, before responding. "I fully believe in grown ass men killing my little ass," She snapped back with a true sense of fear in her voice.

Jessica flipped her hair at her and said.

"Whatever, come on. Let's go back. My mom's dinner is probably ready and she will be expecting both of us by now."

Chapter 5

Tokyo, Japan

Kyle woke up a day later, after nearly twenty-four hours of unconsciousness, only from the random ringing of his cell phone. Luckily he had plugged it in the day before, so it wouldn't be dead. He threw his arm out and grabbed the phone without even having to look to see where it was. Bringing the phone to his ear, he hit the accept icon on the phone.

"Your taxi is outside waiting for you,

Kyle," spoke Mr. Kusama, in a flat tone, devoid of any emotion. Still, Kyle thought that he was enjoying this. 'The jerk really gets off on a power trip,' he thought.

"They will take you to the airport," Mr. Kusama continued. "Once you get to the airport, go to the Delta airlines Terminal and give them your complete name. We have already paid your airfare, so the worker will just give you a ticket and check your luggage. It has been a pleasure young man, I hope the best for your future." Mr. Kusama then hung up the phone abruptly.

It was clear that he couldn't have cared less, Kyle reflected.

Oddly enough, though, Kyle had no expression or feeling about the phone call. Setting the phone back down on the end table, he got up and put on the same clothes, yet again, that he had worn the past few days. That, he really didn't care about. Kyle's hair was matted from sleep, but this time no attempt to comb it down was made.

His ice blue eyes seemed to be brighter than usual, with almost a sparkle to them now. Kyle finished up putting together his few belongings and headed out the door, without a second glance at the room where he had spent so many months living.

Now standing out in front of the Neural Gen building, Kyle watched as the taxi driver put his luggage into the back of the vehicle. Something an American driver wouldn't have offered, but the Japanese were clearly a unique people. He tilted his head to the driver in appreciation, but said nothing. He still carried a blank look on his face, the same one he had woken up with, and that hadn't changed throughout the morning.

His face was still expressionless, and without emotion, as he sat in the back of the taxi. As they began to pull away from the massive building, Kyle took one last look at the place that he had hoped would make his career. It almost looked like a huge castle made of glass. On a bright and sunny day, it glistened, sending its reflection for miles in every direction. Today, it just looked dull and lifeless to Kyle.

The streets were littered with an amazing amount of pedestrians, all walking fast to get to their respective destinations. It wasn't a clumsy movement taking place, though, such as a crowd walking in New York City. It was like everyone seemed to move in Uniscene.

There was no pushing or yelling at one another.

They were all respectful and purpose driven. They all seemed to be very decent to one another. Even in the morning, all the neon signs and lights seemed to glow incredibly bright. Some were hard to look at directly, for fear of being blinded.

"I was told to take you to the airport," spoke the man in the front seat. "We will be there in about fifteen minutes."

Kyle just tipped his head to the driver, yet again, in acceptance. There was no smile, no frown, just an emotionless face. The driver looked at him in his rear view mirror, noticing his eyes. The driver didn't think he was being rude by not speaking, many Americans did this, so their lack of Japanese language was not noticed.

The fact that he had such a bland look to his face was a new thing for the driver to encounter, though. While Kyle was looking out the window at the scenery, as they passed it by, the driver stole another look at him. His eyes almost seemed to be glowing, he thought, with astonishment.

'Maybe he was wearing a special type of contacts,' the man thought. 'These Americans, so unique.' The taxi driver would have chuckled aloud, if it wouldn't have been disrespectful.

Kyle absorbed everything in his surroundings, every minute detail of every person that walked by flowed into his brain, was analyzed, and then accepted. He heard the driver talking about his eyes and how unnatural they seemed. He wasn't wearing any contacts, never did like the idea of touching his own eyes. The curious part was that the driver's lips had not opened or moved, not once since he had told Kyle they were going to the airport. How did he hear all the other things though? His brain was in overdrive, processing this new information. He wasn't getting nervous about it, but was very surprised. What was going on with him?

As he looked out the window, Kyle could easily hear the conversation a small Japanese woman was having on her cell phone. She was angry about her in-laws not accepting her into the family and was very upset that she could no longer fit into her skinny jeans. Yet, once again, the window to the taxi was up and there was no audible sound coming from outside of the taxi. It was very perplexing, to say the least. 'What is happening to me?' he thought again, for the second time.

Kyle's face betrayed no recognition that he was hearing other people's thoughts. Surely a common individual would be freaking out about now. How could this be possible? Is something wrong with me? What do I do now? Not Kyle, though. He sat as calmly as a Shaolin monk.

His mind eventually recalled the accident at the laboratory and things started to come together for him. Mr. Kusama had mentioned the fact that NeuralGem dealt with some of the most dangerous chemicals in the world. Whatever was in the vials on the top belt that had fallen on his face, might be what was doing this, to him. He also thought about what had gone directly into his eyes and had to wonder.

He knew the human eye was notorious for absorbing elements, just like the common flu and how it could get into the body, via this pathway. All you had to do was rub your eye after coming into contact with the flu and you had introduced it into your bloodstream and cells. That's what had happened! It had to have been!

Kyle was suddenly very excited, but he still was a bit worried about whether this was going to be a problem that could be fixed, or, he thought, if he wanted it to be. The vial of mysterious liquid had put something into his body and now he was hearing other people's thoughts! It was amazing!

Kyle's eyes glowed brighter when making this assumption. They almost appeared to have a translucent wave of light coming out of them. The driver noticed also, his own eyes going wide. He could not wait to get this freak of a kid out of his taxi. He started to drive a bit faster, in response.

They arrived at the airport, making a screech of burning tires, as the cab driver slammed on the brakes. He stopped in front of the sidewalk entrance, the smoke circling around the car. 'Wow,' thought Kyle. 'This guy is certainly in a hurry.' But, he knew what was really going on; he freaked the driver out.

Jumping out of the car, the driver went to the trunk and grabbed the luggage, nearly tossing it to the curb, in his rush. The man made a quick motioning gesture, with his hands, indicating that he wanted Kyle to get out of the car. As Kyle opened the door, the driver said, it was time to get out, now. Kyle stepped out and grabbed his bags without even acknowledging the driver again, still displaying his cold and indifferent look.

A cold feeling went down the spine of the driver, chilling in him from the center of his soul. Inside, he knew Kyle had known everything he had been thinking. How that had even been possible, he had no idea. But, a most uncomfortable sensation spread through his body, one that was almost violating.

The taxi peeled out, leaving skid marks on the pavement and sending exhaust smoke into the air. Everyone in the nearby vicinity stumbled away, as fast as they could. The airport was not nearly as crowded as the streets of downtown Tokyo were, but there was still an abundance of people. They all stared at the strange sight that of a city cab speeding away from the drop off point.

As Kyle walked into the terminal, he glanced indifferently at the people, as they passed him. Some were wearing tailored suits, while others were in business dresses. Some were even in dingy torn up attire. Every walk of life in the city was here waiting in line at the terminals for their boarding pass. Kyle could have cared less.

He walked straight up to the terminal desk for the airline. There were a couple of workers at each station, each behind their computers. His line was not as long as some of the other flight companies, which was good, as Kyle wanted to get into the air and head home. Kyle took his place behind a business man that was last in line.

The gentleman carried a leather briefcase and wore an Armani suit that screamed, "I have more money than god, stay out of my way." The look of disdain on the man's face helped to carry that feeling from him. With Kyle right behind him, those feelings were picked up, immediately. His eyes had calmed down now, only looking to be oddly bright, not as if they could shoot lasers anymore.

"Damn this wretched line," the man howled in his mind. "I hate coming to the airport! I hate the children here! I hate the workers for searching me every time! I hate the air here! I hate this damn place!!!!" The last was screamed in the man's head, so loud, that Kyle actually winced. It was good that the man wasn't looking, at that moment, as things would have looked very strange.

Kyle was hearing the man's thoughts. He was actually hearing the man's thoughts! It was wild! Regardless, he was still inwardly shocked at how hateful one person could be. His eyes began to pick up color and intensity again.

The man turned and looked at Kyle with a look of absolute disgust. On the other hand, Kyle still looked as if he had just rolled out of bed, unwashed and smelly. After all, he was wearing the same clothes for the third day in a row.

"Good god," the man thought in his head.

"Now, I have street trash in line behind me! God he stinks! I swear they will let anyone get on an airplane nowadays."

As Kyle heard this last thought, his eyes picked up another level of intensity. For the first time that day, an emotion was beginning to form on his face. The emotion of anger had formed and it was glorious in its intensity. Truly, he did not like this man in front of him. He wanted to destroy this man, tear and rend him to pieces.

The man turned to look at Kyle again, but quickly recoiled back to face the front. The look on Kyle's face and the glow of his eyes immediately deterred him. Fear crept all over the business man, as he started shaking. Kyle could hear the fear coming from his mind and he reveled in it. Completely undone, the business man dipped underneath the line divider and walked with haste down the hall and around the corner, out of Kyle's sight.

Kyle stepped forward, taking his place in line behind another man that wore casual attire. The man looked back at Kyle and smiled at him. The man radiated calm and happy thoughts, all of which helped to bring Kyle down emotionally. Kyle's face returned back to the bland and emotionless form from before, while his eyes also returned to just carrying a sparkle.

"Cool contacts, dude", the man in front of him said, with a laugh.

Kyle simply dipped his head to the man in acknowledgement, like he had to the driver. They both moved forward in the line, as people were slowly processed through and headed to their terminals. Kyle was going home.

Chapter 6

New Orleans.

The mysterious man with the top hat sat at an old desk in a chair that creaked even from the slightest movement. Slowly, he turned the page to a book he was reading. Nicadimus's family had owned the voodoo storefront for over three generations now. Nicadimus Fluei was New Orleans royalty. His family had never made a point of flaunting their money. Instead they had kept to the shadows of society and stayed satisfied with simple living.

Keeping a lifestyle of the ordinary, the townspeople had never realized they didn't go to work. Nicadimus was now the last member alive in his bloodline. Not marrying and choosing to never have a girlfriend, a descendent had not come into existence as of yet. Being that he was twenty nine, though, he figured he still had time.

The book being read had an ancient look to it. Its binding was made of leather and stitched together with horse hair. It had a look to it that would have haunted most, but Nicadimus was fine with it. It was a portal to a different world, for him. It was his entry to his Black Magic.

Nicadimus turned another page of the text, slowly rolling a coin over the bridge of his fingers. He carried out the motion as flawlessly as a trained magician. The coin flipped back and forth over his fingers, while he continued to read. His brows suddenly lifted, as something in the passage had taken his interest.

Flicking the coin high in the air he removed his top hat, then held it out to catch the coin. Smoothly, he let the coin fall into the hat while putting the hat back upon his head, casually, like he had done this a thousand times.

Ripping the page from the book, Nicadimus rose, while stuffing the page into his coat pocket. He walked to face the wall and then stopped and looked at it with a hard focus. Lifting his hand towards the wall he chanted.

"Malik...belandifoo...elephantine...booseee ...." A bright yellow light engulfed him and small red sparks began to appear all over the wall. Within a moment, the yellow light brightened and the sparks shot out all over the room. Then, suddenly, the wall disappeared. He walked through the empty space and into a hidden area that rested behind it.

Then he turned back around with his hand pointed towards the empty area and began speaking, again.

"Malik...belandifoo...elephantine...appop ooosssse....." With a quick bright yellow burst, with no red sparks this time, the wall had reappeared. There was absolutely no way to know there was an office chamber behind the wall, when it was there.

The magic that Nicadimus used had been passed down to him from his mother, who had died tragically in a battle to the death against another gatekeeper, from a different continent. The details had been kept away from him, since he was but eight years at the time.

He walked to the counter and took a seat. He had an uncanny ability to know whenever someone was about to walk into the voodoo store, so wasn't worried about missing someone, or being in the 'special' parts of his shop. Tourists loved the shop. It made their vacation to New Orleans feel more authentic and spooky.

That was especially due to how many of the things for sale were actually usable and practical. Nicadimus carried herbs for healing, wealth, love, and even weight loss. There were crystals for a variety of purposes: voodoo decor, practice grimoires, crystal balls, ceremonial masks, and the list goes on....on lookers would constantly ask him what each thing was used for. He gladly answered them. Nicadimus fully enjoyed spreading the knowledge that was passed to him.

But, this only extended for so far. There was, of course, the sacred arts that he would not share, or show, to anyone, under any circumstance. It was a code that he lived by, something that his mother had taught him. However, for everything else, he figured if you could learn something by a google search on your smartphone, then it would be ok for him to explain it to them. He could explain how to align sticks at your door, while spreading salt around the formation, in order to bring good fortune to yourself the next day. He was not, of course, about to show a tourist how to make a wall disappear.

The store was dark and gloomy, which set the mood all the better. Nicadimus' attire even sold the vibe over and above, increasing the creepy factor for the unsuspecting tourist. A moment later a group of what looked to be college fraternity brothers opened the door. The five of them came in talking and bantering very loudly.

But, all went silent once they entered the store. There was an air of uncertainty about them all, taking away the cocky and preppy college man, and replacing it with a scared little boy. They were obviously feeling a bit of nervousness and it showed, demonstrating how out of place they were.

The young men wandered around the voodoo establishment quietly, looking at all the objects around them. A short, and bit of rotund one, that was wearing a Polo Collar button up, picked up what looked to be a stereotypical voodoo doll. Nicadimus filled in the history for the boy, automatically, "This is a beautiful interpretation of a New Orleans traditional voodoo doll from roughly the early eighteenth century."

"Nice...." the boy grinned. "Does it have any powers, or do anything special?"

"Well that all depends on your intent," came the calm, but serious reply, "It can sense the manner of the soul of who is holding it."

The oversized young man put the doll down quickly, while his friends laughed at him. His face showed more than a bit of fear from what Nicadimus told him. "Gee, Collin," one of his friends, mocked. "I wonder what you are worried about it learning...." They all broke down into braying peals of laughter.

Nicadimus laughed with them, good naturedly. "No worries boy, it is not dangerous. It is but a fun looking doll, until you put the correct spells on it. I'm sure you do not know them, so there is nothing to worry about."

An athletic boy, from the group, was on the other side of the store, looking over a collection of old and bound books that filled a massive oaken shelf that spanned the entirety of that wall, from floor to ceiling. "Wow!" he exclaimed. "This is quite the collection you have here."

"Thank you," replied Nicadimus. He continued watching the boys through slightly hooded eyes. He watched as they perused his shop. It was obvious that none were interested in buying, just in looking at something they thought was scary. It was for bragging rights, Nicadimus knew, they would be able to say,

"Hey, guess what I did in the old and freaky shop?"

The boy, outfitted in a full sports athletic suit, grabbed one that said Beginner's Spell Book. It must have seemed funny to him, that it would just blatantly say this on the binding, since he started laughing. Quickly tossing through the pages, he attempted many different spells and incantations in a deep and scary voice. He ended with a "Whoooo." He thought he was hilarious, Nicadimus saw, as he got the others laughing.

The boy's mannerisms said he felt that these were such nonsense, a supreme waste of time. His attire said what was really important to him, that of quickening his time on the forty yard dash. Replacing the book where he found it, he continued scanning the selections, looking for something else to ridicule, Nicadimus figured.

The other three had also become more comfortable in their surroundings of the establishment, so they had started talking amongst themselves again. As quickly as they had come in, the young men wrapped up their play and left the shop.

Nicadimus sighed, as they didn't show any true interest in his store's collections. He did not need to make the sale, but how he enjoyed speaking with an enthusiastic person about the history and the lore. After all, some of the objects here were world renowned for their scarcity and obscure origins. Oh well, he thought. Maybe next time.

Leaning on the front counter, rubbing the stubble on his chin, he recalled his encounter at the coffee shop yesterday with the two girls. It was funny how people were quick to judge him. They possessed a bit of fear, initially, he could tell, but quickly had felt at ease enough to make fun of his attire. That was the nature of most that crossed his path.

Once a shopper had come into the store and told him that he reminded them of a jovial bartender on their cruise to Jamaica. Such a thing made sense to Nicadimus, he dressed like an attraction. So, it only made sense that clients would relate him to another dark figured worker from a vacation they had had.

He contemplated returning to his study, behind the wall, being that he sensed no one was about to come into the store. But, suddenly changing his mind, Nicadimus pulled the page from the pocket of the leather trench coat he wore. Unwrinkling it, and reading its contents again, a frown covered his face. He had to produce this spell, but he was not looking forward to it.

Dark magic always carried a consequence. Proficient as he was with these practices, but a dangerous undertaking it was also going to be. Once, when Nicadimus was a teenager, he had utilized a dark spell, only to age himself five years older overnight. Those five years had been lost forever. Nowhere in the ancient text did it say that that would be the price for enchanting someone's arm to be broken.

Being a young and absentminded teenager, he had used the spell on someone that had not truly wronged him. Magic truly does know the soul of the spell caster, and so a punishment was dealt. The man whose arm was broken, while being on the other side of town from Nicadimus, surely suffered. Just, not nearly the way Nicadimus had. He had gone to bed as a fifteen year old kid. He had woken up as a twenty year old man. He had become an adult, overnight, never experiencing puberty for himself, missing a full quarter of his life, up to that point.

Having lived through such an experience, he knew that the spell he now needed to carry out could have the same end result. So, he needed to take his time and not be too hasty. He carefully searched his soul to know, within a shadow of a doubt, that he would be in the right. He was older now, as well as a true master of the craft; the punishment would be far more severe.

Reading over the page, he could see how the enchantment mantra looked easy enough, at first glance. The ingredients were even carried in his store. All except for one, he noted, one major ingredient. The last part of the spell asked for the bottled soul of an innocent person that deserved to be punished. He knew that it was laid out this way to protect the spell caster. It was a very tricky thing to attain. The spell to take a soul from a person was not too difficult. He had never tried it, but the procedure was elementary to Nicadimus.

Now he would only need to find a subject that fit this description and then study their day to day life, until he could be sure that he or she would be considered innocent, but also would need to be punished for some reason. Crinkling up the page again, he tossed it into the air. While taking off his top hat, he flipped it over, and caught the crumpled page inside of it. After that, he replaced the hat on his head, like he seemed to have done a thousand times before this moment. He was deep in thought.

Chapter 7

New Orleans

Damion looked over the new stack of papers that Jessica had brought to him. He knew she was motivated. Never had someone brought him over twenty sketches the very next day. The first few he noticed were still rather dark and carried a few erase marks. Though by the time he made it to the last couple, they were exactly what he had asked for. Very light, with an emphasis on base shapes, with absolutely no detail.

"I can tell by the end that you really grasped what I was talking about," Damion said

With a small smirk of self-satisfaction,

Jessica replied. "It took a while to finally let myself loosen up, but now I believe I understand it. I can tell my understanding of what I draw is better using this method. I'm able to absorb the whole object instead of just small bits at a time, ya know?"

"Of course," Damion replied, "that's the whole point." He paused for a second, reflecting on what he was trying to teach her. "Now we will move on to the next step. Out of these twenty, you have two that are good enough to use for step two. Follow me to our sitting area again and let's go over what's next."

They walked to the waiting area and took their seats in the wing-back chairs again. Jessica's chair was facing the skull, which was still where it had been, since the last art lesson. Before Damion began talking again, he took one last long look at the stack of drawings she had brought with her.

Setting them on the end table next to him, he crossed his legs and met Jessica's eyes. Her hazel eyes showed a fierce desire to succeed; yes she was fully an artist. She wanted this, badly. Damion handed Jessica one of the two drawings he felt warranted the next step in the progression.

"After you have finished your base simple sketch and feel that your drawing is conveyed in a believable way on paper, only then should you proceed," Damion continued. "Next you want to look at the perimeter of the subject matter, or contour, if you will. Now, we will start increasing the pressure of our pencil, while gracefully sketching in final line positions. You do not want to stop a lot. This will take away from the flow of your artwork and make it look more amateur."

With a puzzled look on her face, Jessica said, "So you want me to draw the outside lines of the object?"

"Pretty much yes," came the reply.

"Imagine that the object is a completely black silhouette. When a silhouette is done properly, anyone can tell what the image is, with ease.

When someone glances at your art initially, you want them to immediately know what they're looking at. Don't make super dark lines.

Just a few steps darker than your presketch is what you need. Work on that and then I will come check your progress soon." Damion walked away, as Jessica smiled at him, then tilted her head down to begin.

Looking at the skull, Jessica forced herself not to focus on any of the details. She was trying to only observe the outside of the object. Damion talked with one of the artists in the lobby. Apparently there was a money problem.

"So on the waiver, you wrote the tattoo was seventy dollars!" Damion snapped. "It took you all day and it covers the whole side of his arm. That was a 500-700 dollar tattoo that took you all day. What's the deal man? You stealing from me?"

The artist just stood there, Jessica could tell he didn't know what to say. He was a very dirty looking person, covered in tacky tattoos. Not high quality pieces, like the ones she wanted to one day produce. "Man I didn't steal nothin," The artist muttered.

"That's BS!!!!" Damion hollered, he was very angry now. "Get out now, before I call the cops!" Pointing to the door, he shook his hand in the direction of the door, for the artist.

"What about my equipment?" He said, with a bewildered look of frustration.

"That's my equipment now," Damion whispered, menacingly, "and the only reason you're not going to jail."

"Damn man this is wack," spoke the man. "I'll be seeing you around." He stomped to the door and swung it open so hard a few paintings fell off the lobby wall. But, then he was gone and the shop was quiet again. Luckily there were no clients in the studio at the time everything happened.

Damion went and sat back across from Jessica. She was more than a little apprehensive now. Seeing that side of him had put him in a different light, to her. She wasn't afraid of him, but she surely didn't want to piss him off!

"I'm sorry you had to see that," Damion said. "That was the third time Zeke had done that to me. Thinks I'm stupid or something. You see all the artists pay a percentage of their tattoo work to the studio. That is how we cover the rent, power, cable, licensing, advertising, and other silly stuff. Everyone here knows what standard pricing is, and what Zeke did multiple times was plain stupid. If you are going to steal, at least try a little harder not to get caught...." He shook his head in frustration.

Damion rubbed his face slowly with both hands in exhaustion. She could tell today was not going well for him. "So, continue on with your drawing, I'm sorry for the interruption. I will let you work for a few more minutes then we will critique."

"Cool," Jessica said. She was relieved that he actually seemed to be able to come back to normal, so quickly. When her parents got angry like that, they stayed mad for weeks.

She continued to diligently focus only on the contour of the skull. Jessica lightly shook her head, in an attempt, to move a few strands of hair that blocked her vision from one side.

With the attempt failing, she pulled the strands behind her ear by hand. The skull was beginning to take a more detailed shape and she was curiously surprised. There had been no detail drawn yet, but just from the under presketch and semi-dark contour lines, a skull was clearly visible.

It even resembled a more painterly style than she had ever drawn. An understanding dawned upon her. From all the sketches done the night before, only two of them had yielded a good base. Now, with this second step, she could see they would almost certainly turn out great in her final drawing. Damion hadn't moved from the chair during this whole time.

He was keeping himself busy, while Jessica drew, with his phone. His face was a constant changing pallet of emotion, while he scrolled on social media no doubt.

"Show me again now what you have," he said, suddenly, as he looked up from his phone. Jessica tipped the drawing in his direction, so he could see it fully. Nodding his head in approval, he continued, "Now go ahead and do the same thing on the inside of the skull, only focusing on the main lines that define the major shapes of the skull. Like the jaw line, eye socket, nose socket, and whatnot. Give it another fifteen minutes working with that."

Jessica brought the paper back to the drawing position in her lap and said, "gotcha." Time seemed to fly for her at this point. Learning this new style had made her invigorated. Jessica didn't want to stop at all. All she wanted to do was practice, over and over and over until it was second hand muscle memory to her, which is exactly one of the things Damion had suggested to her.

He had said that this would become second nature to her, the pre-sketches would begin taking shape in a minute or two with greater clarity. That was something she so desperately aspired to. She now loathed the amount of time her drawings always took in the beginning. So often, Jessica would get lost in the most minute of details, only to toss the drawing to the trash, because it felt off or wrong in some sort of way. Now, with this new style, she would know if the drawing was trash within the first five or ten minutes, instead of wasting days before she would know.

The urge suddenly hit her to use the restroom, and she realized she had not used it yet since getting here. Standing up, while taking a good stretch and reaching to the ceiling, she looked down to Damion. "Where is the bathroom?"

"Right down the hall there," he directed. "Walk to the very end of the hall. Hang a right and you will run right into it. If there is no toilet in it, then you went to the wrong room." Damion chuckled at his own wit.

Walking down the hall, her pace slowed while looking at the art on the walls. It seemed each artist had hung their art in front of, or around their perspective working booths. The first she passed was mainly pencil art. It was sooooo good, she thought, while her mind fluttered. It mainly consisted of dark imagery; skulls and dragons and what have you.

The next group of art was extremely colorful and completed in colored pencil with markers, she gathered. These ones made her stop for a moment. The color schemes were compelling, while the drawing matter was abstract. This was a very smart twist in Jessica's opinion.

Now coming to the last group of works, before the hall ended, she had found her favorite pieces. They were pencil drawings, like the ones at the start of the hall, but they were on a whole other level. A couple were hyper- realistic portraits of people and the other few were animals completed with an intimidating level of detail.

Jessica was starting to think more about what Damion had said with realizing you can always get better. You can't just think your art is perfect, because you did it. Jessica now saw there were many levels to aspire to in art. She wasn't even at the level of the first pencil artist in the hall, much less this modern day Davinci in front of her. Pulling her gaze away, she went in the restroom around the corner and shut the door.

Damion had become infatuated with an article on his phone, found while scrolling. Apparently, Trump had sent more soldiers over to Iran, in retaliation for the US missile attack on one of their generals that had led to an attack on a military base. It seemed Damion's timeline was full of others that were ranting in disdain, or ranting in approval of the president's actions. He always chose to stay out of such controversy. So much bickering over things they had no control over. He had to admit it was all very intriguing, though.

Finally, he continued to scroll and an advertisement for a special kind of razor popped up on his feed. A feeling of unease fell upon him. He was currently thinking about where he would get a new razor. Never did he bring it up in a conversation, or search it on his phone. Yet again, it seemed as if the phone was reading his mind! It was impossible, but that is what it seemed like.

"How the hell do they do that?" he muttered, as he sat the phone down on the end table, like it was a piece of alien technology.

Jessica returned and sat down, while continuing her drawing. Both of them exchanged a smile in a cautious way, but did not speak this time. To Jessica's surprise, she felt this phase of the drawing to be completed. Not wanting to sound arrogant, she did not say anything. She only continued lightly over what she had already completed.

Damion reached out, "Hand me your drawing, please." Handing it over to him, Damion studied the drawing again, for what seemed like a very long time to Jessica. "This looks great, you are coming along fast. I wish I picked up these art theories as quickly as you, when I got started. It took me years to grasp the pre-sketch."

Grinning Jessica blushed a bit and broke eye contact for a moment. "Now we get to the part you were already good at. Find the major details now and begin sketching them in. Make sure to be slightly lighter than your contour lines, but a little darker than pre sketch lines. Continue to hold the back end of the pencil, so your marks are not harsh and are allowed to flow. You have been doing well with that part; most struggle with holding the back of the pencil loosely, while sketching."

He took a breath from the long speech, but then continued. "It is almost like an act of submission to your mind. Taking the power away from your hand, while relying on your mind truly guides the strokes. In the skull, for instance, you would now want to focus on the teeth and maybe some of the cracks.

No shading yet; we will get to that in time. Shading is like the finishing touch to a piece. We are building the foundation to be worthy of that finishing. We don't want to polish a turd." Damion again snickered at his sense of humor.

"Certainly, not," Jessica said, while taking the drawing back from Damion and moving on with her work.

Chapter 8

Bradenton Florida

"I just can't believe he is back," grimaced Kyle's father. "How could Kyle make a mistake like this?" Irritated, Kyle's father paced the kitchen floor, talking with his wife. "He had a specific job to keep his scholarship and room and board. Now he is back here with nothing. He didn't even finish a full year, before getting kicked out!"

He took a large gulp straight from a bottle of whiskey, without even a grimace from the liquid's harshness. His wife only listened, as the man went on with the verbal assault upon her baby boy. While pacing, he stubbed his toe on the edge of the kitchen counter, which caused him to drop the bottle he held. Curses flew from his mouth, as he danced in pain, trying to grab the stubbed toe.

The bottle hit the ground and instantly shattered everywhere. The liquid jumped into every crevice of the kitchen, along with bits of broken glass. Their house was an old Florida home that the family had lived in for the better part of fifteen years. Being there for such a long time was how they were able to live close to the beach. Now anyone trying to buy a house, currently in the vicinity, needed to be rich to afford it.

"Go, sit down, honey," spoke Kyle's mom. "I'll clean this up." She said this, while prodding him to his favorite recliner, in the living room. Blood trickled from the man's foot. All the dancing around had only succeeded in wedging multiple pieces of glass into the ball of the foot. He hemmed and hawed in agony now.

"You calm down, right now," Kyle's mother protested, while pointing her finger at him. "Kyle hasn't said a word since he's been back. The boy is traumatized, or something, and we don't need you to make the situation worse by making him shut down even more."

He decided to shut up after she said this to him. She was right, like usual. He loved his son, but his temper had gotten the best of him, again. Wrapping an old shirt around the throbbing foot, he cradled it, while applying pressure, in hopes of lessening the pain.

As this was occurring, Kyle was residing in his bedroom, standing in front of the window on the far side of the room. Looking out the window, watching the palm tree leaves sway back and forth, he wondered if his parents' conversation was over. It was easy to hear them from his room, but now it was becoming increasingly difficult to differentiate their conversation from their thoughts.

He believed that the thoughts came to him much louder and clearer than audibly hearing someone speak. He didn't know if this was true, or not, but it seemed to make sense. So, that was the method he stuck with to tell the difference.

He knew that they were obviously upset with him, or at least his father was. Because he was able to hear their thoughts, even though his father was mad, he knew that they still loved him. Just being upset at the moment, Kyle's father was not very good at channeling moments of despair. His father always seemed to come across in a vulgar, angry sort of way.

His mother, on the other hand, was great at keeping her emotions at bay. Not a single word in the negative came from her mouth. Interesting though, by listening to her thoughts, she clearly carried more anger at the situation than did his father. Quite the arrangement of foul language seemed to flow, like an endless stream of obscenity, from her consciousness.

Making his way to his bed, he leaned back onto a couple of pillows, while using the remote to turn on the television. Another important discovery for him was that when he concentrated on television, the thoughts of those around him were blocked out, sometimes to a dull hum, other times they were completely gone. This was a peacefulness that he was slowly starting to desire.

Sometimes Kyle was repulsed by how nasty the thoughts were that came into his mind. Some of the most outwardly beautiful and kind human beings often had the worst attitudes towards life. While the people who outwardly appeared evil, more times than not, were very kind. The evil facade was but a barrier to protect themselves from the pain or heartache from others. Kyle wondered if this was common knowledge amongst the public, or a revelation that he alone was shown through this bewildering change in his mind.

The television had been left on a news channel. For what reason, he didn't know, because Kyle never watched the news. Still, it did the job he needed. Since being home, he had snapped back into a few common traditions, such as taking a shower, brushing his teeth, wearing clean clothes, and brushing his hair. He also now realized that his eyes had become an extreme focus to people. He didn't want that kind of attention and chose to wear sunglasses whenever leaving his room.

He also hadn't spoken much, since he had passed out from the convulsions. Now, though, Kyle had started to think he should be speaking more. Might as well not make his mother any more worried or inwardly angry than she already was, he thought. He hadn't even talked to the flight attendant at the airport, only showing his ID, then allowing her to do the rest. But, his mom was different and he figured he should act like it.

The news program had some sort of craziness going on in the Middle East. Watching the violent footage taking place, he was so relieved that he couldn't hear anyone's thoughts through a television.

Suddenly, something dawned on him and he sat upright, bolting into position. He knew that the mysterious chemical in the vial, which spilled on his face, had done this to him. Up until now though, he had forgotten about the second vial that had spilled into the tattoo ink on the lower conveyer belt. His mind raced with the possibilities of what could happen from someone injecting a chemical into their skin with needles.

'Maybe the same thing that had happened to him?' He wondered. 'Or something far worse, or something far better.' Kyle hadn't decided if this new ability was a gift or a curse. He only knew that finding where the contaminated ink bottle resided was a priority.

How would he accomplish this? That thought swirled round and round in his mind.

Until he remembered, 'I can read people's minds now.' Surely that was a better way to attain the information needed…..

His thoughts were suddenly broken by an insistent 'tap tap tap'... a soft knock that was coming from the closed door. Looking over at the Jurassic Park poster taped to the back of the wooden door, Kyle decided to speak. "Come in." As he sat up and turned down the volume from the electronic, he immediately regretted the decision.

As soon as the television was off, the voices started creeping back into his head. Of course, this was his mother's voice, being that she was now standing in his room talking to him. "Are you hungry?" she said, with a plastic smile. "I made some homemade pizza, your favorite."

'You better eat it, you little shit,' Kyle also heard from her mind.

He held back the initial reaction to be angry at this, instead replying, "I would love some." Grinning and standing at the same time, his appearance was slightly startling. He was emitting a sort of psychotic aura. Kyle now felt he had a sort of power over others. There were no secrets to be kept from him. No one could hide their true face from him. "I will be there in a few minutes, thanks mom."

She backed out of the door, while looking at him in confusion. His mother was not sure how to read him, which was new for her. She always knew what Kyle was thinking or felt by intuition.

Oddly, Kyle was drawn over to his desk. Opening it, he grabbed a bottle of hair gel and squeezed out an uncomfortably large amount for an ordinary person. Then, he proceeded to smear it all over his hair, while looking in the mirror and smiling. The blue eyes shimmered bright, almost as if they knew Kyle was starting to transform into someone or something else.

Thinking about the ink bottle, Kyle decided as soon as dinner was done, his search for the location of its origins would begin. No one else could have the power......this gift... yes

Kyle now considered it a gift. Not holding back the voices, he now welcomed them and hoped for more. They gave him a new power, one with which he did not want to share.

With his blonde hair slicked back, which gave it a darker look that he enjoyed, Kyle went to the kitchen for dinner. Both of his parents were having a piece of pizza, but froze for a second as he came to sit down. "How's your foot, dad?" Kyle asked, as he grabbed a slice off the table and took a huge bite.

"It will heal fine, I'm sure," his father replied, "There is no need to worry about that." Kyle listened, while chewing slowly on the hot cheese pizza.

His dad's eyes, however, bugged from their sockets for a beat. How did his son know he was at that moment thinking about how the foot would heal? His father wasn't even sure how Kyle knew that his foot was injured, much less about his insecurity of it healing properly. His father sat back from the table and asked, "How did you know that?" He dropped the pizza slice back on the plate and stared intently at his son.

"Oh," responded Kyle slightly later, "I heard you yelling and screaming a bit from the bedroom. I also heard something shatter, so i figured something broke and you must have stepped on it." Kyle said this all plainly and matter of factly, as if it was the most obvious answer in the world.

'I also heard you whining like a baby, in fear of your wound becoming infected,' Kyle thought.

"I will be fine, it's just a tiny scratch." As he said this, he swiped up the pizza, taking another bite with a grimace across his face.

Kyle looked over to his mother. "Pizzas great mom, thanks?" he said, as genuinely as he felt he could. Seeing her smile, he knew it was what she had needed.

"Good, honey, I'm glad you like it," She answered. "We were starting to worry about you. We haven't heard you speak, since returning home. You seem fine, now, though."

She smiled genuinely

"I'm feeling a lot better. Can I use the car and go for a little drive to the library? I won't be long.

Sure, why the library? I thought you liked to read on your tablet thingy." His mother rubbed her stomach, a sign that she had become over full from eating too much.

'I can't tell you why I'm really going, or both of your heads would explode,' Kyle thought.

But, instead, he said, "Just to get out of the house for a little while. Maybe read a little and use their public computer." He continued eating another piece of pizza while talking. *'I need privacy to find that damned ink bottle,'* he raged in his head. *'No one can have this power but me!'*

"Well, that sounds good honey," his mother replied. "Why do you have those glasses on? I haven't seen you without them since you got home."

His father then chimed in. "Ya......I have been wondering the same thing…"

'Well a mysterious chemical fell into my eyes,' Kyle thought, with an *inner smile, 'now they glow and I can read minds. What do you guys think of that?'* But, of course, he didn't say anything. It would have been like the moment that Iceman shared his freezing skills with his parents, on the XMen. His brother called the police! No, the conversation with his parents could wait, if it ever even happened.

He had explained that all the lights and street signs and billboards had been the brightest, most vibrant things he had ever seen. He thought his eyes had been shocked or made more sensitive, just from looking at them. "I think they are slowly getting better," he had said. "But, having the shades on relaxes them."

That was the best excuse Kyle could come up with in short notice. He could hear his parents considering what he had just said. They were buying it. Good.

Freaking fools! Kyle inwardly laughed at himself. Was it actually this easy to trick someone? His whole life he played by the rules. No more.

As they finished the pizza, his mother went and grabbed the keys to her car. An old Buick century, it rode like a dream, but looked like a pile of trash. Soon he could have any car he wanted, all the money, girls, fame, the sky was the limit for him now. Both his parents stayed in their seat, while watching him walk out the door. They were slightly skewed by the conversation that just happened.

Kyle's father looked questioningly at her. "Did he seem strange to you?"

"Strange and a little scary," she replied. "I hope he is really alright. I'm not totally sure he's telling the truth." She stood up while collecting some plates to bring to the sink. She continued to talk, while cleaning the plates.

"Something happened at that school in Tokyo, I just know it!"

"Well, we will keep an eye on him. At least we are seeing some improvement, since he's been home. Thank god he is actually speaking again. He's coming off a little psycho, but that will fade I'm sure."

Kyle drove down Manatee Ave, slowly observing the surroundings. Things had changed here, over the years drastically. What used to be a charming beach community was now bustling with tourists and over population. Hell, it took 44 minutes to drive to the beach now, when it only used to take 5-10 minutes. Kyle was happy he wasn't in a big hurry, so the traffic did not concern him. Passing store after store and looking at all the drivers whose faces wore frowns, Kyle couldn't help but to think many people were depressed.

'They shouldn't be,' he thought, 'it's beautiful here.'

Instead of going to the town library, he opted to drive another thirty minutes and go for the island library. A barrier island named Anna Maria was just over the bridge. Now considered one of the top vacation spots in the USA, Kyle figured the library may have had a few upgrades.

He had a hankering for a tropical setting also. The town had palm trees everywhere, but the island carried the smell of ocean air. Maybe he would take a quick walk on the beach. The sounds of small Gulf of Mexico waves crashing were so soothing.

He never took advantage of being around it, before he left for Tokyo. It was funny how once he had left, after only a couple of months, the sounds of the ocean were the main thing he missed.

He now had made his way all the way to the causeway, after only twenty minutes, with only ten more minutes to a public beach.

Luckily there were no boats passing at the time.

He had always hated when a boat would come through, due to the delays. Traffic would be stopped, the bridge would open, letting the vessel pass, then the bridge would close again, while letting the traffic continue. This process took far longer than a red light, but today no boat was in sight. '*Thank god!*' *he thought.*

Making his way off the bridge, traffic had slowed, as the speed limit on the island was twenty miles per hour slower than the city. This was no doubt a way to collect more speeding tickets. Now, there was also sand on the sidewalks, with the palm trees. Welcome to Anna Maria Island, a wooden and painted sign read. '*Welcome indeed.*' *he thought.*

He was amazed by how many beach and tourist stores were now on the island. '*How many places do you need to find a bathing suit…geeeezz,*' *he thought.*

Growing up here, he knew not to go to the main public beach if you wanted some privacy. Anyway, the parking lot there was packed to the brim, he observed, while driving by. Kyle continued down the small three mile long island, until he saw the White Ave Street sign. It was a spot many locals used to enter the beach. There was always perfect sand and usually there were never any screaming and crying kids.

Seeing the sign coming up on his left, Kyle turned after letting a few cars pass that were coming from the other direction of traffic.

While driving down the street, it seemed that he was truly on a hidden island. There were overpriced houses on each side, of course, but that was to be expected of such a nice area. He parked illegally in front of a private property, before getting out of the car.

'I won't be here long,' he thought.

'Screw them, I'm parking.'

Walking down the small opening, he stopped for a moment to take off his shoes. The soft white sand engulfed his feet, while he walked. He had to work slightly harder now, to move forward in the sugar sand, because a small amount of sinking took place with every step. After being engulfed by tropical plants and palm trees on either side of him, on the narrow passage, it finally opened up to the beautiful beach.

There were a few people on the beach, sporadically, but nothing like the main beach just a mile down from there.

Kyle walked to the water break, and took his time, taking in the smell of the salty air and the crash of the waves. Deciding it was ok to get his feet wet, he wandered down a bit farther, so the water could rush on to them. For a while, he felt at peace.

Chapter 9

New Orleans

The dust flew out from beneath the tires, as the car sped down the highway. Nicadimus was on his way to St. Francisville, a smaller Louisiana town, just about an hour north of New Orleans. The landscape was dark, but the wooded tree line on either side was still visible. The bitter pattern of rain bounced from the top of his new Challenger SRT Hellcat.

Nicadimus made every attempt not to overtly display his financial situation, but having a nice ride was one luxury he was not willing to dismiss. His radio rang loudly with Creole music, native of the area. It was a familiar beat that put him at ease. Smiling and waving his hand around to the beat of the tunes, he navigated down the road, feeling at ease and happy.

A green highway sign came into view on Nicadimus' right..... St. Francisville next right. He continued on then took the exit, the sweet and salty smell of the bayou breeze filling his open windows. As soon as he came off the highway he was bombarded by huge ancient trees that surrounded the area. This created a much more picturesque Louisiana scene to him. He was dwarfed on both sides by huge and towering Cypress trees, the leafy and vine filled limbs hanging over the top of the road, creating an oppressive, but to him, very relaxing look. Now this was what home should look like, he thought. Driving a bit farther, he made it to his destination.

Pulling into the old plantation home of the Myrtles, he slowed while driving the curvy path to the parking lot. As he glided the powerful vehicle to a stop, he gunned the engine several times, before switching off the key. After that, he just lay his head back and listened, as the echoes from his engine rolled across the ancient landscape.

With a smile on his face, he got out of the car, but he took his sweet time about getting anywhere. Not walking to the guest services center like most visitors would, he made his way to the back of the property. Behind the Myrtles plantation stood a large statue of a beautiful woman, with her arm extended to the air.

Standing in front of the statue,

Nicadimus looked at her with awe. How he enjoyed coming here. An immediate peacefulness settled upon him, whenever he stepped foot on this property. So much history. But, that was to be expected after a house stood for two or three hundred years.

Now, lifting both hands, he waved them in a melodic fashion at the statue. Doing this for about a minute, whispered a chant...."Timbuyannnn...elephantine....askinwa aaaaa... over and over again.

Not long after this practice started, a faint glow seemed to come over the woman's statue. Then, without warning, the human form of the woman stood leaning against the statue of herself with a smirk on her face. She emitted a glow herself, signifying she was not human, but a spirit.

"Nicadimus," she said, "always you summoning me from my slumber. To what do I owe the pleasure handsome? She walked a couple steps toward Nicadimus, an inviting smile on her face.

"I need help with a spell I am about to attempt," he said, quietly. "It is ……. tricky."

"Aren't they all?" she said, with a snicker.

Nicodimas pulled the one parchment paper from his pocket, an old and yellowed piece, full of arcane symbols. He held it up to show to the spirit. "I don't want to be on the receiving end of any punishment after doing this…."

After holding the text where she could see if for a bit, the woman walked a slow circle around him talking. "Well, don't steal the soul of an innocent who doesn't deserve it of course," she began.

"Well, I figured that much." He gestured sarcastically.

"The point of the spells is to be tricky," she said, as if lecturing a school child. "So that not just anyone can attain what will result from a successful spell." Stopping behind him, she moved her hand slowly to his shoulder and let it pass through his body. A chill went across him, with instantaneous goose bumps from head to toe.

"I hate it when you do that….," he complained, bitterly, while walking forward a bit to get her hand away from him.

"Well you should get used to it," she replied, with a small smile. "Once you die, this will be the feeling you live in forever." Making her way back, stopping next to her statue, the woman peered again at him. "You must search for the lost Grimoire of Sharakana. It is hidden in New Orleans somewhere. I'm sure you can find a spell to bring it to you. Inside that book is a spell that will show you what you need to see."

Throwing his hands in the air with frustration, "It would have been nice if it had just said that in the other book to begin with!" he complained.

"You want everything so easy,

Nicadimus. Completing this spell will bring you more power. To achieve this power, a little work should be had, don't you think?"

He shrugged his shoulders in agreement, more in resignation, than in understanding and acceptance of her reasoning. "I suppose."

"Is there anything else you need from me boy?"

It always scared him a bit, when she referred to him as "boy". It showed him how old she must really be. The apparition was that of a young woman, no more than eighteen. In reality, though, she was probably over three hundred years old.

"No," he said, softly. "I appreciate your guidance." He bowed in gratitude.

Her glow accelerated to a brightness now, as she vanished. He looked up, watching the glow now slowly leave the statue. It was again a dirty, white, moss covered figure. Beautiful as it was, no one paid any attention to it. It was truly a shame, he thought. No one knew the beauty that rested within it.

Now that he, Nicadimus, had the next step of the plan, he moved away, with a purpose. His worn leather coat flapped in the calm breeze, as he turned to walk back to the front of the plantation house. Someone came from inside the guest services building with a concerned look on her face. She must have seen him coming, and knew that he was not a paying customer. *Great, I don't feel like talking to this moron,"* he thought, grimly.

"What were you doing out there?" The heavy-set, ethnic woman yelled from across the parking lot.

"None of your business," Nicadimus yelled back, while climbing into the muscle car. He pulled out, while spinning the tires and creating marks on the pavement as he drove away at a higher than recommended speed. The woman waved her arms at him, in a not so friendly way.

Nicadimus laughed out loud, looking at her in his rear view mirror. As he drove, the rain began to fall, soon building into a downpour. Driving further down the road and stopping at a few red lights, he decided he was now hungry. Conjuring up voodoo ghosts would always do that.

A local Cajun cuisine and fine dining restaurant was still open, he saw, as he drove into the town. Pulling in and parking as violently as he had left the plantation, Nicadimus jumped out of the car and hurried inside of the building. Summoning a spirit filled him with a great amount of energy. It was a rush every time, because the spirit could attack him if it felt like doing so. But, he also had to admit, it was very scary, at times.

The door chimed, as he walked through the door. More of his zydeco music carried to his ear drums from a corner speaker. Yes, he liked it here. A foxy middle aged woman came to him and asked if he would like to be seated.

"I would, indeed," he said, in that deep voice that often startled people. He followed her to a table in the center of the restaurant and slid into the seat. Handing him a menu, she left as swiftly as she had appeared.

Looking around his surroundings, Nicadimus noticed the cleanliness of the establishment. They took pride in this place. Photographs of famous jazz musicians hung on the walls, with small lights shining on them. The dim lighting in the restaurant made the picture shine in a magical sort of way. The ambiance was perfect, Nicadimus thought. He scanned the menu, immediately seeing his favorite meal, Crawfish etouffee. It was a most delightful treat for Nicadimus.

A portly man made his way to the table, outfitted in a fancy suit to fit the upscale surroundings. "Good evening, good sir," he nearly purred. "What may I get you to drink?"

"Your finest wine, two glasses," Nicadimus, said. He also decided to waste no time and directed the man with his order.

"Bring me the etouffee also, good sir. I have had it most places, and am looking forward to how your stacks up, in comparison."

"Well, let me be the first to say," came the reply. "You won't be disappointed." Almost gliding, the rotund man elegantly went to then back to get the drinks for Nicadimus.

Nicadimus watched him leave, smile, slightly. This should be interesting, he thought.

Leaning back in the chair, while rotating his head in relaxation, Nicadimus began to calm down from the previous encounter. Coming to the restaurant was the perfect decision; fast food would not have given the same sort of feel. It was lucky that money was no hindrance for him; he could make these decisions at a whim.

Nicadimus sat back and recalled everything the woman had said. Somewhere in New Orleans, there was another book that held the secrets he required. Luckily, finding this book would be far easier than finding an innocent person who also deserved to be punished. He figured this book would have a spell that would make it easy to see the merit of one's soul.

Reaching in his pocket, he pulled out a beautiful gold coin. Whenever he would become restless, juggling the coin along the bridge of his fingers always eased him. This coin, unlike the one he moved along the bridge of his fingers earlier, was solid gold. The coin was a solid ounce of pure gold, giving it a heft that felt great on the top of one's finger.

Nicadimus had a case full of these coins at home. He never had to worry about their safety, for he kept an invisibility spell on them; never would these coins be stolen by the likes of anyone. As the coin manuevered from knuckle to knuckle, it shined bright, catching the eye of the waiter, as he came back to the table with Nicadimus's two glasses of wine.

"Two glasses of our finest, good sir," the man said formally, taking a slow bow. "Your food will be ready promptly. I would say 10-15 minutes."

"Thank you, I can't wait," Nicadimus said with a grin on his face. He actually couldn't, the effort of bringing the spirit into this realm had really taxed his energy, this time.

The waiter kept his eye on the coin, when Nicadimus flipped it on his fingers. He was still looking, as he turned to go back to the kitchen. Pondering more about the book, Nicodimus knew exactly how he would find it. In his grimoire, he had read that it also carried location spells. Into his trusted and cloaked office he would go, and summon the spell. Yes, before the end of the next night he would have the book in his possession and all the secrets there with them.

Returning, the waiter had a jovial look on his face. "And here it is, good sir. I am bringing your étouffée myself and the cook guarantees you will love it."

"Bold assumptions," Nicadimus said, while lifting his brows.

The smell of the Cajun spices was invigorating. As the smells entered his nostrils, his sinuses were almost instantly cleared. A true southern Louisiana delicacy, Nicadimus thought, as he readied himself to partake. The waiter awkwardly stood there, waiting for Nicadimus to take his first bite. He didn't really like the idea of somebody standing over him while he ate, but Nicadimus figured the waiter would leave as soon as he took his first bite and showed some sort of approval. Lifting the spoon with a heap of shrimp and red Cajun sauce, he took the bite and slowly chewed, taking in all the flavor.

"Absolutely, delicious," Nicadimus smiled, his eyes closing in delight. "You were right this does not disappoint."

The big waiter made two small claps, pleased at Nicadimus's approval. "I will go tell the chef at once, he will be so happy to hear this. We haven't had a guest order the étouffée in over a month. Which is quite surprising, being that it is one of the best in the state of

Louisiana."

Finally the waiter carried on and left Nicadimus to enjoy his meal. Taking in spoon after spoon, Nicadimus was making short work of the cuisine. He was able to take him no less than ten minutes, consuming the entire meal. He reached over and grabbed the first glass of wine, drinking it in one large gulp. After replacing the cup on the table, he then took the second glass and made short work of it, as well.

Standing up and pushing his chair, Nicadimus made his way towards the door. "Leaving so soon, sir," The waiter said, palms facing up in question.

"I am," Nicadimus didn't even turn around, while tossing a gold coin to the waiter. Catching it, the man grinned a scary smile. He held the coin up to the light for a good look. One side of the coin had a skull engraved with seven circles around it. The other side of the coin carried an engraved sickle, like a grim reaper would carry. 'Such a marvelous coin,' the waiter thought, 'with such dark imagery.' Putting the coin in his pocket, and turning to Nicadimus to thank him, the waiter was too late. The mysterious man was already gone

Nicadimus was relieved to see the rain had stopped. Being wet had never bothered him, but his car didn't deserve that sort of treatment. Slamming the door shut, while getting into the car, Nicadimus pulled out and raced down the street, heading back to New Orleans in search of a mysterious and ancient text.

Chapter 10

Bradenton, Florida

Kyle paced like a lunatic on the back porch of his parent's house. He was staring at his phone, never removing his eyes, while walking to and fro. Working at NeuralGen, he had been given sign-in information to the company's main website. Remembering this, Kyle had been scouring the website for information. He needed to find where that contaminated ink bottle had been delivered.

"Crap!" he hissed, shaking the phone in frustration. Reading a new page on the website, Kyle found out that that particular batch that contained the contaminated bottle had been shipped last week. But, the problems came when the web page was not saying where the bottle had been delivered.

Sitting down on the outdoor patio furniture, he clearly was very agitated. Even though it was only ten in the morning, the sun was already assaulting his back, with force, from the distant horizon. He allowed his mind to wander, in order to calm down his emotions. Scanning the backyard, he took in his parents efforts at gardening.

The landscaping in the backyard was elaborate, Hibiscus flowers showing all throughout the design of the foliage. His father had become infatuated with gardening a couple years ago and their house reaped the benefits. It looked like something from a Southern Living magazine. The assortment of colors was captivating. He had had small palm trees delivered also, to break up the amount of flower bushes. After all, when not in bloom, they mostly appeared to be large bushes all over the place.

He was suddenly snapped back to the present, as a thought dawned on him. This was great news! If the bottle had been delivered in the US, it would be far easier for him to get to it. Kyle did not want to make another flight to Japan. That many hours in the air was not for the faint of heart. Coming back had been even worse....trapped in a flight cabin with that many people and their inner conversations had nearly driven him insane.

His parents were both at work, leaving the whole house to himself. Walking back inside, Kyle plopped down onto the comfortable couch. Fully stretched out, he flicked the tv on with the remote. His parents had left it on a news channel. How he hated news channels, but this time his interest suddenly peaked.

Currently a special was taking place on NeuralGen industries in Japan. The same company that had just sent him home! Turning up the volume, his focus zeroed in on the news special. He listened intently to the news woman while she talked. The program showed Asian scientists in a lab, working on a project.

The NeuralGen industry in Japan has just made a major breakthrough. I'm on location in Tokyo, Japan, as we interview key figures here at their headquarters. Yesterday, the NeuralGen announced a breakthrough in medicine to treat the brain disease Alzheimer's.

The television showed scientists and doctors administering the drug via a needle to patients in a laboratory, then being put through

a battery of tests. There was one, in particular, an older woman. The aging woman appeared to not even know her name any longer, Kyle observed. They asked her a series of questions. All of which she failed miserably.

After administering the drug, though, the results were near instant, a change that was utterly remarkable. Her answers were suddenly correct and with an extreme mental clarity. All of a sudden the elderly woman knew her name, birthplace, where she was, even the name of her grown children. All of these questions may have seemed mundane, but only thirty minutes ago, she had been unable to answer any of the same ones.

Kyle was astonished. Had this been the same drug that had fallen into and had been absorbed by his eye. This might just be what happens when someone with a perfectly functioning brain takes the drug, he thought. Or, maybe not. Maybe it was a freak accident, since it was absorbed by his eye. The questions swirled in his mind, like a storm. There were so many things that he wanted the answers to. He continued to stare in amazement, as the woman on the tv glowed with happiness.

Standing, Kyle ran his hands through his short blond hair, getting left over oil on them from excessive usage of gel. His mind was running wild. His eyes seemed to be open overtly wide and shimmered bright blue, as they seemed to be in conjunction with his brainwaves. This is crazy, he thought.

The reporter closed the newscast with a final word about how they could revolutionize the pharmaceutical industry. NeuralGen has not decided on a pricing for the drug as of yet. But, it is expected they will be charging a handsome fee. This, the reporter continued to say, may cause turmoil in the medical insurance sector. Kyle jumped to his feet. The company was really taking off in the world scene. They had no idea what had happened to him.

He stopped and stared at himself in the mirror, whispering, "They can't know."

Who knows what NeuralGen and that asshat Mr. Kusama would do with this knowledge, Kyle thought, while he continued pacing again in the living room. He grabbed his phone off the couch and began reviewing the company website once more. He would find where the bottle had gone and close this loose end.

Peering over the site a section jumped out at him. It was the shipping manifest schedule! It was written in very tiny print on the lower right area of the website. "How is someone supposed to see that?" he grumbled.

Clicking this hyperlink, the computer opened up a new screen with list after list of shipment locations and times. Scanning down the list Kyle came over what he had been looking for. "Tattoo ink bottles. ...." he whispered. "Yes!!!"

The batch number corresponded to the date of manufacture, making it easy for him to find the right one. Now that he had found the correct batch, he used his index finger to follow it over to the right side of the screen, underneath the shipment locations....New Orleans.

He had found it. Kyle threw his fists in the air, shaking them in victory. Not only was the bottle shipped from Japan, it was now in Louisiana. That was only a fourteen hour drive by car from Bradenton,

Florida, where he currently was. If the bottle had been in California, he wasn't sure if he could make that trip by vehicle or not. New Orleans was doable, for sure. Although, he did not have a car.

His first thoughts were to steal one of his parents' vehicles. It wouldn't be that hard. They would go to sleep and he would grab the keys off the counter and off to the races he would be. But, why do that. I can read people's minds now. Kyle had already been pondering how to use his new power a few days ago. Now he had an idea.

"I will blackmail a rich dude, cheating on his wife," he whispered. "That would be cool!" There were always rich middle aged guys at the beach and boat harbors, drooling over younger females. It wasn't hard to tell the ones that already succeeded in their endeavor He would find one of those guys. He would read their mind to find out the wife's name, then threaten that he would tell the woman, unless he could borrow their car for a few days. Hell, if they refused, he would tell on him anyway; the assholes.

Kyle didn't want to wait any longer to get started with the scheme. He walked into his parents room and over to the nightstand, on the right side of the bed. He knew his father always kept a few emergency twenty's in there. Walking back to the living room, Kyle sat looking at his phone one more time.

Quickly, he found the Uber app and began the process of getting a ride to the island. Being that it was only six miles away, it wouldn't cost much. He finished the process over the app quickly, and then the Uber driver was en route to him. Soon, Kyle would be at the boat harbor and yacht club to find himself a vehicle. He had no doubt the plan would work.

As he sat waiting, his eyes fell onto a family portrait on the wall of their family. Inwardly, he mocked his shit eating grin in the photo. It was a family portrait done on a family cruise they took, before he left for Japan. It was his big going away party at sea.

Kyle's family had been so proud of him, then. Anger festered in him, thinking about how disappointed they were now. Soon, he would show them the new gifts he had. If they acted right, he would help them also become rich, making their life a bit easier. Looking down to his phone, he saw that he had ten more minutes until the driver would arrive.

He made his way back to his bedroom and changed clothes. He wanted to look a bit more respectable, so whomever he approached, took him seriously. Anyone wearing a suit on a beach community would surely stick out and be taken seriously. Right? Or, he would just be very hot in a monkey suit.

Either way, it seemed like a legit idea. Kyle opted for the same suit he wore to the prom, senior year. It was all black with a teal button up dress shirt. Not wearing the coat of the suit would save him from a bit of the heat.

Soon, Kyle arrived at the boat harbor. Getting out of the car, he slung a twenty dollar bill to the Uber driver, without saying anything. The old driver looked at him with disdain, then drove away, down the street. Seagulls littered the sky, while squawking their horrible tune. They circled like vultures, in hope of any scraps that may be on the ground.

In front of him was a massive steel building, a structure with a large opening in the front to drive vessels in for maintenance. On each side of the building, there were large boat bays that had stacked boats, two high in a row on either side. These were no little dinghies. These were all massive, beautiful boats that surely fetched a pretty penny.

Walking towards the building, sand shell particles crushed underneath his dress shoes. The farther from the ocean you got, the rougher it felt, treading the ground. The back of the structure was built directly over the water. Kyle figured boats could be pulled in by vehicle, from the front, or drove in by water from the back. There were rows of docks besides the building on the backside. Each dock had a bench with which to sit.

"I guess rich people needed a break, every now and then," he said, with obvious sarcasm.

Kyle walked a few docks down and sat on the bench. From here, he could easily see everyone at the location and decide upon his mark. He had expected to see more people than were here. Unfortunately, that made his options limited. The whole plan revolved around blackmailing a man. But, currently, there were only a few females at the different boats. They were each working, it seemed, on different things on the decks. He couldn't tell, being so far away.

'Screw it,' he thought. 'I'm going for it. I don't have to make a move on them, anyway, unless I get some good info.'

Kyle decided to go for the oldest of the three women. The younger ones would only think he was hitting on them. From experience with grandparents, they were often excited to chat with anyone, really. That would make the opening of the conversation that much easier for him.

Walking up to the vessel named 'ole Betsy', which was painted on the stern of the boat, Kyle looked at the woman. She hadn't noticed him at first. She wore khaki shorts, with a horrible Hawaiian shirt.

Horrible as it was, Kyle could still tell it was Tommy Bahama, so it probably cost a fortune. She looked to be possibly in her mid-seventies. But, she was still as athletic as a twenty year old, Kyle noticed, while she rolled rope and moved anchors around the deck to her liking.

"Hello, maam," he said, with the most pleasant voice that he could muster.

"Good morning." He kept what he felt was a pleasant smile on his face.

Turning to look at him, the woman didn't respond at first. She wiped the sweat from her forehead, studying him, before moving to the back of the boat. She sized him up and down, just like a shark. "What do you want, boy?" she finally said, with a touch of bitterness in her old and cracked voice.

Kyle hadn't expected to encounter any hostility, much less this level of anger from an old woman. Luckily, her thoughts began to pour into his head, making him feel more at ease, and instantly in control.

'Look at this little bastard,' she was thinking. 'I dated one that looked like him in college. He was a waste of space.'

Kyle grinned at her. This wasn't the response she expected either, as her eyes narrowed and she took a step back in surprise. His shades were on to hide the glowing of his eyes, which was probably a good thing. She would have gone running, then.

"I like your boat," he said, leaving the conversation open ended.

"Thanks…." she said, just as dryly. "Can I help you?"

'Ya little shit,' came her thoughts. 'I got a man's retirement to steal, before lunch. The lawyer is waiting on the paperwork. Gotta meet him at the boat gas-up station, a few miles down the coast. No one will find us there. I Love my boat.' Her thoughts betrayed her at that moment.

Kyle laughed in her face, jumping on the boat and sitting on the small couch by the steering wheel. "What in the Sam hell are you doing boy," she cursed. "Get off my ship!"

"Or what?" he laughed, again. He was really starting to enjoy this. There was nothing that anyone could hide from him. There was nothing that he couldn't have. The world was his oyster.

"Or I will call the cops to arrest your ass," she replied, smugly, sure of her own power and control of the situation.

"Go for it," responded Kyle, smartly. "When they get here, I will have to tell them about your meeting with that lawyer. You know lawyer Thompson who works downtown. It would be shameful if you were late to give him all that paperwork you tricked your new husband into signing. Gonna steal the retirement he worked twenty-five years to earn, huh. I've heard that shit is a felony."

Her mouth went slack, as her face went white. She was speechless.

"Ho.....howwwww...how. Did you know that?" Her skin became even noticeably paler.

"Well now, I can't tell you that," Kyle replied. "I do have evidence, though, of your nasty little business." Kyle grinned, while having another idea. New Orleans was where he needed to go, another coastal city. He would take the boat.

"I want you to fill ole Betsy up with gas," he continued. "Then I will borrow her and your credit card for about a week. I will bring it back. I'm not stealing it. I just need it for a trip that I want to keep a secret."

She just looked at him and didn't respond. Her mouth was still hanging open, in shock. It was clear that his power of mind reading was going to have the desired effect. He was in control.

"Or, I guess that I could call Detective Henry at Holmes beach PD and tell him about what you're planning. Then you won't see this boat for, ohhhh, I dunooo, 30 years. I suspect at your age, you would die in prison."

"You little asshole," she finally replied, with fierce venom in her voice, the hatred she showed for him literally dripping out of her with every word. "I outa beat the shit out of you!"

"You could certainly try," Kyle answered, evenly. "But, there are other people here and I would scream so loud and even put on a little fake cry. Maybe I could tell others that you were trying to make me take off my pants…." This is too easy, he thought. It was crazy how the plan just flashed into his mind, while it unfolded.

She walked up to the bow of the boat and sat on another plush sitting area. A single tear trickled from a wrinkled eye. Kyle knew that he had broken her. "How will I know when you are back," she finally asked.

"What, are we in the Stone Age?" he answered, in jovial good humor. "I will call you silly. Give me your number. That's simple. But first I will ride with you to this gas station and you will fill this bad boy up, while showing me how to drive it on my own."

What choice did the woman have? She didn't want to go to jail and he wasn't lying, she would have her boat back in a week. Then, she could continue her plan of stealing her husband's pension. He really didn't care about any of that, anyway. It certainly wasn't his problem. But, he didn't have any problems with using it to his advantage, though.

The foaming ocean water sprayed over the boat and into the air, as they raced down the causeway. Red and green signs, mounted on large wooden posts, showed them how to stay in the correct channel. She told him exiting the waterway could make him run ashore and destroy the boat engine and possibly hurt himself. The wind knocked Kyle's short hair and the woman's long red hair around pleasantly. 'I could get used to this,' Kyle thought.

His shirt flapping violently in the wind, Kyle felt a sense of freedom. It felt as if they were flying over the water. The ocean spray kissed his cheeks making him smile.

The woman, however, wore a frown the whole ride. She wasn't having a great time. Being blackmailed, of course, wasn't fun for anyone. She pondered trying to think of a way out of the predicament. Coming up with nothing, short of killing the boy. She was not willing to take anything that far, though. Finally resigning herself, all the woman could do was hope Kyle actually returned with her boat.

She whipped into the water bound, boating gas station. "Get out and catch the line," she called, "tie it up to that peg." Jumping out, he waited on the rope from her. She tossed the rope, while Kyle caught it and tied it to the peg, which anchored it to the dock.

"You're doing that wrong, but it will hold," she continued. "Just make sure you tie it like that, if not more loops. Don't want my baby slipping away from you."

"I gotcha," Kyle responded.

She jumped out and went up to the gas tanker. She showed him wear to insert the nozzle to start filling up the boat. "Remember not to leave it unattended when filling. Most of the boat stations are very old and won't cut off when full. You will pump gas everywhere if you're not around once it's full. And that could be a major explosive danger."

"Oh, wow. Thanks for telling me. So far, this all seems to be pretty straight forward."

The woman stopped to look at him sideways. "Don't think it is because I give a damn about you coming back in one piece, kid," she said, with an evil gleam. "I don't. I just want my boat back." She said all this, while walking to the small shack at the base of the dock. She continued staring at him for a moment, before continuing. "Stay here, while I go pay."

Kyle was ready for this. The boat was easily navigated, he had learned, and he was in possession of one of her credit cards. It carried a 10,000 dollar limit. Rich old lady Hen, he thought, while wondering how many husbands she had swindled in her past.

She returned right as the tank was full and overflowing a bit. "Pull it out, dummy," she hissed.

"Oh, my bad," he smiled sheepishly. Kyle released the trigger for the nozzle and the gas stopped flowing, immediately. He handed the nozzle to her, which she returned back to the tanker.

"Well, I am going to leave now," Kyle said, relishing the moment. "I have my GPS on; my phone will even guide me on the water. Thank you for showing me what you have. I will return your boat within the week and I will tell no one of your secret. Believe me."

Still speechless, she stood with her hands on her old hips, shaking her head in disbelief. 'This was actually about to happen', she thought.

"Does the shack up here have a phone?" Kyle said, while looking at it.

"Yes," she said, softly. Never in her life had she been so dominated, so controlled by a man, especially one that was barely old enough to start calling himself, such. It was a new feeling to her, one that she didn't think she actually minded, surprisingly. She was used to being the one dominating men. 'If only this little shit was a bit older', she thought, with a ghost of a smile.

"Well, call yourself a ride," Kyle continued. "I have your number. I will be in touch. I am going to start it up, you untie me and toss the ropes back." He jumped back in the boat and powered the engine up, while the woman unhooked him from the dock. Throwing the ropes back with aggressive force, she turned to walk back to the small shack. Apparently she didn't even want to see him leave.

'Well, that hurt,' Kyle thought, chuckling out loud. Yes, today was living up to be a wonderful day. He leaned back and enjoyed the morning sunshine, as it warmed his exposed skin.

Chapter 11

New Orleans

"Are you sure this tattoo thing is what you want to do with your life?" Jessica's mom leaned on the kitchen counter with one hand, while staring at her, intently.

"Yes, mom," replied Jessica, trying to keep the exasperation out of her voice, but figuring that she was failing. "I have told you over and over again. This is what I want to do."

"You are such a great artist, honey," her mom continued, attempting a soothing and placating tone that never failed to get under

Jessica's skin. "Is there no other way to use your talents?"

Jessica always got infuriated when this conversation popped up with her mom. Now that Jessica was eighteen, they would have to let her pursue whatever career she wanted. But, because she still lived under their roof, her parents, especially her mom, felt more than free to offer her advice. She was not happy about the idea of tattooing.

Jessica's mom had paid for a slew of art classes for her growth, when she was younger. Other parents always had told her to nurture their child's interests. She certainly would not have, Jessica was sure, if someone would have told her that her precious daughter would want to be a tattoo delinquent. Jessica kind of liked the sound of that, a "tattoo delinquent". Sounded kind of cool.

"Mom.....tattooing is a great career and very accepted in our modern age," Jessica said, calmly. "It is hard to find people that don't have tattoos, actually. This is the best way for me to make a career with my art. Body art is expensive and the only purchase a person can make that no one can take from them. You keep your art forever and carry it wherever you go."

Her mother wanted to be accepting, Jessica could tell, but it was hard. "Well I suppose you're right about that. I just worry about who you see, there. I have seen some very unsavory characters around those tat shops."

"They are called tattoo studios or body art establishments mom. They are just artists making a living. The workers in those places don't have to live by "normal" work guidelines. So, sometimes people can get confused by their appearance. But, believe me, they work their butts off. Staying up all night, making designs for their clients the night before they work. Then they work all day, executing said tattoo designs in a professional fashion, so they can be paid well. It is exciting mom. All these art classes you put me through are actually going to pay off big for me."

Jessica knew exactly how to butter her mom up, and she could tell, immediately, that it was working. Tilting her head in a way of understanding and submission, her mom finally said, "I guess you're right hon. I just want you to be safe and not to go down the wrong path. Heck, I have seen those shows on tv about the artists competing to do the best tattoos. I figure they have to be making some sort of serious money to get on tv."

"Mom," Jessica said. "Most of the artists in the studio I work at charge one hundred and fifty dollars an hour, or more, depending on skill and how in demand they are, given you only make that money when you're actually tattooing. It's not guaranteed money, but still.

One day, I could have a huge clientele and be making really good money."

"Wow," Jessica's mom exclaimed, eyes widened. She was obviously shocked by the amount. "I had no idea." She just stared at Jessica, in amazement.

"Ok, ok, ok," she finally continued. "I guess there may be something worth pursuing there, then. You're eighteen now, so you can do what you want of course, career wise that is. You still live here, so no acting like a crazy person. If you need to feel out your wild side, you will have to move out."

"Nawww," Jessica simple, feeling a sort of warmth, towards her mother. "I'm good. I don't want to pay bills yet. I would rather get this career thing up and rolling."

"Very smart, young lady," came the reply, with a grin. "Well it sounds like you have a plan and that's all I wanted to hear. Come take a ride with me."

"Where are we going?" asked Jessica, not really caring, but making conversation.

"I just need to get out of the house and need some company." Her mom was already heading to the door, figuring that Jessica would be right behind her.

She grabbed her purse from the counter and headed for the door looking back to Jessica. "You coming or what?" She called back. Jessica hopped off the counter stool and went to the door also. They both exited the beautiful antebellum home and jumped into her mom's Range Rover. The air had a moist feel to it and a stickiness you could almost inhale.

Not even five minutes driving down the road and the area changed dramatically. It went from gorgeous homes, now to run down, inner city dwellings. Homeless vagrants walked up and down the street, begging for money. Jessica felt sorry for the people, but could tell her mother didn't care for them.

As quick as they had entered this area, it was gone again. Now, they were driving through pleasant shops and businesses that surrounded them on all sides. Signs with jazz players hung on the lamp poles, setting the mood for the New Orleans feel.

"Turn here, mom," Jessica said, enjoying the ambiance of the city. To her, it was magical.

"I really don't want to go onto Bourbon

Street, honey," her mom said. "It's almost seven. It will be busy right now"

"Since we are here, I want to show you the studio I'm apprenticing at," Jessica answered. "Come on, mom." Jessica's expression was pleading, but showed that she was not going to back down a bit.

"Ok, ok." Her mom said, giving in and turning onto the busy road. The cars were bumper to bumper, quickly blocking them into a snarl of congestion. Some sort of festival was happening in the street, dancing people filling it from end to end. Jessica had an oops sort of expression, on her face, since they were dead stop in traffic. Her mom looked over to her with that 'I told you so' look in her eyes.

"Well...." began her mom.

"Maybe it will be over soon," Jessica answered, still embarrassed that she hadn't listened and had gotten them stuck in this mess. She shrugged her shoulders in a questioning way.

"Not likely....look at them partying their asses off," she replied. "The police have the road blocked for them, so this must be an organized event. It will last a while. Oh, well. Let's roll down the windows, so we can at least listen. Might as well enjoy it. One of the perks of living here." She settled back into her seat and tried to relax.

Rolling down the window, they were instantly transported into a different world. The moist air caught both their breaths, while smells engulfed the SUV. Street vendors, serving food, were all over the place. Jessica loved the smell of street food. It was always so good, compared to her mother's homemade meals. But, she had resolved to never mention that fact, to her mom.

A few cars ahead of them, the two of them could see groups of people dancing, as they walked down the street. Several men were playing saxophones and trumpets, while waving them in the air, as they moved to the hypnotic beats. Looking behind her, cars had already blocked them in, making the same wrong turn. Yes, they were officially stuck here for the duration.

A boy came walking by with a box in his arms, with a winding strap around his neck, holding everything in place. "Popcorn!" he yelled.

Jessica waved her hand around to get his attention. Noticing her, he started a bag. "Five dollars," he said. She cocked her head sideways, like a German Shepard, looking over to her mother, who rolled her eyes in annoyance.

"Fine, here," she finally said. She handed her ten dollars. "I want some too." The boy walked away, as they sat there enjoying the buttered and slightly stale popcorn, watching the parade. Luckily, only about fifteen minutes later, the parade passed them, and the police opened the street back up for traffic. They slowly got up to a measured ten miles per hour, but they were finally moving.

"It's just right up here, on the right mom," Jessica said, finally. She was pointing out the window in that general direction

Her mom was nodding her head. Not a bad location, she appeared to be thinking.

Jessica smiled, knowing her mom was coming around more to the idea. It was no secret how pricey this location must be. She was sure to be thinking of that, as she observed the rich surroundings. They pulled up to the curb, in front of the studio.

Walking up to the front window of the shop she let her mom take it all in, without saying a word. The custom lettering on the front window was a sight to see. Looking in, she could see there were quite a few people inside, still.

Jessica's mom put her hands on her hips, taking it all in, at a glance. "There are quite a few people inside, maybe we should come back later," she finally said.

"Its fine, mom," Jessica replied. "The owner is a nice guy. You will like him." Practically pushing her through the door they finally got into the building. Jessica's mom was clearly taken back by the amazing artwork on all the walls.

Damian walked up to the two of them with a wide smile. Jessica took a step forward to introduce her mom, equally smiling at Damian. "Hey there, this is my mom Karen Shaw. We were in the area and I wanted to show her where I was going to be working."

"Welcome, Mrs. Shaw. I have enjoyed your daughter's company and teaching her. Bringing his hand out to shake hers, Karen accepted the shake and was pleased at how gentle and pleasant the man was. She thought this might work out, after all.

"Jessica is catching on quite fast to the art principles that I'm teaching her," Damian continued. Looking over to her daughter, Karen smirked.

"Well, I guess a few hundred art classes as a kid will do that," Karen answered. They both chuckled for a moment, while Jessica blushed red.

"I would offer you a seat in the waiting area for us to talk, but we have a few clients waiting right now," he mentioned, with satisfaction. "Busy day, thanks to the parade. It makes folk want to decorate their body. I love it." He clasped his hands and smiled wide, showing how happy he was for the extra and unexpected profits to come into his store.

"No worries about that," Karen answered. "I'm glad business is good. But, I have been a little skeptical of Jessica pursuing this trade. I have to say that your studio is not what I expected. It is clean and classy. Very traditional New Orleans feel here. I actually feel right at home. I have raised Jessica in an Antebellum home in the French Quarter. That is probably why she feels so comfortable here."

Damian smiled his broad grin, again, bowing his head slightly. "Thank you for the great feedback," he said. "I really wanted to pull off exactly what you described. However, I need to work with some of the people waiting in here. Feel free to walk around and check everything out. Stay as long as you want."

"Thank you, Damion," Karen tipped her head back in gratitude. The two of them continued to slowly walk the perimeter of the shop, as Jessica showed her mom all of the art that had fascinated her. After a while longer, Karen looked to Jessica and spoke softly. "Ok, it is quite nice here. I will let you continue this for a bit. I'm interested to see where it leads. That Damian is also kind of easy on the eyes, huh?" Her mom elbowed her softly in the shoulder.

"Mom!" Jessica replied, horrified. Not only did she have zero interest in discussing this with her mom, but Damian was a *lot* older than her.

Her mom smiled, as all moms do, when they see they have embarrassed their children. "All right, let's go. We need to go where I originally had planned to stop today." Getting back into the silver Range Rover, they moved along the road, turning on Quarter Ave, then another left onto Broad. Following this road for another ten minutes, they came up to the famous New Orleans cemetery.

Jessica looked bewildered by her surroundings. "What are we doing here?" She looked genuinely puzzled, when glancing at her mom.

Pulling her hair back into a ponytail and checking her makeup in the mirror, her mother began. "I didn't think you remembered what today was. It is the anniversary of your

Grandmother's death."

Karen's family had paid a vast amount of money to have her mother buried her. It was a status symbol in the role as tourists flocked from around the world to see the famous cemetery. Recent hurricanes and storms had caused major damage to the establishment, now making it almost impossible to have a loved one buried here. It was lucky, in a way that Karen's grandmother had passed before the storm had started battering the location.

Groaning unpleasantly, Jessica pleaded with her mother. "Do we have to? This place is so dreary and morbid. I always get an uneasy feeling here.....it's creepy!!"

"Yes, we have to," Karen replied, with a tone that said there would be no further discussion. "Now get out and come pay your respects."

Walking slowly, though Jessica was going even slower, they observed the surroundings. Bit by bit, Jessica was becoming happy that she was there. She just took in the haunted feeling of the place, but usually forgot the incredible architecture, sculptures, and art this place had, everywhere. Being a student of art, it should have been a Mecca to her, but they were so creepy.

There were normal tombstones of course, here and there, but the majority looked to be fit for kings and queens. They towered in the air, with sculptures attached. Everywhere she looked, she could see the like of angels, saints, and Christ. There were crosses of small and large on nearly all surfaces. Then, there were the Mausoleums, which looked like one could live inside, they were so substantial.

Making their way, almost half way into the cemetery, Karen stopped in front of her mother's tomb. It was not a small tombstone, but also not a massive monstrosity. Her grave stood about head high to Jessica. Most of the graves here were raised above the earth, because of the ever climbing sea level. If you dug a couple of feet you would be standing in the Gulf of Mexico.

Karen rubbed her fingers slowly down the name upon it, feeling the nicks and breaks in the stone. Jessica watched her mother, wondering if she was in pain. She thought she might have been a bit selfish when she refused to come in here. This was obviously important to her mother.

"You know, she really loved you," Karen finally said, "I wish she could have made it a bit longer. You were so young when she passed."

Hugging her mother from behind, Jessica said, her voice choking now, "I know mom. I'm sure she was great. I know you loved her."

"Oh, I soooo did. She was amazing, an excellent human being. The times have changed here in the south. Hospitality has become a notion of the past. She wouldn't like it here anymore. She is in a better place." She grasped Jessica's hand and bowed her head, with her eyes closed.

Jessica stayed quiet for a minute after her mother had reminisced about the past. They stood in silence... A gentle wind hit Jessica's ear, while standing there. Turning to the left, she saw the man from the coffee shop! The same man who stood tall with the aged leather jacket and dreadlocks was walking behind him.

Watching him still, he appeared to have just walked out of one of the mausoleums they passed when walking here. She was confused, as she didn't think anyone was allowed into those places. 'What the hell is going on?' she thought.

Her mind was in turmoil, as she stayed quietly standing there with her mom. Looking over again, the man had disappeared. Possibly into another tomb, or back to the parking lot, she had no idea. It was so strange. 'This is why I don't like coming here mom.' she thought.

Chapter 12

New Orleans

Nicadimus brushed the cobwebs off of the brown coat sleeves, as he walked back to the Challenger. He had never really liked coming to the cemetery. There was too much bad history here for him.

But, this was where the book at his office had led him. It had been buried underneath the tomb of one of Louisiana's most famous murderers, Marie Laveau. It had been laid with her, the spirit had told him. As he was sitting in his powerful car, flipping through the pages, Nicadimus noticed that the words were in a different language.

'Great......another obstacle', he thought, with disgust. He was frowning at the book, wondering how he was going to be able to get past this one. But, as quickly as he had gotten mad, the emotion left him, realizing that he did know a solution. Fortunately, an old friend could help him. Not one he especially enjoyed calling on, but desperate times......

Peeling out, as he usually did, Nicadimus made his way back to the store. He thought about the girl that he had passed, coming out of the cemetery. He knew that he recalled the girl from somewhere, but he couldn't quite place where he remembered her from. It racked his brain like a probing ice pick, burrowing deeper and deeper into his mental essence, sure to drive him insane, from the agony it was causing. He was sure that it would come back to him.

He felt he had to know and that was why his head pained him so greatly. Nicadimus felt a power emitting from the girl. Not many carried such an inner power, and the ones who did, usually had no idea. They never would. Most people didn't go bumping and prodding around the occult to discover such things. It would take a major event, or catalyst, to propel her power to the forefront of her mind.

It didn't take long, with how he drove, before he came back to his store. But, immediately, his face creased in anger. Smacking the top of the steering wheel, he growled, "Took my damn spot." How he hated when someone parked in the spaces in front of his store, when he wasn't there. Now Nicadimus would need to park around the block, just to go to his own place of business.

"Bastards....." he mumbled under his breath. Usually he was quite sparing about how he used his powers, but annoyed as he was, there was a fix for this. After parking, he looked all around the vehicle, to see if anyone was watching him. There was no one.

"Elephantine...invisigaloooo...basnechaka....." he chanted, while sitting in the vehicle in a praying type position. His body then began producing a slew of yellow lights, swirling around his body. Slowly, he seemed to be vanishing, until he was gone.

Like a thunderbolt, he reappeared in his hidden office chamber. "Ahhhhhh!" he groaned. "Shit that hurts every time." Knowing that the spell carried a slight bit of pain, he still followed through with it. He refused to walk to his business, out of plain stubbornness. Spinning around in the chair, as he appeared, the power of the magic propelling him with an unnatural force. His dreadlocks slapped him in the face before settling down to his shoulders.

He dropped the book on the table with a loud thud. The noise that came was substantial, nearly shocking him into falling out of his chair. He didn't, instead opening the manuscript to a random page, he tried to decipher the language. It was no use, he realized.

Nicadimus swiftly leaned back, while sighing one more time. Pulling out his cell phone, he judged again whether a call to the man for help was warranted. Unfortunately, it was, he realized. How else would he read this damned thing?

Hitting the speed dial, while holding the phone to his ear, he took the plunge and gave his former friend a call. A voice answered after only one ring.

"Well..well..well," came the deep and gravelly voice. "Look who it is calling me.

Haven't heard from you in quite a while young man."

Rolling his eyes, Nicadimus held back a curse. He hated it when Professor Arthur Magnusen referred to him as a young man. Hell, he had been through things people couldn't even dream of.

"How are you Arthur?" Nicadimus asked, resting his chin in his large hand.

"Very, well," Arthur replied. "Just doing some research and grading papers for these students here and there. I have some very interesting things I'm working on right now. I think you would be intrigued. Will you come down here? No need to drive. I know that little teleport spell you have. Might hurt quite a lot to come this far with it, though." Arthur said all of this with a chuckle.

"Ya, I think I would drive," Nicadimus replied. "A teleport that distance could put me in a coma."

"Oh, poor little baby," Arthur mocked.

"So, what do I owe the pleasure of this call, Mr. Voodoo man? You're not a chatty Kathy if I remember right."

Posturing to the point, Nicadimus closed his eyes and just spoke, "I have a manuscript I need you to translate. It's about, I dunno....220250 pages."

Scoffing at the number, Arthur continued, "Oh, well, is that all. That is a lot of work, Nicadimus. Why would I do that for you? It would take up all of my free time for over a week. That is, if I can even understand the language.

"I will make it worth your while. You like gold don't you?"

"Oh, yesss. The sorcerer's coins. I had forgotten about those little lucky things, quite heavy if I remember right. I would do a job like this for five of them."

The cost didn't bother him slightly. Hell, a simple spell and he could conjure more up at any time that he needed. "Five it is, then. Two up front to start the job and the rest once completed. Deal?"

"Deal," came the satisfied response from the Professor. "What is the manuscript about, if I may ask?"

"It's an old grimoire," answered

Nicadimus. "I need a few things from it. But, I cannot read the language. I know you like old relics, so this should be fun for you, in a way."

Arthur sounded excited, while talking on the phone. "Yes, I would indeed, very much enjoy a task such as this."

Arthur Magnusen, over the years, had collected a large number of old memorabilia, like very old. Some had even given him a few special abilities of his own. They were nothing like the magic that Nicadimus could produce. But, it was impressive to the average person's standards.

For instance, whenever he got sick, an old skull from the Mayan culture would heal him when he acted out some required steps. That particular skill came in handy quite a bit, as Arthur found himself getting sick, quite often, as his age climbed.

Arthur bore a striking resemblance to Indiana Jones, except his hair was fully grey, even his beard. He was constantly dressing like he was on a safari, even though he worked at the Harvard Anthropology department, as a tenured professor.

Arthur had come across Nicadimus on a trip to New Orleans, when looking for an artifact. Knowledge of local lore had led him to Nicadimus's shop. Being in the right place, at the right time, he saw Nicadimus do a teleport spell from his car and into his voodoo shop.

The tall dark man hadn't thought anyone saw him. Yet, Arthur had been peeking from behind a large bush, at the time. Bold as Arthur was, he had decided to confront him. Nicadimus didn't have the heart to kill the old man, since he had vowed to not speak of what he had seen to anyone. The fact he had a healthy understanding of the occult had also helped to spare his life.

Now Nicadimus called on him for random jobs such as this. Arthur, the old fool, was marvelously well schooled. The five coins that Nicadimus would pay him would fetch more than the man made in six months at the university. Just a quick bit of magic for him to gain more coins had been the one of four spells that carried no punishment upon using. It was a gift bestowed on Nicadimus's bloodline.

With a serious look on his face, even though Arthur couldn't see him, Nicadimus spoke, "Finish quickly and I will give you an extra two coins."

"Bully, ole mate," came the reply. "It will be done soon." Arthur hung up with a deep smile of satisfaction.

After the call, Nicadimus continued flipping through the pages of the text. It was all just a random bunch of gibberish. It was in no known language that he could think of, nothing being recognizable. It was probably a code, he had deduced, which was what had led him to contacting Arthur.

Nicadimus was happy that the book had been found. Soon he would have what was needed to complete the spell. Reaching under the desk, he found a small hidden button.

Pressing the button, a flat screen tv descended from the ceiling. It was massive. Though the establishment had a look to be rundown and sketchy, this vibe helped with business. People liked creepy. To keep this guise in place, Nicadimus had a fun time hiding things of value out of sight, even his office chamber, which not a soul knew existed.

Scanning through the channels of the huge television, he stopped on CNN, his favorite news channel. He could tell when people were lying and telling the truth. It was nice to be a sorcerer. On the tv a special was taking place about a company in Tokyo. He had never been to Tokyo, but it sounded nice, though. The company was NeuralGen industries.

It seemed boring, so he turned the channel to ESPN. Sport center was on and all the commotion was about the LSU tigers who won the national championship. The streets of New Orleans were abuzz with celebration. Now he saw that even the tv carried the same excitement for them. It was a good time to be a Cajun apparently.

Still internally conflicted about having to carry out the dangerous spell, he rubbed the side of his arm, while watching. He had no choice. Weeks ago, the creeping feeling had come upon him. Something was coming...something big and deep down, he knew that his current powers would not be enough to stop the force. Nicadimus had no idea what was coming, but this intuition had never failed him before, at any time.

Whatever was coming would require more power to defeat. So, unfortunately, this spell would need to be completed. It was an intense challenge being the sorcerer gatekeeper of North America, but it was a job that he took very seriously.

Every continent had a gatekeeper. There had been generations of Nicadimus's family that took on this responsibility, but now it fell on him. Once a year, all the gatekeepers from around the world convened to go over the year's happenings and discuss any possible threats. He liked most of them alright. Everyone that was, except the Russian gatekeeper. Nicadimus couldn't stand the sight of him.

He was an arrogant prick that claimed he was a direct descendent of the mad priest Grigori Rasputin, the holy man that had advised the Romanov family of Russia. Nicadimus had a less public heritage, but he figured the man probably was being truthful. He was certainly crazy enough to be of that nut job's family.

It was the job of the gatekeeper to keep any being with special abilities in check. If a gatekeeper found someone with abilities that were beyond what he or she was capable of, they had to be watched, and, in the most extreme cases, eliminated. They could not be allowed to get out of control and hurt innocent people or bring attention to the invisible world that hid in plain sight. Nicadimus was a protector of his continent and he took it seriously.

"Busanti......elephantine.....loosenliiiii," Nicadimus chanted, as the yellow flame surrounded his body, making his eyes glow. The glow seemed to project from the sockets like a laser, projecting like a ray of brilliant bright light into the air around him. Red sparks started to crackle all around him, bouncing off of his body like burning embers....then poof! He was gone. He reappeared almost instantly, in the front of the store, behind the counter.

Nicadimus stood straight and twisted his head, making his neck crack several times, creating a profound sense of relief. "Damn," he groaned. That hurt every time he did it. He didn't really want to even think about what was happening to his body; every molecule being stripped apart and transported instantly through space, to be slammed back together again. It was no wonder every joint and muscle ached furiously.

He had had to come back to the shop for some much needed cash for errands. MOST places didn't take gold coins worth $10,000 apiece. So, off he went to his favorite pawn shop.

He never had bothered to keep much on hand, never saw a need for it. Why keep tens of thousands in the bank, when he could create hundreds of thousands out of thin air. Taking several of his coins, he walked out of his shop, this time, and headed down the street, at a fast clip.

He was heading for a place that asked no questions, and gave him about three grand for every coin. They made a huge profit off of him, but he didn't care. He could go and there would be no requirements to know where he got them or a record that he had ever been there. He was able to just walk out with plenty of cold hard cash. Little did the pawn shop know, but the coins were old and worth far more than just their weight in gold.

So, they would think their profit of a couple of thousand dollars was fantastic. But, they could have been earning at least seven grand, or more, on each coin. Always made Nicadimus smirk, as they thought they were getting over on him, when he could just make more, at any time.

After he had walked out of the store, hanging the 'be right back sign', and locking the door, he had moved away quickly. Walking around the corner to his car, he suddenly stopped in place, so fast, that he nearly tripped over his own feet. What he saw stunned him more than anything he had seen or done in his unusual life. Frozen in place, staring like a marble statue, he saw a boy. He looked to be no older than sixteen, Nicadimus thought.

The kid was walking down the sidewalk, looking at the shops. From a far distance still, Nicadimus could actually see the boy's blue eyes. The odd part, Nicadimus realized, was that the kid was actually wearing glasses, but his eyes were still detectable. Nicadimus could still sense the color of his eyes, due to the eerie and unnatural glow that softly emanated from around the edges of the glasses. Nicadimus knew that he was able to see the color, due to his own powers and that a normal person would never know the difference.

The eyes were not natural and he knew it. What was this kid? Something was different about him and it was very unnerving. Looking at the thin blonde boy, Nicadimus shut the door to the Challenger and walked back to the sidewalk, staring intently at the boy.

The sensation of whatever power lay inside the kid hit him like a ton of bricks. The sense of raw power emanated to him like the outer edges of a hurricane. There was a frightening level of an unnatural sort of strength in the boy, but what? Was this what his intuition was warning him of? Was the boy the threat he was preparing for? His doubts took over, as his rational mind battled with his inner power.

No way, Nicadimus finally decided. The boy had power of some sort; that was obvious. Nicadimus had come across others, in his life, but not often. Just because a person had power, it didn't mean they were a threat. They had to be watched, of course, but most often, more intense and severe intervention was not needed. Sometimes it was, but Nicadimus felt that that probably wasn't the case with this boy.

'I don't think he threatens the balance,'

Nicadimus finally concluded. As he walked, Nicadimus's coat flapped in the air, trailing behind him like the probing tendrils of his mind. His presence always carried an air of mystery and strength, stoic and silently powerful. Reaching into his leather coat pocket, he pulled out a gold coin and began rolling it over his fingertips, while walking. All the while, he continued staring intently at the boy.

Chapter 13

New Orleans

The streets of the place enchanted Kyle. It was nothing like the home he grew up in and had known all of his life. New Orleans had a sense of mystery to it, and an excitement that captivated him. It seemed to be an endless party, a party dancing and flashing lights that spilled out from the numerous bars and clubs, creating a pulsing wave of happy, and drunk he saw, people that flowed throughout every space of the road.

Kyle felt the pull of the energy, nearly allowing himself to join in the dancing. But, somehow, he managed to restrain the impulse. He took the time to look around further, and realized how hungry he actually was. Seeing that the street had a small beer and taco stand, he moved towards it. The aroma was intoxicating.

Surprisingly, he loved it. He figured most would be nauseous from it, since you never knew how long the food had been in the serving tray, but he wasn't. Exhausted by the walk from the New Orleans port, where he had parked the boat, he looked on with salivating lips at the street cart. He was famished.

Walking up to the street vendor, almost running, Kyle asked, "Do you take cards?"

"No, kid," the man replied, while not even looking up at him. He was busy organizing the various foods in his tray. "Cash is king baby".

"So, how do I get a taco, or three?" Kyle asked, starting to feel slightly annoyed.

Kyle heard the man's sarcastic reply come filtering into his mind, instantly. 'ATM down the road genius.'

Kyle didn't like the man's attitude. He was just ready to say something, in reply, before more thoughts came to him. He learned that the man had a wife and a newborn child at home. He wasn't getting any sleep and they were months behind on their rent. But, after hearing all that he was dealing with in his head he understood the man's behavior. Selling tacos on the street had to be tough to make enough money to keep his family happy, financially.

Looking closer at the man, Kyle said evenly and with no malice, "I'll be right back.

I'm gonna get some cash."

The street vendor gave a nod without looking up to him. Kyle kept walking, looking around for that ATM that he had heard from the man's mind. A few steps later, though, he realized that he had forgotten to get the passcode for the woman's credit card. He could only use it in places where they only asked for a signature.

"Dammit!!!" he cursed, a little too loudly, as others looked up on the street and gave him a funny look. He didn't realize that his eyes were flashing brightly, at that point.

Forgetting about the delicious smell of the tacos, he averted his attention to looking for a restaurant. There would be no other way to get food, and besides he would get a bigger meal.

The street carried mostly bars, though, he quickly realized. He was surprised that food establishments were hard to pick out, rather than the entertainment. There was definitely no shortage of places to get smashed and make bad decisions!

As he walked past all of the bars, he had a hard time not laughing out loud from all of the drunken, inner thoughts that he could hear. They were so slurred and out of it, that he couldn't understand a thing.

Walking for another couple of blocks, he came across the Orleans. It seemed popular, as there was a steady stream of people heading into the building. It was a big Cajun all you can eat buffet. He wasn't buffet hungry, but hell, beggars can't be choosers, he thought, in fine spirits. After studying the front of the building, he walked inside to see what he could find for food.

Unnoticed, a block behind Kyle, Nicadimus watched his every move. The need to trade coins for cash was long forgotten. The closer he got to Kyle, the heavier the sensation of doom loomed upon him.

The boy had just walked into Nicadimus's favorite lunch spot. He knew that he could not go in, as it would bring way too much attention, since everyone knew Nicadimus around the area. That would cause this boy to notice him. Nicadimus immediately decided that he would wander outside till the boy finished eating and then continue trailing him.

After walking into the restaurant Kyle was pleased to see that it was a dimly lit establishment. Being that it was night time, outside, the lights were on, in the streets. His eyes were so sensitive now, that it was almost blinding if he looked directly at them. He found himself still wearing his sunglasses, even at night. With all of the eccentric people roaming the streets, he fit right into this city.

"Seat yourself hun…" said a tired looking, middle aged waitress, in passing, carrying an armful of dirty dishes.

Walking to a table, close to the meat bar of the buffet, Kyle took a seat. Not a moment later, a different waitress appeared. She was a younger woman with an unnatural look of aging that hinted at a possible opiate problem, Kyle presumed. She scratched at her super short brown hair, while speaking.

"What do ya want to drink babe," she asked, with a dreary look. Her thoughts flooded into his mind, instantly. She was an open book, her needs tearing apart her subconscious and giving him free access to everything. However, what he saw sickened him, it was a poisoned and ugly mind that filtered up to the surface, her thoughts revolving around the singular desire to get the next fix. He jumped away from the thoughts as quickly as he could.

"Mountain Dew," he said, feeling slightly ill in his stomach.

"You got it," she said, with a sickening smile. Kyle found that he could almost envision a bare skull in the place of her face, so sickening were her thoughts.

"Help yourself to the buffet." She sped away, her thoughts trailing behind her like ghostly trails that he could almost see.

Kyle stood up, slightly wobbly from the filth that had circulated through his mind. He was surprised at how much of an impact this whole mind reading thing was having on him. Shaking his head roughly, in order to clear it, and moved over to the buffet to bask in all of its glory. He suddenly found himself much, much hungrier than he had expected.

The first area consisted of meats. There were large sirloins cut thick and stacked in a row. The next in line were the pork chops, chicken breast, and sausage links. The sausage links, in particular, caught his eye. The smells that wafted up from the steamer tray captivated him as strongly as the taco cart from outside on the street. He read the label and saw that it was Cajun Andouille sausage. Everything about it said that it was good!!

Grabbing a plate from the side of the bench, Kyle loaded a few links to the plate.

Continuing on down the line he came to the sides. Overwhelmed by the choices, he could only stare back and forth not being able to decide: mashed potatoes, baked potatoes, green beans, lima beans, pinto beans, steamed carrots, fried rice, brown rice, pasta.....the list went on and on down the line. Finally settling on a sweet potato and spiced corn, his stomach truly started to growl as he carried the plate back to his seat. It was looking better by the minute.

As he moved, he passed the breads, gravies, and seafood. He had heard that the seafood in New Orleans was fantastic, but no room was left. The plate was already full, so he just opted for a piece of cornbread to shuffle onto the side. Even then, he figured he would be back for some fried shrimp and fresh baked bread. This place is off the hook, he thought.

Sitting back down at the table, he immediately set to the food with a frenzy.

Anyone that was watching, would have seen an almost animalistic hunger. He took a huge bite of the medium rare sirloin, ripping it apart with just his teeth. Someone was watching.

Nicadimus couldn't help but look in the window, as the kid tore at his food.

Nicadimus's eyes narrowed, seeing the manner in which the kid was eating. It was absolutely bizarre. He had the sudden feeling that he was watching a creature, rather than a young boy. As he looked in, he saw the boy indulging in the mammoth steak.

As he ate, the boy seemed to pulse with an unnatural sort of energy. Nicadimus couldn't figure out why the boy's eyes were not attracting more attention. They were almost glowing, as he ate. The kids' pupils, themselves, even seemed to be an incandescent sea of azure blue.

'Maybe only those with abilities can see them….?' Nicadimus thought, wonderingly. He had truly never come across anything like this.

He continued walking past the window, so he wouldn't be noticed. Every waitress there enjoyed his company, so he would be seen immediately. They thought he looked like Kobe Bryant with dreadlocks. He didn't want anything disrupting the boy. Making his way to the edge of the building he leaned against the brick laid wall. Arms crossed, he tapped his forearm in impatience, as he waited on the boy.

Kyle had polished off the steak and vegetables, a habit his mother had taught him, to never leave anything behind on the plate. Feeling grotesquely full, he pushed the plate away from him. No seconds after all. He felt satisfied and in control, again. Leaning back in his chair, sighed contentedly, when the waitress suddenly appeared. It was the tired, middle aged one, this time.

"No dessert?" she asked, simply.

"I am stuffed," he replied, with a grin. "I guess my eyes were bigger than my stomach."

That brought a ghost of a smile. "Ya, that happens," she said.

Kyle's comment about his eyes drew her attention to them though. She now noticed how blue they were. So icy.

"Son, you have the brightest eyes I have ever seen. They are simply magical."

"Thank you....I guess," Kyle replied, uncomfortably. He was just starting to receive her thoughts.

'Boy what I would do to you,' she thought. Her inner dialogue rolled into his mind like a toxic miasma of filth. Suddenly, he realized that he could not only hear what she was thinking, but he could also see it! A parade of horrifying images flashed through his mind of what she wanted to do to him in the bedroom.

Repulsed by what he saw, Kyle practically threw the credit card to her. "Put it on that," he said, with no small sense of urgency.

"Be right back, sweetie pie," The middle aged waitress threw what she must have thought to be a seductive smile at him. Kyle was suddenly bombarded with an image that nearly made him fall off his chair in horror. It involved him and her in her bedroom, as well as silk scarves. Kyle simply pressed his hands to his head, willing his mind to clear of this horrifying woman's perverse fantasies.

Kyle had barely been able to catch his breath from the filth that had flooded his mind, before the lady came back, 'Ye, gods...' he thought, 'No more.' But, thankfully, as she came up to him, the only thoughts he could detect were purely professional, all business. He could detect that she was confused and slightly upset.

"So, your name is Marsha?" she asked, her brow creased in rising anger.

"Yep," Kyle answered smartly, "that's my mom. I'm a lucky kid. She just gives it to me and says to take a hike. She needed some quiet time." For a moment, Kyle had to think. He knew he could read minds. But, could he put a thought into a person's mind? He concentrated on that, wanting this woman to believe him.

For a moment, the waitress considered what he had said. He could see that she was struggling with whether to believe him, or not, but his conviction won her. Kyle had learned from his early years. Make your case fast and without stuttering and practically anyone would believe you. He had to wonder, though, about his abilities to influence minds. Something to explore.

"Ok, sweetie," she finally said, back to her usual self. "Just sign there." She discreetly tapped on the tip area. "Don't forget about me though." As she said that, another flood of horrific fantasies of hers battered their way into his mind.

Kyle could only sigh and try to force the images out, closing his eyes for a second. He signed and put down a twenty dollar tip on a ten dollar meal. He figured her happiness with the tip would make her forget about her disgusting thoughts. It didn't work, he saw, as the images just doubled in strength, showing the level of happiness she felt towards him.

It seemed that she wanted to reward his kindness with a very acrobatic and flexible act that Kyle didn't even know existed. "Good, god!" Kyle groaned, as he moved towards the door as quickly as he could humanly run.

He fought back, pushing the images in the direction of the lady, visualizing that he was throwing something at her. It seemed to work, kind of, he thought. As he hit the street, he could only laugh uncomfortably at the awkwardness of the situation. "Wow!" he groaned. "That was weird."

Nicadimus noticed the boy's abrupt exit and turned to face the direction. The energy broiling off of the boy was almost visible. It was like standing on the beach, watching an approaching hurricane. Nicadimus felt like he was on a beach, getting battered by the psychic waves that the boy was sending off of him in furious cascades. It was the eyes that caught his attention, again. They broiled and sparked like blue fire.

Kyle started walking away from the buffet, trying to clear his mind and recapture his good spirits. It was hard, hearing everything that was being said and thought around him. It was getting more difficult, by the second. He fondly thought of the trip here, when it was just him and the open sea. There was nothing invading his mind, then, the experience feeling like a dream to him, now.

As he ambled down the sidewalk, he looked around, taking in the happenings. He didn't even notice the large man sporting the leather trench coat. Nicadimus fit into his surroundings quite well in the south. After passing him, Kyle looked both ways for vehicles, then crossed the street to continue down the block. After a moment, Nicadimus followed again, but from a safe distance.

It was interesting, Nicadimus noted, but it seemed as if the glow from the boy seemed to ebb and flow. When he first watched the boy, Nicadimus saw the glow was subtle, but noticeable. When he reached the busy streets, the glow got brighter, more elaborate, almost like it was pulsing to the beat of the music. But, when he came out of the restaurant, it was almost raging. The boy had nearly been covered with the glow. Now, it was back to a more subtle illumination.

Nicadimus watched as a couple of female street workers passed Kyle, smiling at him. The glow suddenly pulsed, again, nearly a blush. Nicadimus suddenly stopped, realizing what was happening, with a smile. It was emotion….the boy was changing the glow, unconsciously, based on the emotion he was feeling. Based on the company, he could tell that the boy was embarrassed.

Kyle stopped suddenly, his attention grabbed. He read 'Tattoo studio' in giant letters on a billboard that was in front of him. He had spent years of being the perfect son; he had never even considered the possibility. That was, until now.

Swiftly he walked into the place. Rock music filled his ears and gave a pleasant feeling to him. Kyle moved around the studio, looking at all the artwork on the walls. A girl covered in facial piercings came up to him, looking him up and down. For a second, Kyle feared the thoughts that would come from her mind would be similar to the waitress, and he prepared himself, but nothing of the sort came. She was all business.

"Whoa.... bro, nice eyes…" she exclaimed. "I could get lost in them." She looked at him seductively, but nothing too bad filtered over from her mind, which was good, because Kyle didn't think he could take more of what he had just experienced at the buffet.

Blushing at her sexy behavior and fidgeting with nervousness, Kyle could barely reply. "Thanks," he answered.

"Can I help you find anything?" she asked, eyes opened in a questioning manner.

Kyle started to talk, but he was still struggling with the errant thoughts that were filtering into his mind. She was still thinking about his eyes, apparently. "I'm thinking about getting my first tattoo," he finally said.

"Well," she began. "Do you have any idea what you're looking for?"

"None at all. Recommend anything?"

The girl started to talk, "Well it is a pretty personal decision. What are you into? What do you like? You can, nowadays, literally get anything. You can look through some of these books to get the wheels turning. These two are artist portfolios that work here, and the four or five are a bunch of design ideas. Usually after ten minutes staring at all these, you have more than enough ideas."

"Cool," Kyle grabbed the first artist portfolio. It attracted his attention, because the name on the front said Axle. 'Well that's a cool name,' he thought.

Opening the book, he was greeted by a multitude of old school tattoos. They reminded him of something a sailor would have, or something. Not what he was into, so he laid it back down, picking up the other. There was no name on the front of the portfolio. But the artwork was a more realistic style. Some of the tattoos looked like a photograph, so real that Kyle felt himself drawn into it and actually imagined that he was there.

"Wow!" he exclaimed. "I like this one."

"Yeah, a lot of people do," the woman answered. "But, he is pricey."

"Well good thing I have a lot of money," Kyle told her.

She smiled, clearly liking him more, thinking he had a multitude of cash. He started having more images of the amorous natures coming into his head, from her. He didn't mind, since she was much younger, closer to his age, and very attractive.

But, he had to wonder what in the world he was propelling from himself that triggered such a response in women. Even the old woman, back at the marina, had wanted him. Kind of.

"Oh yeah," she replied, "Do you want me to go get him, so y'all can go over ideas. He's just in the back, drawing."

"Sure," Kyle shook his head in the affirmative.

"Take a seat. I'll be right back."

Nicadimus chose to again wait outside, while the boy shopped for ink. Kid doesn't even know a better shop is right down the road. This was the tourist trap tattoo studio, housing second rate artists. Nicadimus only went to the shop in the middle of Bourbon Street. It was classy and artistic. This place made him feel like someone would give him Hep C.

He watched from across the street, as the boy sat, waiting for the woman to return. Nicadimus felt that he was correct in his assumption. The boy was influenced by his emotions and feelings. Right now, he was only slightly anxious, so his blue glow was only slightly visible. The woman came back, and Kyle stood up to greet her.

Kyle had looked and saw the woman reenter the lobby. The artist with her was supposed to be the one who did the realistic tattoos. He was a young Hispanic man in his twenties. Like the woman, he was also adorned heavily with tattoos. Kyle particularly liked the dragon that was soaring over a distant mountaintop on the man's right arm. The tail wrapped around his bicep, like an armband.

"This is Zeke," she said. Turning to Zeke, she continued, "He likes your work, but is not sure yet what it is he wants."

"What's your name, homie," Zeke jumped in, walking over to Kyle.

"Kyle," Kyle replied. He was happy to finally be talking with someone that didn't want to take him into the bedroom. The only thoughts that came to Zeke's mind were genuinely friendly and good natured. Kyle felt better, having talked with this young man. He seemed like a very good person. That was a pleasant change.

"So you have no idea what you want?" Zeke asked, slightly amused. His thoughts conveyed how this certainly wasn't a new thing for him. He constantly got people in here that wanted a tattoo on an impulse.

"Not really," Kyle said. He appeared perplexed.

"Why don't you start off with a universal type image, like a skull, or a rose; you know something cool, that is also timeless," said Zeke. "That way you won't regret it." He lifted his brows in a questioning fashion, as if to ask what Kyle was thinking.

Kyle took that as his cue. While scanning over one of the books filled with designs, one caught his eye and actually filled him with an exceptional level of enthusiasm. Kyle wasn't even sure what the image was, but he was drawn to it, almost as if he needed it. The image was of an abstract nature, clean yet fearsome. It embodied how Kyle felt about himself.

Glancing back up to the artist. "This one....I really like it."

Zeke found himself suddenly very surprised by the kid's interest. "Really?" he asked. "No one has gotten any of those designs. I don't even really know what they are, to tell ya the truth. Possibly they are some sort of voodoo stuff. A local artist drew them that doesn't tattoo. He only sells his design to anyone willing to give him a little cash."

But, Kyle was not to be deterred. "How much would something like that cost?"

"Where would you want it on the body?"

The question took Kyle back. How could he have not thought about where to put it yet? That might be the most important part. So where.....then the first thing popped into his mind.... his hand. Kind of a bold move, but Kyle couldn't help it. The idea of this image laid on his hand flooded his mind. Despite not having had a clue of where to put the image, he found himself now dead set on having his first tattoo on the top of his left hand.

Holding his hand up to the artist, so he could see the top of it, he said, "Right here, on top, cover the whole area."

"Black and grey, or color?" the artist asked.

Here was another question that Kyle had never even thought to figure out. But, once again, the solution rushed him like a tidal wave that smacked the back of his head. "Blue," he said, "as close to my eyes as you can make it." He stared directly at the artist.

"Ya....your eyes are pretty blue," Zeke said, "I didn't even know they sold contacts like that."

That's probably why so many people never said anything about his eyes, Kyle realized, suddenly. People passing him by casually probably thought he wore bright blue contacts. Interesting, he thought. Kyle decided that he wouldn't wear sunglasses all the time to conceal them.

"So you want your tattoo on your hand?" asked Zeke. "I don't see any other work on you..."

"Yep, and nope. This will be my first."

Zeke's eyes opened slightly wide, his expression one of disbelief that quickly morphed into a sluggish shrug. It's your body, bro. You what, eighteen?"

"Yes," Kyle replied cautiously, feeling slightly offended. What did his age have to do anything? But, when gathering in the man's thoughts, Kyle did not detect anything malicious.

"Well..something baseball size in size on that location, would be about two-hundred and sixty dollars."

Kyle was a little shocked by the price, but not for long. He remembered that he possessed a credit card with money he hadn't had to earn. So.....screw it. First he would take a step outside and think about it first. He wanted it, but his common sense was kicking in and stopping him. Kyle didn't want it to, but one can't just erase a life of playing it safe.

Handing the book with the design over to

Zeke the artist, he said, "Get it ready, if you don't mind. I'm going to step outside for a few minutes."

Zeke had heard that before and knew the kid would never be back. "Bro, if you don't want it, just say so...it's not a big deal."

"I want it for sure, man. I just want some fresh air...promise."

"Ok....it'll be ready in about 15 minutes," came the reply.

"I'll be back in just a few minutes," Kyle answered. He walked outside the shop, but not before sending a smile to the cute, pierced, girl that had moved behind the counter, though. Did he have a shot with her? Kyle couldn't tell, but the inner thoughts that she was sending were sure interesting. He never was great at communicating with the opposite sex. He wondered if this mind reading thing was going to help in that area, or the possibilities of putting thoughts into someone's head...

Nicadimus looked up and saw Kyle walking out of the tattoo shop. Starting to get late, he thought. He didn't want to follow him around all night, trying to guess what was going on with him. No telling how late he would be out and Nicadimus wasn't a night owl anymore.

He finally concluded that approaching the kid to feel him out seemed to be the best option. At this point, it was clear that the kid had tremendous power, of some sort. But, what kind and was it dangerous? He didn't know.

Walking up behind the boy, he tapped lightly on his shoulder. Kyle turned around quickly, partially startled. He immediately opened up his mind to receive what this strange looking man was thinking, but couldn't. All he saw, each time, was a door, solidly closed. 'Strange,' he thought.

"Uh....yeah....?" Kyle said, realizing that this encounter was a bit different, from what he was expecting.

Nicadimus had felt a furious onslaught into his mind, when the boy turned. Nicadimus seen the boy's eyes flash, furiously, when he had jumped and turned, confirming that emotion played a part in the pulsing light that was emitted.

But, what truly startled Nicadimus was that he saw that pulsing blue light reach for him, questing like a living tentacle towards his skull. He instantly knew what was happening and put up his mental defenses. 'This one is a mind reader,' he thought. 'But, is he dangerous.

He's just a boy....''

"Sorry to bother you, young man," started Nicadimus, "but I saw you just come out of that tattoo shop. Are you thinking about getting something?"

"I think so," Kyle replied, somewhat ill at ease. He had never come across someone that he couldn't read. "I actually came out here to make my final decision and think about it."

Kyle didn't know what the man wanted. But oddly, he wasn't intimidated by Nicadimus. A safe vibe came from the man, even though his appearance was anything but safe. Kyle was still very unsure of why he couldn't read the man's thoughts. "Should I be worried?"

In a friendly motion, Nicadimus put his

hand on the boy's shoulder. He nearly gasped aloud, when he realized the energy that roiled and tossed, screaming to get out, just under the surface. But, instead, he kept it inside of him. "I wouldn't do that. No locals go here. Kind of a grimy place. Horrible place. I also don't think they ever clean their equipment."

Sneaking a glance behind him, Kyle narrowed his eyes, "Nasty...are you serious?" "Ya man, pretty sure. All the locals go to the shop in mid Bourbon. Only lost tourists get ink here. You are way better off heading to

Bourbon Street."

"Damn...I'm glad I stepped outside to think about it. I had a funny feeling about the place. Unfortunately, you just verified that suspicion. 'I really have suspicions about you, old man...' Kyle thought.

Nicadimus spoke and listened to Kyle. All the while, though, he was entranced by the blue eyes. So bright. The pulsing lights had tempered down, while there weren't any more of the reaching portions towards him. The boy didn't know what to make of him, he thought.

Kyle was appreciative for the advice and said as much. "Well at least I have an idea what

I want now, though."

"What were you wanting?" Nicadimus asked, generally curious.

"It's a design I can't really explain too well," Kyle offered. "The artist inside told me a local guy drew it and sold it to the shop."

Nicadimus poked out his bottom lip and held one hand up stopping him. "Explain it to me, please."

"Okay," answered Kyle. "Well, it has what looked like a long stick with a curved knife on the end. The stick is wrapping around a skull. There were coins in the skull's eyes. There were also some cool geometric shapes and lines mixed into the design.

"Wow, well I would say you described that pretty well. I like the sound of that myself. I may have a little insight about the design. It sounds like a New Orleans magic drawing.

Kyle was instantly puzzled.

"Magic....what do you mean?"

For a moment, Nicadimus could see the questing tendrils appear, again. It seemed like they wanted to come for him, but that the boy felt it wouldn't be wise.

"Well kinda, I guess...black magic....voodoo type stuff."

That was now two people that had told Kyle the image was voodoo related, or magic, or whatever. Oddly, it made him want it even more. Looking up at Nicadimus, his eyes turned up a notch of brightness. A normal passerby would never have noticed, but Nicadimus certainly saw it and more.

"Your eyes are amazing," Nicadimus finally allowed. In his mind, though, he was saying 'holy crap'. The boy was so awash with light, now, that his head was nearly invisible within it.

Kyle was still very surprised he couldn't hear Nicadimus's thoughts. Usually anyone that conversed with him directly, inadvertently sent all their private thoughts to Kyle. This eased and worried him at the same time. Again, he couldn't help but wonder why. The tall man that looked like a voodoo man right out of a movie seemed nice. But was he?

Tapping next to his left eye, Kyle said, "I got em from my momma."

Nicadimus gave a slight laugh. "Me too," he offered, pointing at his eyes, which were a deep brown. "At this time of night, I wouldn't initiate a new tattoo. All the good shops will be closed. Anyone that starts it tonight, will only try to rush it. Just go to Papa Midnights tomorrow. Around 2 pm, I suggest.

Let the artist get warmed up and ready to work.

You don't want to be the first tattoo, either.

Some of those guys party pretty hard in the evening."

"Well thanks for all the advice," Kyle replied. Guess I will just need to find a hotel room and go for it tomorrow."

"Can I recommend one?"

"Sure," answered Kyle. "Why not. Your advice has been good so far."

"Just go down a few blocks, further up," answered Nicadimus. "There is a brand new Hilton that just was built." Kyle just nodded his head, in thanks, and walked up the street in the direction that was offered. Nicadimus watched him go, still thinking about what he needed to do. But, one thing was for sure. He knew exactly where he was going to be, tomorrow, at 2 pm.

Chapter 14

New Orleans

Drawing non-stop over the past few days, Jessica was positive that she now had a solid grasp of the lessons from Damion. She had been diligent about practicing lightly for the pre-sketch, even repeating an image a few times, until it carried a pleasing aesthetic.

After that, Jessica had practiced bumping up the darkness of her lines, slightly, for the contour of the image. This step proved to help her drawings drastically from before beginning the apprenticeship. This, in turn, made her want to practice that much more.

Today would be a great day. They were practicing the next step of the drawing process, base shading, which was her favorite part. She nearly always started too early on it. Before, that's how she would start a drawing, with shading. Jessica shook her head slowly, while grinning at how she once drew. It was a new day and the future was bright for her.

There was no telling how far this art thing would take her.

Too bad it was still morning time. Waiting till this afternoon when she could get back into the shop seemed like an eternity, being that she desired to continue on so badly. Finishing up the sketch of a rose that

Jessica was using for a still life reference, she held it at arm's length away to look at her final product.

The rose looked so authentic that it seemed to glow straight from the page. It was a pretty one at that. She swore that she could almost smell it. Even without the final details and shadings, it looked real.

She was starting to find a whole new respect for line art. It really was the base and foundation of a drawing. Laying the piece down on the table, she stretched her arms and stood up, walking to the dresser. Scratching the side of her leg, Jessica really didn't want to change out of her sweatpants. They were so comfortable.

Can't go outside looking like a hobo, mom always said. Years of that saying had been completely drilled into her psyche. She didn't like being seen looking like a scrub, so she figured she should probably change.

Throwing on some black skin tight jeans and a bright red shirt, she moved to her closet to pull out some shoes. Doc Martens it was today. She enjoyed the extra inch or two of height that they gave her. Strolling slowly down the stairs, she let her fingers glide on the wrought iron handrail. The steps creaked, as there were possibly over one hundred years old. Sturdy though. Things were built to last in that era, unlike the current era.

She cruised happily across the floor, relishing the new skills that she had picked up from Damion. She flopped onto the couch and allowed for it to hiss a bit, as her body weight settled on to it. Jessica pulled out her phone holding it close to her eyes. There were a few unread messages. A couple were from April, as usual. The last one was from Damion at the tattoo shop. He would be leaving the shop early today, so she could come early for their lesson. Wow! She thought. This day just got better real quick, not wanting to wait till the afternoon.

She left her home and hurried away to the shop. Moving along the sidewalk, the traffic passed her by, slowly. This area was a tourist Mecca, so everyone tried their best to see all the surroundings. Jessica decided she would stop by the coffee shop, since she had about an hour to waste. While walking, she came up to a store that she usually passed by. It was a small book shop. The sign on the front glass said, 'coffee inside'.

'Maybe I'll just get coffee here and look around,' she thought, taking in the interesting surroundings of the shop. 'I can't believe that I never have seen this place.'

She began looking over a sales area in the middle of the floor. All the books on the stand were only two dollars. Thinking something might stand out, Jessica circled the stand like a shark smelling blood. The only thing she enjoyed as much as drawing was the occasional great story. As she was looking, an old woman came up to her.

The woman's face was endowed with a sea of wrinkles that looked like a desert plateau, filled with a dry and dusty landscape that almost covered her whole face. She seemed like

the exact type of person to run this establishment. She looked like an ancient librarian. The old woman gestured to the display.

"All of those are two dollars, hon," she rasped. "Not for long though. I am going to end that sale tomorrow. I have had most of these for over ten years. So, every now and then, I will mark them way down to try to get rid of them." "What kind of books do you like?" she continued.

"I'm open to a lot of things, but definitely steer towards fiction," Jessica answered, truthfully, "But, a book from this digital age is always nice."

"Oh right you are...oh right you are...," the old woman wasn't as interested in her, once she discovered that she probably wasn't making a sale. "Well, let me know if you need anything."

"Yes," responded Jessica. "The sign in the window says you have coffee for sale?"

"Sure do...follow me, its right back here," continued the old woman, a little brighter now, as she was going to make some money, even though it was only for coffee, "We have a nice little selection."

Making their way to the back, Jessica was pleasantly surprised to see the list of choices of coffee and lattes. There weren't as many as the coffee shop, of course, since it was for a bookstore. But, she was still impressed. With over ten choices, she scanned the list up and down a few times, before finally making her decision.

"A large caramel latte, please" she said, politely. "With an extra shot of espresso."

"You need all that caffeine?" The woman asked, with a little laugh. "God, in heaven, child. Keep drinking like that and you are never going to make it to my age."

"Well, no one needs it," Jessica laughed.

"But, I really like it."

"Can't argue with that, dear," the woman smiled, "You go look around some more. This will be ready soon and I will bring it to ya."

Coins for the Skull

Jessica was impressed by the service and quaintness. Too many times she had passed by this small place to go to the coffee shop. The small store gave her a feeling of relaxation that she hadn't felt in some time. It was very pleasant and enjoyable. It made her feel good.

This would have to be in the mix as much as a couple of times during the week. There was a line of small couches in the back of the shop. They were all different colors and brands, probably free or very cheap from somewhere. Nonetheless, each still looked comfortable and convenient, if you wanted to read while drinking your cup of hot Joe.

Just about every store cashed in on the city's spooky and creepy fame. From Voodoo and Obeah, to freaky animals, or ghost stories, it was all represented in the shops throughout the area. This store was no different. They actually had a section of books about voodoo, magic, and the paranormal, she found. It was tucked into the back, in a dusty and rarely visited corner she saw, which peaked her curiosity even more.

Jessica wasn't interested in ghosts or monsters. But, magic certainly struck her fancy. She had always been curious about the subject, ever since first reading a book about a young boy wizard. She picked up a small book, almost a Pamphlet.

Curious, she thought, wondering what it was. It was clearly old, the paper was yellow and cracked. She found that it was very brittle, when she tried opening it. On the inside, she gazed in wonder at a collection of drawings. Each one had about a page of description for them. The woman came up to her, just as she started reading.

"Here ya go, sweetheart," the proprietor said, while handing Jessica the Latte. "I see you found something to look at."

"Yes," answered Jessica, dreamily. She was only half paying attention to the woman.

"I love art and I have never seen drawings like these."

"Those were done by an old man that lives here in town. That's how he makes his living, drawing and writing. Then he walks around the town trying to sell them. I sent him away the first few times he came by the store.

But one day, I actually looked through some of his stuff and.... it's quite good. I bought everything he had that day. Goes perfect in this little spooky section I have."

"Yes, it does."

"Ok, I'll leave you to it. She walked away, back to the area she had made the coffee.

Jessica stopped on a page with an image that resonated with her. It was an image of a skull with an ax or something wrapping around it. It had coins in the eyes of the skull, reminding her of the Greek ferry boat undertaker that took souls across the river Styx. She heard stories of the entity that brought the deceased to their respective resting places, but you needed two coins to pay your fare. 'The Greeks had some brilliant imaginations,' she thought.

Jessica went over to the old lady, old pamphlet in hand, "How much for this one?" She tried to not sound too excited, but she felt it. Her whole body was alive with energy.

This collection of drawings were special, she thought. She thought she might have something to incorporate into her artwork. It was awesome.

"Well you seem like a nice girl," said the old woman. "I will sell it to you for what I spent, twelve dollars."

She thought about it for a moment. But, ultimately, Jessica stayed with what she had thought, when originally looking at the book. She decided that the subject matter inside would be great for some future drawing. This would be especially true in the city, for tourists, if she ever got to do tattoos. "I'll take it," Jessica finally said. She handed the woman a twenty dollar bill.

The lady went to go get change, but Jessica stopped her. "Don't worry about it.

Keep the change. You will be seeing more of me, this shop is fantastic."

The woman gave Jessica a warm and genuine smile that touched her, "You come back and see me again now."

"Oh I will. Thank you for the coffee."

After Jessica left the bookstore, she continued her walk to the tattoo shop, now with a new small book and a warm Latte, with which she sipped. The sun was picking up intensity, as it was getting closer to noon, but it was still tolerable. A lifetime resident of the south, Jessica was very used to the weather and kind of enjoyed it.

The air was redolent with strong smells, cooking, the bayou from down south, but particularly interesting was the tobacco. The air smelled of cigars as she passed a cigar shop. She didn't smoke but enjoyed the aroma. It was a sophisticated smell she thought. Her parents would kill her if she started smoking. Nothing wrong with taking in the smells though, she thought.

An elderly black man with a large stogie in his mouth told her good morning while she walked by him. People were always friendly to her. She never knew if it was because of her looks, or the fact they could tell she wasn't a tourist. Either way, she had always loved the people of her city. They were so nice! It always put her in a fine mood.

Her regular meeting with Damion for art instruction was not until 12:30, so she had time. Still some more time to kill, Jessica thought. What better place to do that, then here. Jessica took a seat on a public bench, overlooking a small green space, just a few storefronts down from the tattoo studio. This was a great spot to relax and watch the commotion around you. Not in the evening though. Too many people at night to relax at all.

Her curiosity had been at an all-time high, when she was in the store. From the little she had seen of the old book, she had become seriously excited. The drawings were so rich and arcane, but still approachable. Someone that wore them would feel special and unique, but they wouldn't be labeled as a freak. The pictures, particularly the skull and coins one, had power. She had never felt like that about a picture, before, but she did now. It was a picture that truly spoke to her. She had to practice making it.

She began to look through the book again. It was interesting the amount of information each drawing possessed and that the artist had chosen to share it. That was something she never really saw from anyone. The fact this art was local made it all the more entertaining to absorb the information. It seemed that each picture was filled with history and local lore. It was fascinating. Maybe she would meet the artist someday. He wasn't famous, obviously, but was still a motivated author and artist. Jessica felt inspired.

She looked at the writing and started reading under her breath, "The bird's wings symbolize a change in the directions of wind that is required for magnetic attraction. The orange coloring on the beak and the exterior rain glue symbolize the power of the hemisphere attracted to it.

Each wing has five feathers for the five different regions of magic in the voodoo practice. The two tear drops underneath the left wing, fourth feather, represent the night one can conjure this entity." Jessica looked up and thought, one word, 'fascinating'.

This description next to a curious drawing of a raven was especially interesting to Jessica. Was it all made up? Was it real? She didn't know, but it was positively intriguing. The idea of giving a drawing purpose like this was a brand new idea to her. She began to think about ways she could do the same with her own artwork.

Pulling her phone out and checking the time, she realized that she only had a few minutes left. It was already 12:25. 'Where does the time go?' she thought. Might as well head on that way. She was very excited to get to work on her drawing, this time.

Damion looked over the new stack of papers Jessica had brought with her. Per usual, he was taking his sweet time going over them, as if he was breaking them down into the subsequent parts. It always made Jessica nervous, because she hated being judged.

Finally, he spoke up, "You are ready for the next step. Base shading. Your pre-sketch and contours are looking much improved. Setting all the papers down to his side, except one, he started speaking while pointing to the drawing.

"So, when we shade something, you want to have a point of origin for the shadows," he continued. "What that means is, in a nutshell, is that you need a light source. Remembering to use one from now on will set your art a notch above others, with this step alone. We don't want to randomly shade things.

Every shade comes from a light source. You want to look at your drawing and decide where you want the light coming to originate."

Jessica shook her head in understanding. She was seeing where he was going with this and was picturing what she would have to do.

Damion was still speaking, "Then, take your time deciding what shadows would be cast on the object. I find a very simple way to start this is to lightly draw an arrow that is pointing at your drawing, coming from wherever the light is supposed to be shining. It will help your mind stay on track. Of course, after doing this practice for a year or two, it will be second nature and an arrow won't be needed."

Damion grabbed a pencil and drew an arrow in the upper right hand corner, pointing towards Jessica's rose drawing. "We want to imagine a bright spot light shining down from this arrow on our image," he began.

"While doing so, you want to think of your drawing as a three dimensional object, with different layers on top of each other. This will better help you to figure out where to draw shadowing. With our first pass of shading, we want to keep it light like the pre sketch. If you go too dark, it will be hard to change it later."

"This way, you can map out your shades and then look over them to make sure they make sense. This is a little bit easier with a still life, because you can visibly see where the light is hitting an object and clearly see the shadowed areas. With this practice, you will have to do it all from your mind and imagination. You have a lot of leeway, as long as it makes sense and is pleasing to the viewer."

Jessica had never taken such steps before, when shading. She simply did what looked cool to her. This method or approach would take a lot of guesswork out of the equation when drawing. She felt her initial excitement and enthusiasm from finding the mysterious artwork increasing, due to this. It was a great day for art, she decided, loving every minute of the experience.

Handing Jessica the rose drawing,

Damion said, "Ok, go ahead and try this out. I'll be back in a bit to see how you're doing." He gave her a reassuring smile that made her feel good, feeling that it meant he believed in her.

Damion left her to the drawing. She began to imagine the sun shining on the rose. She tried to believe the rose was real and it had landed on the paper. If the sun hit the top left of it, then there would be a main shadowed area coming from the bottom right. Lightly shading the lower right of then rose, a feeling of confidence set into Jessica. She understood.

Damion came back soon and peered over her shoulder to see the drawings progress. "Wow," he exclaimed. "It looks like you are getting it quickly. This is what I had hoped from you. You see I need to see art potential and growth from you. That way I could feel confident about teaching you how to tattoo. All of these same rules apply to body art, as well. Just instead of paper, you will be working on skin."

Jessica couldn't help but smile, from hearing such praise. Soon her goal of tattooing would begin for real.

"Finish this piece," Damion continued, "Then work on finishing some shading on the other drawing you brought. Since you understand, let's go ahead and go over another step. After the shades are drawn in, you can finally go to the step you were already great at creating, detailing. It is at this point, and only at this point, that you can choke up on the pencil and hold it closer to the tip of the lead. So, you have full control to be exact and can go darker easily.

"But remember that the whole time before this, you needed to be holding the pencil close to the end of it, so you stayed loose and made clean sweeping motions, while also staying light. Everything you need for your drawing is now on the page. So, just detail and tighten up everything as the artist likes to say. Give details hard edges where they are required, clean up your borders, and so on... like I said, you have been doing this step your whole life, so it should be second nature to you."

"Ok, cool..." Jessica replied. She went straight to work on her drawing and Damion smiled while walking towards the back of the shop, his behavior evident in that he was liking her growth as an artist. For Jessica's part, she was thrilled with how she was improving, so fast.

Chapter 15

New Orleans

Kyle couldn't help but think about the man from last night. His mind was plagued by the chance encounter, and the mystery of why he couldn't read his mind. He had certainly been strange, Kyle thought, but was he dangerous? That was the big question. Kyle had a notion that the man was safe, but he certainly didn't know that, for sure.

Go with your gut, he told himself. Kyle took the last bite from the cheeseburger that room service had brought him. Not particular caring for the fries, those were left mostly untouched. He had received little, to no trouble, checking into the hotel with the woman's credit card. The front desk attendant just took the visa like it was a piece of gold and had allowed him into the hotel.

Rubbing his stomach, he was extremely satisfied. He could get used to this life. 'Do I even bother going back to Florida?' he thought. But, then he figured he should, eventually. Otherwise, he could probably find a new mark, for new income. He could always call that old bat and let her know where to come and pick up her boat and credit card. There was only so long that the old woman would tolerate this situation and report the boat and credit cards as stolen, consequences be damned.

Kyle looked over his attire and took in a deep breath. He smelled salty and musky. The dried ocean water had started to make a bit of an odor that clung to him like a toxic fog. That would definitely repel the wrong crowd, in this city, he thought, with a grin. But, he figured he should take care of the basics.

Kyle figured that he would need to get some new threads before going to the tattoo studio that was recommended to him. The heavy gel he had slicked through his hair was gone, leaving the blonde hair standing in all sorts of directions. Bed head. He hadn't even pulled the covers down to sleep, only falling onto it and passing out, immediately. Stealing boats and credit cards takes a lot out of a guy, apparently.

Gazing and typing on his phone, he tried to look up the address for the tattoo studio on Bourbon Street. He searched the listings, hoping to find the place that the man had told him about. The other artist from the place last night was surely pissed at him for not coming back in, so he knew that he couldn't go back there. The drag was that they had the design he liked. He was also still trying to find that bottle. It had to be in one of the shops.

He hoped he could find the design he wanted in the new shop, as well as get a read on where the bottle went. He found that Google Search had given him a shop named Papa Midnight Tattoo. He looked for a location, scrolling down. It read 373 Bourbon Street.

'Perfect!' he thought. That was the place he was looking for. They would be open until 10 pm tonight. He had time to get a change of clothes from somewhere.

Tossing his phone on the bed Kyle, walked to the bathroom for a shower. While he took off his clothes, his attention was drawn to the mirror. Always forgetting about the luminescence of his blue eyes, Kyle was shocked like the first time, all over again. His eyes glowed a bright and shining blue, reflecting off of the mirror and bathing the room in a soft and rolling wave, looking just like the walls of a pool room.

With a grin, Kyle jumped into the shower and turned it on, the steam building up, almost immediately. The 5 star hotel spared no expense, apparently. This was, by far, the nicest establishment he even slept at, even when he compared his short time in Japan. Nevertheless, it was hard to get out and dry himself. As he was slinging the complimentary robe over his half-dry body, Kyle had an idea.

Kyle went to the end table, by the bed, and picked up the phone. Hitting 0 to dial the front desk, he only waited for a moment, before a perky receptionist answered, "Hilton Grand

Orleans, how can I help you."

"I forgot to bring clothes with me and I have somewhere I need to be, soon," Kyle replied, with an equal level of enthusiasm.

"Would you guys happen to have anything I could wear?"

"Why, yes," she replied. "Our gift shop has Hilton shirts and hoodies. They also carry a wide array of polo attire. What are your sizes and I can send some things to you. It will be billed to your room, if that is ok?"

Kyle was tickled to discover he could actually hear her thoughts, through the phone.

'Is there no limit to this?' he thought, wonderingly. She was complaining, in her mind, about him.

'What kind of an idiot would go to a hotel without a change of clothes?' she was thinking.

Kyle had to smile. That might have made him mad, on any other days. Not today. He said, politely, "That will be just fine, thank you. I'm a large and a thirty-four waist. I need underwear and maybe some socks also, please."

"Not a problem sir," she replied. "That will be delivered to you within thirty minutes.

"Thank you," Kyle said, sincerely, pouring on the charm. He hung up, but not before he heard the thought come through, 'whatever, you dumbass…' He laughed out loud, as he put the phone back into its cradle.

"Wow," he whispered, amazed. "Is this how the upper one percent live? He could get used to this. First he had had his lunch delivered and now his wardrobe. Life was goood! Even better, the old biddy back in Florida was paying for it!

The knock on the door actually came within ten minutes. That was much faster than he had expected, prompting another hearty smile, from him. Opening the door, he greeted a younger bell boy in a proper suit with a name tag on it.

"Wonderful," Kyle exclaimed. "His good cheer was showing through. "That was fast."

"We try to be as fast as possible sir," this was with an obvious sense of faked sincerity.

Kyle knew this was true, as the boy's feelings bled through in his thoughts. 'Little rich boy forgot his nice threads….to bad!' He all but thrust a stack of brand new and folded clothing into Kyle's face.

"Sweet!" Kyle shut the door in the attendants face. He was going to be polite, but the thoughts filtering over made him not really care too much.

"Bastard!" The bellboy quietly muttered, as he walked away down the hallway. He had expected a tip, only to have the door shut in his face.

Kyle quickly slipped the clothing on and stood in front of the mirror. He was pleasantly surprised how well everything fit and danced a little jig. It was the type you do when no one is there to see. Grabbing his phone and the key card for the hotel, he left the room, making it down to the lobby. It was tattoo time. Kyle was going to Papa Midnight Tattoo.

The streets of the city were filled with people. As soon as Kyle walked out of the hotel, he could feel the energy broiling over, an auditory beat that rolled across the city in waves. The sound of laughter and yelling filled the air. 'This place is off the hook!' he thought.

He could see where folks were already starting to get inebriated, even though it was just barely five in the evening. But, it was New Orleans and Bourbon Street at that. He was in the Mecca of drunk idiots.

Every other person carried around a large cup that had an alcoholic slushy in it; a hurricane as they called it. These drinks were sold all over the place. He was curious about it, but didn't think he would try it out anytime soon. The drunken thoughts that came to his head were ridiculous.

Suddenly, his attention was drawn to a Gothic styled, ornate street lamp. It was like nothing he had ever seen before, in anywhere he had visited. 'They really take you back to a different time, here,' he thought. He shook his head and continued walking along the path that his phone recommended. It wasn't like before he realized he had arrived.

He found a rather fancy store front. On the front were large letters in an old fashioned font that read Papa Midnight Tattoo on the large paned glass. Kyle could see the waiting room through the window. There was only one girl inside from what he could see. She was an edgy looking girl with shoulder length brown hair that was drawing feverishly. She appeared to be very focused and on a mission.

Kyle's cheeks heated, instantly, as her appearance caused a reaction in him. It hit him so fast that it felt like a tidal wave. His reaction was near complete. He could only stand in the doorway and stare. It was an inner turmoil, as he was awestruck by the lovely girl. He almost didn't go into the studio, feeling an awkward sense of embarrassment. Shaking that feeling off and focusing on the fact he wanted a new tattoo, Kyle walked in the studio.

This shop was noticeably cleaner than the one from last night. At first glance, Kyle thought it was really quite pleasant. The music was not blaring, but soft and pleasant, as background music should be. The walls carried fine paintings and sconces. The mood was very elegant and spooky at the same time.

The man behind the desk looked at him and smiled, but did not engage. Kyle could tell he was letting him check out the space first. His heart fluttered, while making his way over to the waiting room. The girl was still sitting there, whittling away at the drawing that he could now tell was a rose. Kyle wanted to talk to her, but was still hesitant.

Looking closer at a painting near him, Kyle didn't want to make it look like he noticed her. He didn't want anyone to think he was a creep. He noticed a small book next to the girl. The same small booklet he found the drawing that he loved last night at the other store!! Suddenly, all of his inhibitions were gone. "Damn..." he whispered.

He would have to talk to her. He needed that book, if only to take a picture with his phone of the one image. It was such an easy thing to ask. But it would require him making the first move. He would know, instantly, what she thought of him, due to her thoughts transmitting.

Maybe it wouldn't be construed as a move, since he actually needed to see that book. Would she believe him? Would she say yes? Kyle's mind raced with questions. Inwardly, he thought it would have been very helpful if he had practiced pushing thoughts into people. It would have been helpful.

Damion could clearly see that the young man had an attraction to Jessica. Something she was probably used to, being a decent looking girl, he thought.

But, the young man hadn't done anything out of line so, Damion let it go. Instead, he approached Kyle. "Thanks for coming in today," he said. "Anything I can show you?

Thinking about a tattoo?"

"Yes, I am," Kyle replied. "This shop was recommended to me. It is way nicer than the one I stopped into last night."

"The one on Spruce Street?" Damion asked, with a slight smile. He was well aware of what that place was like.

"Ya, I think so. It didn't have a name anywhere that I could see. It was just a real big sign that said tattoo

"It was good that you got out of there," Damion replied. "That place has a sort of bad rap. Eventually, all the rumors have to have a little truth to them. So, what kind of tattoo are you interested in?"

Kyle leaned closer to Damion, hoping the girl drawing on the other side of the room couldn't hear him. "Well, I found my design at the other shop, but had to leave it there. It was in a little book they had.

But, believe it or not, that girl over there has another copy.

The book sitting next to her, is the same one. Crazy coincidence, huh. I was thinking about asking her to look at it for a second, just to get a picture of the design I liked.

"Small world," Damion postured. "That is Jessica, our new apprentice. I will ask her.

Wait here." He moved over to her. Jessica can I see that book you brought in with you?"

Without looking up from her diligent drawing, she said, "Sure, I bought it from a little bookstore on my way in today. It had some cool concepts in it for artwork." Damion picked up the book and looked through the pages, while going back over to Kyle.

"This the one?" he asked. "Sure is," Kyle replied, enthusiastically. He was so excited about the moment that he hadn't even thought to look into either of their minds, especially the girl. But, she didn't seem to even notice him, so he figured that she would probably only have thoughts of drawing in her head. He also hadn't even thought to look into the man's mind and see if he could learn about Tattoo ink shipments. Instead, Kyle just took the small booklet and turned to the page with his design. Sure enough, there it was.

"I like the coin laden skull with the knife wrapped around it," Kyle said, enthusiastically. "It's trippy."

"That's unique," Damion said, with undisguised interest.

Kyle handed the book back pointing at the design. "I want it on my hand in blue ink, mainly to match my eyes."

Up until this point, Damion had tried not to focus too much on the kid's eyes. He didn't want it to seem like he was staring. They were oddly bright blue, unnaturally so. They glowed like a bioluminescent sea creature. Damion shook his head clear, trying to focus. "We have a guy that can make that happen for you. He is just finishing up a small one. He can make it bright blue, but it won't have that same glow that your eyes do... is that ok?"

"That is fine," Kyle answered, "Just the best he can do. It is my first tattoo, so I want it perfect."

Rolling his eyes a bit, Damion couldn't help but shake his head inwardly. Kyle caught a fleeting glimpse of his thoughts, but couldn't quite make it out. "Don't they all. Damion said. Striding to the back he went to find the artist for the job.

Kyle took a seat in a posh wingback chair in the corner. It was a luxurious seat, thick and fluffy. He felt like he had sunk into a cloud, as he perched himself upon it. He sat fairly close to Jessica. He still was continuing his mental struggle of whether or not to say anything to the girl.

He also couldn't get anything of interest from her mind, as she was very, very focused.

She had an edgy style to her clothes, without too much makeup and just a little mascara. The bright red shirt she wore tugged at his attention. At any moment, he thought that he might start sweating. With a pulse that was beating like a racehorse, Kyle finally decided to make contact with Jessica.

In a dull and sheepish tone, he asked. "What are you drawing?"

Jessica stopped drawing to look up at Kyle, really seeing him for the first time, or even noticing that anyone was even there, so intent was she on her work. Her first reaction was to ignore, but he caught her eye. There was just something about him that drew her attention in, kept her enthralled.

She noticed his jock or preppy attire, not really agreeing with it. Jessica never really liked the look of pretty boys. At least he was clean though; the clothes looked to be brand new. His eyes though........ Jessica had never witnessed such a miracle of light originating from the eyes. The blue was shining like a light. Her heart began to speed up, as she realized he was a living example of that light source she was trying to learn.

"A rose," she replied, thoughtfully. "The owner here has been teaching me drawing tips and tricks. I will be tattooing soon hopefully."

"Oh, cool," Kyle answered. Although, he wasn't really saying that, because of her artwork. He was saying that, because of the thoughts she was giving about him. It gave him chills to hear what she thought of him. "Well the rose looks perfect. I'm sure you'll do great with the tattooing, once you get there. You are a great artist."

"You're not from here are you? I'm not picking up any accent, at least not a southern one."

"I'm just here for a little work," Kyle replied, truthfully. "I'm looking for something that got lost. But, you are right. I am not from here. I'm from Florida, and came up on a boat. It was awesome. I was touring the city last night, when I met some guy last night that recommended this place for my first tattoo."

"I don't have one yet either," Jessica said, seriously. "I still live at home. I figure that if I can't pay my own bills, yet, then I don't need a tattoo. That's my parent's viewpoint at least. I'm surprised you're here on business.

"You look my age. I'm seventeen. How old are you?

"I'm eighteen," Kyle answered. "My parents probably wouldn't be happy about me getting ink. But lately, I just haven't cared. Crazy for me. I have always done what I'm told, but now…..eh." He said the last with a shrug and a smirk that Jessica kind of liked.

Damion walked up to them. "The artist will meet with you in the back," he said. "He is going to go over some things. He will get a measurement of your hand and some specifics on the design with you. He's the 2nd door on the right."

"Great!" Kyle answered. He fired off his biggest and broadest smile to Jessica as he left. There was a bit of awkward tension in the air. Damion went to his seat, as he left to see the artist.

Damion nodded to Jessica. "So…you two were getting along huh?"

Jessica blushed…"Ya, he's nice."

"Sure, he's nice," Damion replied. "But, a little naive. Kid doesn't even realize his first tattoo is a voodoo drawing. And he's getting it on his hand. I don't know what his future plans are, but this will majorly limit the options. Did you see his eyes? I've never seen anything like that."

"They were crazy blue," Jessica joked.

"Like the blue of a lightsaber in Star Wars. The

Force must be strong with him."

That brought a ghost of a smile from Damion, as he grabbed the drawing of hers.

"Nice..," he said. "Bring me a few more like this the next time you come into work. If they are good, we will move on to tattoo setups and technique."

"Sweeeeet..!" she squealed, in genuine enthusiasm, clapping her hands and bobbing her head in happiness. "They will be good enough. I won't sleep until they are."

Later.......

With a bandanna wrapped around his head, to hold back the sweat from the humid room, the tattoo artist carved away on Kyle's hand. The tattoo was almost complete. As Kyle sat there, taking the pain with ease, he could hear the thoughts of the chubby artist. The guy was tired, his back hurt, and he was overheated from concentration.

Kyle never realized producing tattoos could cause a struggle like this in an artist. He had a new respect for them. To make new art day after day carried with it a mental and physical struggle that took much resolve to pursue year after year. It was impressive.

The round cheeked guy leaned back and sighed a bit. "We are done," he said, tiredly.

"You sat great. And for a hand……. your first one…. good job buddy. The owner up front will give you an aftercare sheet."

Kyle gazed at the swollen hand. He could feel his heart pump through it. He loved it, the excitement bursting inside of him. The artist executed the drawing far better than he'd expected. There was a realistic quality to it. The finished tattoo was clean and polished. The coins in the skull's eye somehow looked like they were glowing. The knife, which the artist had told him was a sickle, looked sharp enough to draw blood.

He had talked Kyle out of all the geometric shapes and lines, saying that they were cool, but too busy and confusing for a hand tattoo. He was right. Taking them out left all of the focus on the main image. There was a black coloring that surrounded the image to help give it depth and add to the realism.

"Wow," Kyle replied. "All I can say is wow! It looks so real."

"Thanks man," he said, "I appreciate it….you pay up front also." The artist tapped on a sign next to them. It read, if you tip your waiter, tip your artist. Kyle thought that it was a little direct, but the man definitely had earned it. Kyle's hand looked powerful. The artist patted him on the back, as Kyle left the room.

He handed the card to Damion at the front counter. "Please put an extra fifty on there to tip that guy. My hand looks killer!"

"You got it," Damion said, as he ran the card. He thought that it was funny it had a woman's name on it. Hell he wasn't a cop. He and the artist needed to get paid for their time. 'Not my problem,' he thought.

Kyle looked back to see if the girl was still there, hoping to go talk with her and show her his tattoo. Already gone, he noticed. "Damn," he whispered. "Probably never see her again."

Bitter disappointment set in, as he came to this conclusion. Maybe it was a good thing. He couldn't make an ass of himself now.

Damion gave him the credit card back and an after care sheet.

"Make sure you read that dude," Damion spoke. "You paid good money for that piece.

Don't want to mess it up just from not taking care of it correctly."

"I will," Kyle replied. He felt happy, really ecstatic. The hand throbbed, but he enjoyed every beat. Kyle felt complete now, having made a decision of his own accord. Unknown to him, but on the other side of the street, staring through the glass, a set of deep brown eyes watched him intently.

Chapter 16

Cambridge, MA

Harvard University

His magnifying glass was heavy with a brass frame and marble inlay on the handle. The man's eyesight had deteriorated over the past years, so the tool helped aid his work. He could have used one on a stand, so he didn't have to hold it. But, Arthur Magneson was pretentious and always wanted to look sophisticated.

Arthur was constantly rubbing his nose, after sneezing for the umpteenth time. The book had come in the mail yesterday from Nicadimus. Arthur had figured it must have been buried, because each page was covered with a layer of dirt and light mildew. This was something that his allergies did not appreciate, as his nose had begun turning red from all of the friction.

Although Arthur didn't enjoy the dust and dirt, he was thrilled with the contents of the book. This was another rare find. Not too many people got to look at such things. It had been lucky for him that he knew an honest to goodness sorcerer.

Once he had told his eldest son about some of the objects and books that had crossed his path over his career. After telling these stories, though, his son and family had written him off as a quack and a loon. He worked at Harvard for crying out loud. Did that not give him any credibility? After receiving such a negative retort, Arthur now kept all his work and findings secret. He didn't tell anyone, figuring that they didn't deserve to know anyway.

Once he had settled in, he had quickly found himself within his element. He had started from the middle of the book, just to mix things up and keep it interesting. What he was going for was to see if he could even read it, first, before seriously digging into the text. After studying the page for a few minutes, relief came over him. This would be an easy job. He actually had another book with this same language already.

He already knew that it was early African Voodoo speak. Every tribe had had a practitioner of Voodoo or the healing arts. It was not uncommon for them to be the only educated ones in a tribe of a hundred or more. Of course, this system of beliefs had been brought over to the colonies by enslaved peoples.

This particular book had been written in segments, as they called it in those days, not chapters. Arthur could see that each segment started with a list of some sort. Surely these were ingredients. The rest of the segments most likely explained how to carry out the spell or ritual, while giving special descriptions, as well. He knew that Nicadimus must need a spell from this manuscript. Exciting!!

Without his help, a sorcerer couldn't even carry out certain spells. A sense of accomplishment, and he couldn't help but admit to himself, pride, came over him as he eyed the page. He continued looking through the eye loop with a sense of bravado that you could feel across the room. Practically skipping to the bookshelf on the wall, he grabbed another book that had the same language in it, already transcribed to English. This would be short work for Arthur.

He laid the book next to the one he just received. Most of these ancient books were written by hand, of course, which left a lot of extra room on the page for more writing. Under each sentence, he wrote the English translation in a 4h pencil that could be effortlessly erased. As he worked, the words flowed onto the page, creating the story that was hidden underneath the ancient text.

Nicadimus didn't realize that he took photo backups of all of his work. He had hired Arthur six times now, for the same type of job. Arthur had a picture gallery of every page he translated. It was, in fact, from one of these books, that Arthur now had the ability to heal himself from any illness.

There were other spells, but most came with strict punishment if used the wrong way. Arthur was smart enough to use a spell that came with no negative consequences. Sure, it was nice not having to worry about the flu anymore, especially at his age of mid-fifties., but….. Arthur couldn't help but think of what other mysteries were locked in these books and how they could help him.

Arthur was interrupted by a student intern that entered the office. "Mr. Magneson," he said. "I have graded all the final papers. Can I go now?"

"Yes you can, Petrie," Arthur replied. "On your way out, shut all the lights off in the lecture hall and make sure there is no trash on the floor."

"But, I really need to get back to my apartment, professor," he said, "I have plans tonight." The boy's voice was urgent, but that didn't matter to Arthur.

"Being my intern is your first priority, Petrie," Arthur replied, coldly. "You do as you're told, if you wish to keep this position."

"Yes, sir," Petrie said, quietly. He quietly shut the door and started walking down the hallway. From the safety of the closed door, he cursed at Arthur in a soundless fashion, while waving his middle finger in the air. After this mild level of defiance, he left to do as he was told.

Arthur had been working for hours now on the translation. He really pushed himself during these jobs. It was a contest for him to see how fast he could get the gold coins. Just getting paid was not only great financially, but he got to see magic also. He was particularly interested in seeing if something valuable to him would come from this book. He would love to find something like the healing spell.

Nicadimus didn't drive to him in person, to pay. Apparently, Nicadimus possessed special abilities, specifically tied to the gold coins. After Arthur finished working, he would let Nicadimus know. Nicadimus would ask to make sure no one was around him at all. No one could be in the eyesight of him. Then, on a table in front of wherever he was, sparks started to pop in a circle the size of a softball followed by shining yellow lights that got so bright that it was hard to look. The first time that Arthur had seen this miracle, it had blown his mind.

The sparks always disappeared, just as quickly as they started, leaving behind a pile of coins sitting where the display had taken place. It was a simply marvelous spectacle to watch. Sometimes Arthur took the jobs, only to see this. Boy, was he ever hooked! He loved the extra money, but to see real magic was always a treat. The average individual wouldn't even believe such a thing was possible. Modern movies had made skeptics of everyone. That was probably why his family thought him to be a fool.

Leaning back, Arthur pulled open the drawer on the bottom of the desk. He grabbed a bottle of Scotch, an uncomfortably strong liquid to most. Arthur enjoyed knowing he could muster the strong drink easily. It took some practice at the cost of his liver's health, but now it was as simple as drinking water. He had taken on the hobby, after acquiring the ability to heal himself from any sort of ailments or damage. Perks. You had to love them!

Arthur took a big gulp from the glass, then refilled it with more. He took another long drink, feeling it burn all the way down his throat. Refreshed and ready for more work, he put the bottle back in the drawer and shut it. He felt like a rebel for drinking, while at school. But, even if the stodgy old dean happened to wander in, Arthur wouldn't have given a damn.

Looking down, Arthur could see that he had almost half the book translated. He had already seen several different spells that he would have to look back upon, at his convenience. Some of them looked very well worth the time to practice. But, mostly, he just wanted to see the coins reappear. Soon, Arthur would get to see that magic trick again and get to go on another free vacation to the tropics.

Petrie had been Arthur's main intern for over a year now. After scoring perfect grades on his entry test in his freshman year on campus, Arthur quickly approached him for the position. Petrie's parents were thrilled, of course, but he felt the old man to be a bit arrogant. But, having the title on his resume would help with job placement and connections in the future, so he took the position.

A couple months ago, Petrie had noticed strange behavior from Arthur. The old man would be deathly ill when arriving at school, full of snot dripping from his nose, a violent cough, and pale skin. But, only a few hours later, he would see the professor before his lecture and he looked of perfect health. He had brushed the incidents off the first few times, but now it was positively intriguing.

The old man worked oddly late and had questionable conversations with strange people. Petrie had found a spot in the lecture room where he could hear all of the professor's conversations. To say the least, something was fishy. He overheard the conversation with somebody named Nicadimus recently and heard the men debating on payment of gold coins to read and translate a book.

Or, that is what he took from the conversation. Petrie found it odd to get paid in gold coins and not cash or bank transfer. Also, the fact the professor never did this work in front of anyone, proving it must be other than kosher. He walked up and down the lecture hall, picking up trash from the students' class. 'Why must they be so damn messy,' he thought, with no small amount of disgust. They all had backpacks; couldn't they just put the trash back in them?

He made his way to the classroom door and turned the lights out, while leaving. He figured Professor Magneson would be staying late in his office, again. Flags were draped in an elegant fashion, showing off the school color of crimson. In his mind's eye, Petrie always imagined the school to be futuristic.

When he had been at home it was a famous school that must have unlimited money. When arriving though, the school had reminded him more of a mix of an old castle with an attached large dormitory. It was quaint and nice for sure. But, it had also been a slight let down for him. Surprisingly, the university didn't have unlimited money.

This was something he had found out when trying to borrow a laptop from the campus library. They were constantly unavailable. Even his community college, in the small Russian city that he had grown up in, had a large supply of computers for students. Not that he would ever leave here. A scholarship to America and Harvard was a huge achievement in Petrie's country.

Another student saw Petrie moving down the hall and met him. "Yo, you coming tonight?" he asked, throwing his arm over Petrie and slightly squeezing his neck.

"I can't," Petrie responded with only a portion of the glumness he truly felt. "I have papers to grade."

"You have been here two years already and never have I seen you at a party," the other kid responded. "Man, you're only young once.

You are missing out. The lady's would love your young Dracula looking ass." "Look, I don't have rich parents like you. If my grades drop they send me back home. Do you want that for me?"

"Of course not, but one night a week or every other week will not hurt. It may even make you feel better and work harder.

"I don't know Thomas," Petrie answered, seriously. "My family warned me of young American treachery like this." Both of the young men laughed at that a bit, thinking it was hilarious.

"Just come one time. If you hate it, I won't bug you about it again....ok?"

Petrie hated it when Thomas used logic against him. Thomas looked at him with those thoughtful eyes and friendly body language. Everything about him suggested that he just wanted to have fun. 'What am I doing, thought Petrie. 'This is not what I came here for.'

But, ultimately, he relented. "Ok, I will come ......," he finally said. "But, only this once. What time, tonight?"

"How about eight?" he questioned.

"Eight?!" responded Petrie, incredulously. "I'm normally in bed by nine.

Why don't they start earlier?"

"Well most people our age are up till midnight through 3 am, Petrie." replied Thomas, with a confused look. "It is a bit strange that you are asleep by nine Petrie. I will see you tonight."

Thomas left Petrie, walking away in victory. It had been a year of working on his friend, slowly whittling him down, but it had finally worked. He was going to come out for a little shindig. Now, he could show his Russian friend a very good time.

On the other hand, Petrie held his head down a little while walking. He found himself to be a bit ashamed that he submitted to the peer pressure. He grabbed onto the leather strap of his bag tighter in frustration.

Arthur continued working, unaware of any of the difficulties of his young aide. But, truth be told, he couldn't have cared less, even if he had known. Anything past what he was wanting was not important to him, anymore. He was deep within the text, enjoying every minute of his work.

Reading the passage he had just translated, Arthur stumbled onto something. "Oh, my god," he whispered, in shock. He pondered if he would ever have the courage to use such a spell. The temptation was substantial. With this particular incantation, Arthur could make himself younger. Turn back the clock. Oh the possibilities!!

He favored the aged salt and pepper look he'd acquired over the years. He had the air of a gentleman, and most could tell by looking at him, that he was an intellectual. Most of all, he loved the power that he had, the people that he was able to control and bend to his will.

But there were decisions he would like to take back, things to be changed. What does every person on the planet want, but a do over! This magic came at a price though. If not correctly followed through, the practitioner would meet certain death. Wow! Either successfully complete this task, or you would die.

As Arthur dreamed of the possibilities, he couldn't help but think of the risks. Never had he undertaken such a risky procedure. He certainly would with this spell, after all he wasn't a sorcerer. But, this book would be secretly cataloged with the rest for whether or not they ever became useful. Arthur stroked his grey and brittle beard in contemplation.

Chapter 17

New Orleans

'When will this old fool call me back' thought Nicadimus. 'I'm tired of waiting.' Inside the voodoo shop, Nicadimus threw a large buck knife at a wooden section of the wall. It was a physical representation of how he felt, the throwing of the knife. This particular spot was riddled with dagger markings and scratches, many having been recently done. It was a favorite area for knife throwing practice, and it showed.

Thud.....the knife struck the wall with a velocity that was unreal. Moving so fast, it was almost invisible, a blur that nearly passed through the worlds that Nicadimus was able to see. He could, he supposed, actually make it pass through the worlds, if he wanted. Nicadimus had thrown knives his whole life. It was a fun pastime that his mother had gotten him into doing. She pushed him to practice every day.

She would always say, "It's a fun and an effective means of self-protection. Only cowards use guns."

Nicadimus listened to his mother, as always. He had done this, day after day his whole life. He chucked various styles of knives at everything and anything he could. Now being a man, Nicadimus knew his mother had been correct. He could send a knife flying at an assailants head or chest faster than he or she could lift a gun to point at him. The knives left no trace of evidence behind, as long as he took them with him. Also, he never needed to reload.

While throwing the knife, Nicadimus had found it so easy that he started moving one of his gold coins across the finger bridge of the other hand. But, now that too, was easy. So, now it was a mechanism for mediation. He found that tossing the knife, while juggling a coin with the opposite hand, helped him to think.

He currently was thinking of the boy that he had met a couple of nights ago. He had stood silently outside of the shop, watching, when the boy was inside, getting a tattoo. His eyes were unnatural. Nicadimus had been the most curious, when watching the kid's glow. It had flashed the brightest, when he had seen the young girl. Nicadimus would have brushed that off as teenage hormones, if not for the fact that he had suddenly realized that it was the same young girl he had seen in the cemetery. He had sensed a power about her, then, as he did now. 'What is going on, here,' he had thought.

Yesterday, he called the owner of Papa Midnights. Damon, being a longtime friend, was happy to answer a few questions for Nicadimus. He found out the boy had, indeed, received a tattoo, one on his hand. He had gotten a Voodoo ritual image tattooed on him, unbeknownst to him. Inadvertently, the kid now was vulnerable to any sorcerer. He would also carry a couple of special abilities with the mark carved into his flesh.

But Nicadimus knew that he surely didn't know any voodoo. He was just a kid. Because of the mark, Nicadimus could now find him, no matter where he was. Nicadimus figured this would be a very valuable asset, in case the kid went the way he thought he might. Since Arthur had not called him yet with the information he needed, to further his spell, he decided to see about finding the kid. Following a mysterious newcomer to the south would be easy. Hanging in the shop on a wall, was an old map of New Orleans, dating back over one hundred years. "Locatiomaaaaaa.....elephantine......banis himaaaa......" he chanted loudly, while pricking his finger with the edge of one of the throwing knives. He wiped some onto another finger and then placed the smeared blood on the corner of the map. The red streak on the map coagulated back together into a large drop and then started moving slowly, leaving a light streak of red behind it. It moved until stopping at a location not far from Nicadimus. Interesting, he thought.

The spell had a way of looking into his mind, by way of his blood, to search out whom he was looking for. In this case, he wanted to find Kyle. He wanted to learn more about the kid with the glowing eyes and a voodoo tattoo on his hand. Maybe this was the one he sought. He waved his hand slowly over the blood trail on the map, making it disappear completely. He didn't even need a spell to make this happen, as it was part of his birth magic passed from his mother.

While moving for the door, his cell phone buzzed in his pocket. Looking at the caller, he saw that it said, "Arthur". 'Perfect timing,' he thought sarcastically.

"So what do you have for me old man?" Nicadimus asked.

"I am finished with the book," responded Arthur, with undisguised glee. "This was an old one, for sure. It wasn't easy, but I got it done. I will need double the amount we agreed on for the information."

Nicadimus grimaced. He had expected something like this and was surprised Arthur hadn't tried it sooner. "Greed doesn't look good on you Arthur. I figured you above something like that."

"I'm not above money, Nicadimus," Arthur replied, with an obvious grin, despite being over the phone. "I realized I'm the only person that can do things like this for you. So... I want more. It's as simple as that. Will it be a problem?"

"No....it won't....but it may be a while till I request your help again.." Nicadimus said, through gritted teeth. "Do you still wish to proceed with the pay increase?"

"Oh, I do indeed....and after I have the gold, I will put the book in the mail, like usual."

Nicadimus didn't even need to say the spell aloud to make the coins appear in front of Arthur. He simply closed his eyes and concentrated for no more than thirty seconds. "Yesssssss......" Arthur spoke with great glee.

Nicadimus didn't need to see what was happening, to know what it looked like. In front of Arthur would be a yellow light in a small area that would begin to swirl like a mini tornado. Sparks would be jumping a few inches out of the whirlwind. Then as the whirl slowed and came to a stop, the mask of a cloud would clear. Nicadimus knew that, then, he would be looking at a pile of coins. A pile of large and heavy gold coins.

Nicadimus also got a brief glimpse of Arthur, in his mind's eye. It was a face of monstrous greed, while the old man grabbed at the coins and held them in the air in victory. He looked more like a troll than at any other time, Nicadimus thought. "So, Arthur," Nicadimus continued. "You have your payment. Send the book. Nicadimus hung up the phone abruptly. Looking back to the old map on the wall, he recalled what he was about to do, before the call interrupted him. Find the boy.

Leaving the door locked, and making his way to the car, he revved the engine. He didn't need to search long, because he knew the boy's location from the spell. The location on the map was now a coffee shop that he frequently visited. A little late for caffeine, though, he thought.

He drove by the store, looking inside, while moving at a turtle's pace. There he was, sitting at a table near the window, gazing out into the street. He was by himself, Nicadimus noted. Not that he was surprised. He had always seen that people with true power were often loners, like himself.

Nicadimus could see the young man's eyes from the road; they glowed like an unholy fire that truly unnerved him. Something was probably going to have to be done, he reckoned. Pulling around the side of the block, he parked the car. The thunder cracked outside, the moment he turned off the ignition. Rain was becoming a daily thing lately, the stormy season obviously starting. It annoyed him, not wanting to get wet anymore. Once or twice a month was one thing, but every day…

The sky flashed, making him mask his eyes even from the safety of the vehicle. The storm was right on him, not even being able to count to one, before the rolling crackle of the thunder split the sky. The hairs all over his body started to stand up, goosebumps covering his arms, even in the humid conditions.

Looking out, he suddenly saw Kyle walking down the street. The rain drops slapped the car windshield. Then……. a beam of light from the heavens struck, slamming into the earth, right where he had seen the kid walking. For a split second, everything turned white as snow. The visibility was zero. Then the lightning strike was gone, but Nicadimus's vision was still blurred. As it came back, he could see the boy. "What in the hell!" croaked Nicadimus. The boy was now covered in flames, a living sheet of blue fire. But, he was not moving, nor was he showing any emotion. He was just standing there ablaze. The concrete around him was black from the electrocution. The boy's eyes were glowing so bright that they were hard to look at. The tattoo on his hand also glowed bright, the skull and coins dazzling

Nicadimus's eyes with the piercing visage.

"What the hell?" Nicadimus breathed. He watched, as the boy lifted up the tattooed hand, slowly, while still ablaze, and thrust his fist skyward. At that moment, the flames stopped and he poured smoke from all over his body. The clothes he wore had not burned whatsoever. The storm immediately quit, rain ceasing, at the same time. It was as if the weather was somehow listening to the movement of him.

Nicadimus wasn't sure if he was imagining this, or whether it was even real. No, the boy was certainly there, he was moving his head in a slow motion, checking his surroundings. Somehow, the streets were empty. No one had seen what had transpired, only Nicadimus. As Kyle moved in the opposite direction, Nicadimus got out of his car and began to follow.

Kyle looked down at his hand. The bright illumination was now subsiding. For a moment, he had been worried that someone might have seen what had happened. But, when he had looked around, he could see no one present, in the area. 'I just got struck by lightning,' he thought. 'Now, my hand glowed, as well. Maybe it was even brighter than my eyes. What is happening to me?' Kyle even thought that the rain had stopped, because of him.

The sheer idea of it all boggled Kyle's mind. There was something about the tattoo. It called or summoned an unknown power to him. Happiness came over him, as he realized the magnitude of what he could probably do with it. Did he now have more powers than mind reading or maybe mind control? Could he control the weather? It blew his mind.

'I can't wait to find out what I can do now,' he thought. Reading minds was pretty nice, but could he control lightning; who knew?

'I was on fire and didn't feel a thing. The lightning felt like a warm hug.' It was an incredible feeling.

During the previous evening, Kyle had stayed up late researching where the ink bottle had been delivered. The quest had paid off, brilliantly. Not only did he know where it was, but he'd actually been there before, not two days ago. The red tattoo ink bottle had been delivered to Papa Midnight Tattoos. 'To easy,' he thought.

So, now, that was where he was headed. He needed that bottle to destroy it. No one else would be infected by the serum. He would be the one and only to have the ability.....the power. Being an ex-employee of NeuralGen laboratories, he was able to navigate the site easily. He had gone back to the section of the website he had found. This area displayed all of the pertinent information that he required.

Luckily, it had been updated daily with the new info.

Nicadimus spoke loudly, while positioning himself behind the boy. "Excuse me, young man."

Turning, Kyle was surprised to see that the same man he met a few nights before, the one that had recommended the tattoo shop. He still wasn't sure what he thought of the man, whether he was dangerous or not. But, he thought he would go with the moment, while still being mindful. "Hey there stranger," Kyle responded. "Thanks for the advice on the shop to go to." He held up his hand for Nicadimus to see. "They did a great job."

Looking closer at the design on his hand, Nicadimus had to agree. Even though it was a very dangerous symbol, it was still done very well. "Yes, that is a fantastic job," Nicadimus allowed. "Um.......I think I just saw something happen here. There was lightning and you getting hit......and appeared to be on fire...." Nicadimus spoke all of this with a light and concerned tone, but his eyes never strayed from the boy's face, intent on looking for any tell of the untruth.

The body language was not at all lost on Kyle. He read the tone of concern, but knew it to be fake. He saw the eyes. He couldn't help but wonder what this man's play was. It was even more concerning to Kyle, as he could not get into his head. But, he still responded cheerfully, "You saw that? I didn't think anyone was around."

"Right over there in my car," answered Nicadimus. "I was about to get out, but then the lightning came down on you. Are you ok? You looked like you were one fire."

"Actually, I feel the best I have in my whole life," Kyle answered. His eyes swelled with color, making Nicadimus want to back away, but he was not willing to give an inch.

"Where are you going?"

"I'm going back to the tattoo studio where I got this," Kyle answered. "I have a couple of questions to ask."

"Mind if I walk with you?" Nicadimus asked.

Hesitatingly, Kyle answered. "Sure...I guess. Are you going to the same place?" "I'm friends with the owner. I stop by to talk with Damion, every now and then."

"Cool, well let's walk," Kyle said, in reply. He was desperately sending out his mind to see what was happening in this man's head, and why he was interested in him, but all that he could get was the same, closed door.

"We are closer to my shop than Papa Midnights," Nicadimus said. "Care if we stop by first. I need to grab a couple of things."

Kyle's curiosity suddenly peaked.

"Sure...you have a shop?"

"Yes, it is a spiritual business. Nothing fancy." Nicadimus said this so nonchalantly, that Kyle was all but certain that it was only a half-truth. There was far more to this man than he was willing to show on the surface.

The two walked and talked for the next couple of blocks, exchanging pleasantries and getting to know each other better. They talked in a forced level of comfortability. But, it was clear that they both were wary of each other, recognizing it as such.

Finally, Kyle questioned, "I gotta ask.....what is up with the top hat?" Rubbing the brim of the hat in a playful way, Nicadimus responded. "You know, I just get the feeling that it completes me. It's an old style that needs to be brought back, I think. So, I'm trying to make it catch on in the city. Unfortunately I'm the only person wearing one still, after seven years. Now it is a trademark of mine."

"That's cool how you are not scared to be different," Kyle said. "I'm just now learning to do that, in my own way. This tattoo is my first step. Well...." He paused, with a slight smirk. "I've done a few other things recently that are uncharacteristic of me."

Nicadimus could tell the boy was referring to some sort of negative happenings that he had caused, most likely. Finally, they found themselves standing in front of the voodoo shop.

Pulling out the old key and sticking it into the door lock, Nicadimus said, "Here we are...." He let the young man in and shut the door behind him. Kyle marveled at the collection in the store. The man had told him it was spiritual, but this resembled more of a witch doctor's dwelling.

"So....what kind of stuff is this?" Kyle asked, genuinely interested.

"Well, it goes by a few different names," Nicadimus began, "Spiritual, magic, voodoo,

Obeah.....whatever you want to call it really." He swept his arms around the room and continued. "All of these things are old and original New Orleans bred magical relics. Everything in here has a purpose."

Kyle nodded his head in understanding. He moved from left to right taking in everything. He was obviously fascinated, that Nicadimus could see. He, however, was not looking at anything in his store. He was paying attention to only Kyle.

He looked intently at the kid's hand. The fresh tattoo was swollen, but bright as can be. The blues that the artist had managed to sculpt in it were impressive. After seeing what Kyle had done with the storm and with being hit by lightning and surviving, Nicadimus had finally concluded that he would need to intervene. Until more was known of the boy, he would have to put a stop to things progressing.

Kyle had picked up a solidified chicken foot, with bead and vines flowing from it. He held it in the air, shaking it a bit to get a better look at it. The kid smiled with a near childlike enthusiasm.

"Elephantine......transfersiiii.

Monoassssssiii..." he chanted, while looking at the boy, holding his hands toward him, palms out. Kyle looked over at the man mortified.

What the hell are you doing?" Kyle asked, in terror. He sent out his strongest probe, yet, but only found it batted away, surprising and scaring him deeply. Kyle looked down to see that his hand had begun to glow. They both looked at it, surprised, but it caused Nicadimus to start chanting louder to speed up the spell.

The kid's new tattoo got brighter, almost as if it were actively trying to resist the man's chanting. Kyle started to walk towards him, like a ravenous beast seeking its prey. He seemed to be almost possessed by something. But then yellow light circled them both, making vision hard for them. The sparkles cracked and ...poof....they were gone.

They reappeared almost instantly, on the inside of Nicadimus's private studio. They looked at each other, Nicadimus in curiosity, Kyle in absolute hatred. He tried to act, to lash out at this crazy individual, but he found himself thoroughly stuck. He couldn't move his legs at all. He tried to lash out with his mind, but was batted away again, as if his power was nothing.

"No point in struggling kid, "Nicadimus said, after he had planted himself in his favorite seat. The spell takes away movement of the lower half of your body. You are not going anywhere until I let you. There is something strange about you. I need to find out more about you, before I let you walk my streets any longer."

Kyle was bewildered. "Did we just teleport?" he asked, in shock. "How is that possible? And did you say you put a spell on me? What are you?"

"So many questions," Nicadimus said, with a frown. "I will answer some of them, but then we move on to things about you. Magic is real....let that sink in for a second....I'm a sorcerer from a long line of sorcerers. Yes, I made it to where you can't move. But, I won't keep you here long, if I like what you have to say."

Kyle was still in a state of shock, as he looked around the office. There is no door. I don't understand how that is possible. Kyle was still sending out probes of the man's mind, trying to figure out what was going on here.

Nicadimus looked at him seriously.

"You can only enter this room through magic," he said. "I am in control, here. Tell me what I want to know. Tell me about your eyes. They are far too bright to be natural. Did you know that you glow, as well? I think it is when your emotions get elevated, but I am not sure. Something is going on in there. Not to mention your choice of a first tattoo, on your hand and of a Voodoo nature."

"Okay, okay," Kyle finally whispered. "I was on an internship and scholarship in Japan. I was working in a lab and something fell in my eye, then they started glowing." Kyle was talking, but he was doing everything in his power to send out probes. He tried everything that he had been able to learn he could do over the past few weeks. Everything was batted away with ease. 'What in god's name was going on?' he thought.

He kept talking, trying to gain time.

"That is not the only thing though." Kyle tiptoed around the next sentence. "I can also.....kinda.....read minds....well maybe not read them...but hear what others are thinking.

Except you that is. You are the first I haven't been able to pick anything up from."

Nicadimus looked at him sternly. "I know of no magic that would make that ability possible," he said. "Whatever fell into your eye made that possible. Which is incredible by the way. But the lightning hitting you and doing nothing at all to you? That was magic.

Brought on by that tattoo on your hand.

The symbol you chose brings death from above. That is one of the meanings of the image. It has others, but that one stands it most. Its magic must have sensed whatever is different inside of you and protected you from the lightning. You somehow knew that subconsciously holding your hand towards the sky would stop the storm, as well. We have a blend of science, magic, and supernatural occurrences happening inside you. You see my concern."

Kyle was beginning to get irritated by his immobility. Ya! I get it! But do you always kidnap people to figure this stuff out?!!"

"Only ones that could be a danger to others," Nicadimus responded, calmly. "It is my job to protect the innocent from humans with abilities." He stopped to look at Kyle with his most intense and penetrating stare. "People like you...." The look he gave could have frozen stone, but Kyle was beyond caring.

He struggled, bending and swaying as far as possible, trying to reach anything in the room with his hands. It was no use though. Nicadimus had perfectly placed him where he could grab nothing. Without his mind reading, he could do nothing."

"Settle down," Nicadimus snapped, his command breaking through. He had gotten directly into Kyle's face. "You are stuck here, until I feel it is ok to free you. So you had better start impressing me or at least convincing me that you are harmless."

Kyle discontinued the quest to try to free himself. It was obviously no use, but he couldn't bend to this man's will. There were principles, after all.

The man went behind the century old desk and took his seat, again, while reclining back a bit and looking at Kyle. "What are you doing in New Orleans?" Kyle didn't answer, pretending to not have heard the question. "Apparently we have stumbled upon a subject that you don't like," Nicadimus said with interest. "I will ask again. What are you doing in my city?" Kyle rubbed his eyes in an exhausted fashion. There was no point in lying to the man.

Kyle finally responded. "The accident in

Tokyo started all this," he said. "When I was on duty, it was my fault that the vial dropped. While one fell into my eye, the other fell into a bottle of ink that was being produced on a conveyor belt. The type of ink being produced is for body art. So, whoever gets that bottle of ink may potentially inject it into someone else, possibly giving them my same abilities. I don't want that to happen. So......I'm in search of that damn bottle to take it and destroy it." He said with disdain.

"Are you trying to save other people from this? Or are you trying to keep it for yourself?"

A look that resembled a thieving troll came over Kyle. It was one of lust and greed.

"I'm keeping it for myself. No one will have this gift but me," he said, his eyes gleaming with absolute malevolence.

Nicadimus was severely taken aback by the intensely creepy response. He turned his head away from the boy to think. The kid was obviously going down a dark path that would lead to the death of himself or someone else.

"My name is Kyle by the way," Kyle said, with disgust. "Stop calling me kid and boy. I hate that. I tracked the bottle to the same shop I got this tattoo from yesterday. Can you help me retrieve it?"

Nicadimus continued to ponder on what

Kyle said, without responding. This meant that Nicadimus could consult with Damion about the whereabouts of the bottle. He would leave the boy here for the time being. He stood up and moved to stand in front of Kyle. "Thank you for your honesty. I'm leaving you here for now, while I find out more about this bottle and some more about that tattoo on your hand."

Chapter 18

New Orleans

Nicadimus watched Kyle as he struggled against the invisible bonds set by the magic.

'What in the hell was he going to do with this kid,' Nicadimus thought. It was clear that he was incredibly powerful and probably growing more powerful by the minute. How to break him of this? Nicadimus knew of a lot of high level spells, ones that could do some amazing things. But to remove powers from someone? That, he wasn't sure how to do. He sighed, heavily.

Getting to his feet, Nicadimus approached slowly towards Kyle. The young man looked up at him with ill-kept fury. The emotion was easy to read in his face. He wanted to harm Nicadimus. That was very clear. "What are you going to do with me?" sneered Kyle.

"I don't know yet," replied Nicadimus, truthfully. "I have to find out some more information. But, for now, you have to stay here." He looked seriously at Kyle, while the boy glared at him, daring him to touch him. Nicadimus could feel the push in his mind, as the boy tried to read his thoughts. It was a nagging, stabbing pain, but one that he could easily resist. "I'll be back." "You do that….." replied Kyle, smartly.

Nicadimus stood up and walked away from Kyle, without giving him that benefit of showing how uneasy he felt. Murmuring under his breath, Nicadimus flashed away into a shower of orange sparks. He had vanished into nothing.

"What in the hell!" cursed Kyle. He had been trying desperately to get a read on

Nicadimus, but couldn't batter his way into the man's mind. Kyle was starting to get very worried, as he realized he could do absolutely nothing. His feet were firmly planted into the ground, no matter what he did, he wasn't moving anywhere. The anxiety started too well, as he tried to decide how he was going to get out of this. He was terrified that the man was going to come back and kill him….

Nicadimus had reappeared in a flash, just on the other side of the door and into his shop. 'I need more information,' he thought. He was thinking about the book that Arthur was supposed to get him. It was set to be delivered via overnight service. Nicadimus looked at his watch and saw that he had roughly ten hours until delivery. That translation was crucial, he realized. He knew that the spell for increasing his power would be in there. He figured he was going to need that extra power to do what he would probably have to do.

'First things, first,' he thought. Let's track down that bottle and tie up that loose end. He walked out of the store, and headed towards his car and the short walk it would take to get to

Papa Midnight's Tattoo. As he walked, he couldn't help but be pulled deep into his thoughts, trying to figure out what to do with

Kyle. He did want to help the boy, but he wasn't sure there was going to be a way to make it happen.

He was troubled, there was no doubt. Above him, as he passed through the old quarter of the city, the skies were dark and cloudy. Once again, he heard the distant crackle of thunder. The rain was coming back, again, he thought. Another part of his brain was questioning whether this was Kyle doing this, or not. He was certain that this might be him, as he was certainly in an angry and brooding mood, when he had left. The walk wasn't far, as his shop was fairly close to Papa Midnight's Tattoo shop.

So, it didn't take long, before he was standing in front of the shop. He hoped he could find some answers. As he stood out front and stared in through the heavy plate glass windows, Nicadimus could only stare at his friend, Damion, on the inside of the shop. He had no idea what he was going to say, once he got in there. But, he had a responsibility to attend to.

Walking in, he could see where Damion was helping a young girl, with a drawing. Nicadimus was again, stunned, with the sight of her. It was the same girl that he had seen in the cemetery. "What is going on, here?" he whispered, to himself. He suddenly realized where he had seen her, before this, as well. She had been one of the young ladies that had stared at him in the coffee shop.

'To many coincidences,' he declared, in his mind. Once again, he wondered at the power this girl seemed to have. She wasn't like Kyle, at least not yet. She had the potential, but, as far as he could see, she was still normal, and therefore, not a threat. He just stood to the side, waiting for Damion to notice him. Behind him, another gulf storm started, again.

"Okay, Jessica," Damion said, as

Nicadimus listened into the conversation. It is getting really late and we should probably get you out and home. We don't need you being exhausted for your first day of learning about the tattoo gun, do we?" He said the last with such a big smile, that Nicadimus almost felt like reciprocating....almost.

"Oh, I am so excited," Jessica gushed, happily. Her expression and face showed exactly what she was thinking and feeling. She was close to getting to help a person, she knew it. "Could I take a kit home tonight, and practice on one of the training cloths?"

Damion almost said no, but he couldn't resist her enthusiasm. She was eager, that much he knew. "Okay," he finally relented. "But, promise you won't be up all night with it, practicing, okay. I want you at your best, tomorrow."

Jessica agreed, wholeheartedly, grabbed the kit and a bottle of ink, and headed out the door with a smile at Nicadimus. She barely glanced at him, as she rushed into the blossoming storm. It was then that Damion saw Nicadimus, for the first time. His wide and genuine smile fell in an instant.

"Nicadimus..." said, Damion thoughtfully. He had known the man for years. He was literally infamous in this part of the world. Being fellow shop owners, they had come across each other frequently. Nicadimus was a very nice man, but truthfully, he had always creeped out Damion. It was the shop and his manner of dress. If he had to admit it, Damion would have said that he was just simply uncomfortable being around him. "What brings you to my end of Bourbon Street?" Damion said, after a near awkwardly long pause.

"I am simply needing information," Nicadimus replied. "I have recently made the acquaintance of a young man that came through your shop. I want to know more about him."

"Nicadimus," Damion responded, tonelessly. He wore an intense frown on his face. "You know that I cannot give that information out to people. It is confidential."

Nicadimus waved that away with a brush of his hand. "That doesn't interest me," Nicadimus said, with intense seriousness,

"Besides, we have been friends for how long...? You owe me some help, Damion."

Damion looked at him intently. He was afraid that this was where the conversation was going to go, from the moment that the Voodoo store owner had walked into his Tattoo shop. Five years back, Damion had been accosted by several street thugs, when he had locked up the store. They had beat him severely, trying to get his keys to get back in and at the till.

Damion had thought that he was finished, that he was going to be murdered by these people, but then, salvation had come, in the form of Nicadimus and his walking cane. He had beaten every one of the men to the ground and subdued them. Damion owed the man his life, but he was still very uncomfortable around him. Now, it seemed that the marker was coming due.

Damion sighed heavily. This was going to go against his principles, but it had to be done. If it hadn't been for Nicadimus, Damion would not be where he was today. He never could have gotten here, he would have been dead five years ago. "Okay," he finally said, "What do you want to know?"

Nicadimus looked at him, still wearing the same serious tone. "This young man is dangerous. I think you made him even more dangerous with the Tattoo."

"How is that possible?" Damion asked, confused. "How would you even know of these things?"

Nicadimus paused, in serious thought. He knew that Damion would want to know more. But, divulging those true secrets of his would be costly. Nicadimus was known as the kindly, but eccentric, shop keeper of Voodoo and other "creepy" stuff from the area's lore and mythology. Nobody knew that he was intensely powerful, but Arthur. No, this one had to be played delicately. "I do know a lot about what I sell," he began. "The symbol that you carved onto the boy's skin was a very dangerous summoning script. Witch doctors use it to control."

"Control?" asked Damion, "What does it help them to control?"

"Everything?" Nicadimus whispered, eyes wide. "I must know where he got this symbol and if there are others around? This is very dangerous Black Magic."

Damion had to think for a minute. "The only copy that Kyle would have seen was in a book that my intern had. She bought it from a bookstore, she said." He looked over in the direction that Jessica had left to, not too far in the past, but snapped his head back quickly.

"Wait. I have seen that picture before! It was in a collection of art that my secretary bought. Stay right here. I'll go and get it."

Nicadimus was shocked at the revelation. Why would anyone be drawing real Voodoo symbols and selling it as art? He suddenly realized he had far more serious issues to deal with, and in his own backyard!!!

He had to find all of this art. He looked up as soon as Damion came into view. He was holding a manila folder that seemed to be brimming with old parchment paper.

"This is it," said Damion, as he handed Nicadimus the file. He immediately opened it up and started flipping through it, his heart immediately skipping a beat. Every page he looked at was filled with the worst possible examples of Voodoo power. It was absolutely sickening. There was a resurrection glyph, a demon summoning glyph, and a mark of power that would give you the ultimate control over someone's thoughts.

Nicadimus was beyond shocked. Why in god's name would someone do this? How would someone know of this, this level of power? He had to stop the creator and burn all of these papers. He stopped to think. 'Why was so much happening, all at once?" he thought.

"May I take these?" he asked. This was necessary. If Damion did not let him have them, he would have to take them.

Though Damion looked a bit surprised at the request, he didn't think he was going to be given much of a choice. He figured he might as well just let it happen. He silently shook his head in agreeance. He hoped that this meant he could safely see Nicadimus out the door, but he was proved wrong, very quickly.

"One more question, if you please,"

Nicadimus said, thoughtfully. "That was some amazing and vibrant ink that you had used for Kyle's tattoo. May I see it? I wondered what chemicals were used. It was amazing."

Damion was expecting something far worse than this, another demand that he might not be able to accomplish. But, this was easy.

"Sure," Damion replied. He was a bit surprised, but if he could get Nicadimus out of the shop by only getting him an ink bottle, then that would be nothing. "Hang on. I have to look up the serial numbers and find the right one."

Damion searched for it, but came back with a look of surprise on his face. "That is odd," Damion replied, with a perplexed look on his face. Nicadimus cocked his head, asking for some clarification. "I found the right serial number, but it is not in the stock of supplies, or anywhere else in the store." He shook his head. "I guess I can't help you, Nicadimus. I don't know where it went."

Nicadimus nodded his head and shook it off, accepting the reply. He thought he might know exactly where the ink was, having seen the young girl carrying one in her hand, as she had left.

Chapter 19

New Orleans

Voodoo shop

Kyle stood right where Nicadimus had left him, directly at the middle of the floor in the hidden office. "What in the world is going on, here," he spoke aloud. "This just can't be happening." There was no way that the man could do this. It just wasn't possible. 'But, neither is reading minds, Kyle,' he thought. The world had gotten far stranger over the last couple of weeks.

"Okay, Kyle," he whispered to himself. "How are you going to get out of this?" There was no way he was going to let himself still be here at this shop when the crazy man got back. Kyle just knew he was going to be killed, probably in a very brutal fashion. But how to do it.

Kyle had been watching when Nicadimus had cast the spell that was holding him in place. It had been done from across the room, near an antique desk in the corner. Even from here, Kyle could tell that the desk, and the adjacent shelf, were filled with old and probably very arcane books. Could they be of help? Probably, but they were too far away and he wouldn't know what to do with them, if he could reach them.

He looked around himself, hopefully, trying to think of a way out of this predicament. There was absolutely nothing in reach, he could see, in despair. But, even if he could reach something, there was no way that he could possibly know how to use it to break this binding. He was dead! Looking in the far distance, he could see several large knives stuck in the wall, big and savage looking. Kyle cringed, thinking of what that would do, as it seemed to be the logical choice for his demise.

"How do I get out?" Kyle sobbed. He was trying desperately to reach something, anything. Outside, the distant crackle of thunder started to sound, signaling another change in the weather. As Kyle's emotions sunk, the sky darkened, showing an ominous connection that he now had, but one he hardly knew how to control.

Kyle's face was contorting in a spasm of grimaces, almost as if he were having convulsions. The part that would have disturbed Nicadimus was that Kyle didn't seem to be aware of anything. The fact he was causing physical changes in his world, without his knowledge, was terrifying. No, Kyle was a danger to himself and everyone around him.

That was when Kyle glanced up and saw the knives, again. 'Maybe,' he thought, with a whisper. He tried to think of how he would do it. The knives were about ten feet away. Kyle thought crazily that it might be that his shoes were the part that was attached to the floor. "If I can cut my shoes loose." The thought signified his rapidly declining mental state. The possibility of simply taking his shoes off had never occurred to him.

Rapidly, a plan now forming in his mind, he stripped off his belt and held the end opposite the buckle. He estimated that he had about three feet, which was not going to be enough. 'My shirt,' he thought, suddenly, removing it quickly. He tied them off, seeing that he now had a reach of about six feet.

"Yes," he whispered. He just had to reach it. Coiling it up, above his head, he visualized exactly where he wanted it to go and threw with every bit of his strength. So, it was to his complete shock, when the collection of makeshift rope hit the knife directly and knocked it to the floor.

"Well I didn't see that coming," Kyle said, suddenly in a cheerful mood, his mournful attitude shifting in an instant to one of near happiness. He could see a way out. He could also see, amazingly, that the knife was caught up in his clothing. There were no obstructions in his path. He started pulling on his belt to draw it back to him.

"Yes!" Kyle exclaimed happily, a peal of thunder sounding outside. The rain was falling heavily now, having picked up to match his mood.

Kyle reached for the knife, before realizing that he couldn't even bend over at the knee. "What the hell!' he cursed, his happy disposition gone in an instant. He could do nothing and he fully realized it, now. He raged, he cursed, and he flung himself about in every direction. His glow was massive, a light blue aura that filled him in his entirety, bathing the room in a pulsating cascade of blue spears, almost like lightning strikes. The center of the storm was upon them, directly overhead. Lightning spears the landscape in time with Kyle's pulsating.

Then, just as suddenly, Kyle stopped, his mood changing in an instant. He nearly collapsed upon himself in his grief. "This is so unfair," he whispered. "I never hurt anyone....." He was nearing tears, at this point.

"I would never hurt anyone." If Nicadimus could have seen him, he would have finished him off immediately, at that point. He would have been so startled at Kyle's ever changing appearance and mannerisms, that he would have felt he had no choice.

But Kyle, an inner voice spoke. What about the old lady at the Marina? You definitely hurt her. "NO!" Kyle exclaimed, loudly, through his tears. "I didn't!"

Yes, Kyle, you did, spoke that same voice. You are a taker. You stole that woman's boat and her credit card. She was old, Kyle. The stress of that, and what you threatened to do, gave her a heart attack.

"I didn't cause that!," Kyle yelled, his face switching in an instant, from a quivering and crying mess, to one of absolute rage. "I didn't! Whoever you are, you shut up! Or else!"

Or else what, boy! The inner voice yelled back at him. You can do nothing! You were trapped by Nicadimus. He is more powerful than you ever could be! All you can do is just stand there like a worm. That is what you are, a

WORM!

"Don't you call me that!" Kyle suddenly screamed. "Don't you call me that!!!" Kyle's face was livid, almost demonic in its appearance. His appearance was nearly primeval in its anger and rage. "He surprised me. He will not do that again."

You can do nothing, WORM! The voice screamed back at home, so loud that books started to fall from the shelves. You are weak. You are a coward that preys on those that are weaker. You would never be able to defeat a powerful person like Nicadimus.

He had been getting very mad by the time that Nicadimus had left. Before that, Kyle had only been scared. But, that had changed. The more he struggled, the more he raged. Now, after several hours of fitfully trying to figure out how to escape, he was in a mental state that was incalculable. The taunting and evil voice was just too much; too much stress combined with the fragile state of his mental being.

He couldn't see it, but he was positively glowing. His eyes sparked icy fire, sending a cascade of dancing blue flame across the room.

He fought and he fought, but it was to no avail. Suddenly let loose with a blood curdling scream, "Ahhhhhh!!!!!" he shrieked.

It was that moment, that he felt something let loose in his mind, something physically changed and he realized that he no longer felt mad, he was calm, and icy calm that flooded his mind. It was a physical feeling, nothing in his imagination. He felt as if ice water had invaded his skull and was soaking into his brain tissue. It would have been a very disturbing image if he had stopped to think about it. As it was, he simply relaxed and enjoyed the calming sensation that it brought him.

What he didn't realize was that he had just suffered a small aneurysm, brought on by his raging blood pressure that had been exceeding nearly 200 beats per minute. It wasn't enough to kill him, but it did flood his brain with some of his blood, a very potent and contaminated mixture that was filled with the modified chemicals of tattoo ink.

He hadn't known it, but the ink from his tattoo had been slowly leaching into his bloodstream, enhancing all parts of his body that it touched. Now that it was literally soaking into his brain tissue, he felt his body surging with the energy and power that it provided. "Oh, my….." he whispered deeply, as he ran his hands across his head, literally feeling the pulsing of his own heartbeat through his skull.

When he opened his eyes, he was shocked to see that some of the littlest things had changed, things that you tend to take for granted. He opened his eyes and saw color, not the typically pattern of assigned colors to objects, that we would see. Instead, he saw a free flowing blur of colors that floated around the room, like clouds chasing each other in the sky. "Wow!" he breathed. "This is amazing."

He looked to the wall and saw that he could literally see the electricity circulating through the wires. He looked to the floor and realized, with a bit of shock, that he could even see heat marks, from Nicadimus's feet, as he had walked from the room. Looking down at his own feet, his face split into a grin, seeing the predicament that he was in and realizing how easy it was to fix.

It seemed that Nicadimus was manipulating actual energy around him! Now that Kyle could also see it, he realized what was happening. He had been secured from roughly the waist down by a large block of energy that had solidified around him, much like ice. Ice was easy to take care of, he realized.

Concentrating hard, he focused his energy into his hand, knowing that the Tattoo was very powerful, now, and lashed out. His hand positively glowed with energy, the skull staring back at him with a fire that was not of this earth. The moment that Kyle slapped at the restraints, they shattered into dozens of pieces, falling away to the floor. He stepped away with a triumphant look on his face.

Outside, a violent stab of lightning crashed into the city, not too far in the distance. The storm stopped, immediately, though the sky still ruled in a darkened and haunting manner. A resident looking up would have said, "It isn't over yet…"

"Not bad, boy," came a voice from behind him. Startled, Kyle turned around, not sure what to expect. What he saw was surprising, but he was beyond shock, now. It was a figure, a figure of a woman. But, he could not see a large amount of detail. He could only see a vague outline, as she was silhouetted in a corona of light.

"Oh," answered Kyle, calmly. "It's you." He continued staring at her calmly, almost coldly. "So, I'm not a worm anymore; I'm back to a boy?"

All Kyle heard was a throaty chuckle.

"Well, you are not as much of a disappointment as I thought. There is hope for you, yet!"

"For what?" Kyle asked, seriously. "What do you want with me?" Kyle wasn't scared anymore. He looked on the apparition with mild amusement and scorn. What could she do with him? He could bend the environment to his will. She was nothing....

"Power...." she said. "What else?" The light shimmered brightly, radiating a strong glow that Kyle felt drawn towards powerfully. "Come and find me."

Kyle felt in her thrall. The power that surged through him and ignited his brain with its radiating cold was nothing compared to what he felt she could offer to him. He wanted more.

"Yes," he replied eagerly. "Yes! Where are you?" But, she was already starting to fade from view, the vibrant colors disappearing rapidly.

"St. Francisville...." it whispered. "You'll find me." Then, she was gone. Also, the lurid colors had faded away `in his surroundings, until it was just a room again.

"St. Francisville," Kyle murmured. "I'll be there." He walked over to the wall, the one that he figured was the entrance to the rest of the shop. As he could see, there was no exit. He smirked mildly, knowing that was nothing to him, now. He could feel the power in his head, as his mind pulsed heavily to the beat of his heart.

Raising up his tattooed hand, he saw it was glowing heavily, his hand encapsulated in the halo of power. In the end, all he had to do was simply lay his hand on the wall. It exploded outwards in a fusillade of wood and plaster, leaving a gaping hole in the middle. "Yes….." he breathed. With a smile, he walked away and into the night.

Chapter 20

Jessica's House

After leaving the Tattoo shop, Jessica had hurried home. She wasn't terribly worried about being home so late. She figured that she would be able to sneak in through the back door, without her parents seeing her. She didn't want her mom getting excited over having been out so late, due to her work at the Tattoo shop. She had just gotten settled over the idea of Jessica having work at such an establishment. There wasn't any reason to disturb her.

She hadn't bothered to get a bus, though there probably wouldn't have been one this late, anyway. Instead, in her excitement, she had practically ran home. She had run at a fast clip down Bourbon Street, which was still very much active at this hour, despite it being nearly eleven at night. Clutching the Tattoo kit and her bag closely, she made excellent time to her house, which was only about a dozen blocks away from the shop.

'Oh, I can't wait,' she thought to herself. She was brimming with enthusiasm to be able to get a start on the Tattooing, despite it being incredibly late. As she walked onto her parent's property, she couldn't help but admire the large Plantation style house that she lived in with them. It was a gorgeous building, full of southern charm.

There was a large wrap around porch that spanned for the majority of the house, on all sides. Bouncing up the steps, Jessica could see immediately that her dad had been up to some work. "Oh, dad," she remarked. Her father had been talking about updating the house, due to all of the heavy storms that had passed through the area, recently. It had greatly unnerved him to be in an old house, without ensuring it to be properly grounded.

She could see large piles of debris and work equipment scattered across the porch. Her parents could easily have afforded to hire out the work, but her father wouldn't hear of it. He said, "I cannot pay someone to do something that I am more than capable of doing myself. So, he did, much to her mother's and her dismay.

As for Jessica, she thought it best to contribute to the small businesses in the area, but her vote didn't count. It didn't matter that her father really wasn't the best at this sort of thing. He just plowed ahead and got into it, consequences aside.

Looking at the porch, Jessica was able to see the evidence of it right in front of her. She didn't think her father was doing a good job of improving the safety conditions of the house. In fact, she thought he might actually be making things a bit worse. But, she would keep her mouth shut, as her father would eventually get fed up and hire someone.

As she walked into the home, the first crackle of thunder sounded in the distance, and a brief flurry of rain hit her in the back. "Not again," she grumbled. It seemed that this season of weather would never be past them. She closed the door gently and headed to her room, without alerting her parents.

Once there, she settled into her desk and pulled out all of the equipment, really studying it. This had been her dream for as long as she could remember, being able to create art like this, for people. Looking at every piece, intently, she reviewed the lessons that Damion had given her.

He had spoken of taking things slow, at first. He wanted her to remember the lessons he had drilled into her thinking for the last week. 'Remember the steps, girl,' she told herself. She couldn't go back and erase someone's skin, if she made a mistake. She had to be perfect, in everything that she did. She planned to do just that, she reflected, with a smile.

She looked at the tattoo gun that she had pulled out of the box that Damion had let her take. It looked just like a large and very fat pencil, she thought. Holding it was an almost religious experience for her. She was reminded of the time that she had first picked up a pencil, when she was probably five or six years old. Even though that had been some time ago, she still held a memory of the events.

She remembered how she had felt. It had been fascinating to her, even then. When her mother had shown her how the pencil could be scraped across the paper and pictures could be created. The magic that the long ago pencil had held had been amazing to her, opening worlds that she never had known existed. She was hooked.

Now, holding the tattooing gun, she had the same feeling. It was an awakening. She was ready for this next evolution in her work, as an artist. This first tattoo would be an experience unlike any other.

But, Jessica was suddenly rocked with indecision. She knew that she should be practicing on the canvas, first, before moving to skin.

However, it was so hard to resist the pull, knowing the absolute pleasure that she would get from practicing on real skin. She was good enough, she knew. It would be just like the work she had been doing on paper. Her confidence was at an all-time high.

Suddenly, she knew exactly what she had to do. "I'm ready!" she whispered, fiercely. "I've got this." Jessica knew that she wanted to give herself a tattoo. She knew how to work the tattoo gun and she was a heck of an artist. She pulled out everything, including the ink that Damion had given her.

'Interesting,' she thought. She held up the bottle of ink to the light, seeing the glow that was cast through it. She could see, immediately, that it was a fiery blue that sparkled and danced in the moonlight that shined through her open window. It was the exact same ink that was used on that cute boy that came to the shop the other day, she realized.

That was what gave her the idea, firmly cementing the plan in her mind. She was definitely going to give herself a tattoo and she knew fully what one it was going to be. The kit was ready, she was ready. She reached for the small book that she now carried everywhere she went and flipped to her favorite picture. Outside, the storm raged.

Nearly an hour later...........

"Oh, wow!" Jessica breathed, in amazement. She was staring at her thigh, right on the side of the big muscle. The tattoo stared back at her, flawless! It was a bright and shining blue that perfectly mirrored the picture inside of the tattooing book that she had bought. It glistened with an iridescent glow, even without the light. There was even a slight glow from under the skin. Amazing!

She looked at the picture and grinned wildly. It was the same skull, with coins in the eyes and a blade wrapped around the back. It was beautiful! She had done it! It had taken longer than she originally figured it would, but she was able to create the tattoo, perfectly. It stared back at her with malevolent intent.

"Good thing I put this on my leg," she whispered to herself. It was high enough up that she knew no one in her family was ever going to see it. She would be safe. It was of concern, only because she knew her mom and dad would never approve. Her mom had just gotten used to the idea of her working at a tattoo studio. A tattoo! Never!

Jessica had been so focused on her work with the tattoo, that she had barely noticed the noise from outside. It had faded to a faraway drone. The clap of thunder was as rapid as her beating heart, but it didn't penetrate her consciousness. It was almost as if she was on a different level when she was inking, so focused was she.

While she had been working, the storm outside raged. The wind had reached a fever pitch as it beat against the frame of her house, shaking the windows. The thunder cracked and rolled across the sky like the ripples of a rock thrown into a pond. She didn't know it, but no fewer than a dozen lightning strikes crashed into the earth over the course of that span of time. It was almost as if something was alive out there, speaking to the city about dangers that were coming.

That was when it happened. She had been looking at the tattoo in awe, when there was an ear splitting explosion, just outside of her window. Time seemed to slow, as Jessica looked up in time to see the lighting crack across her sightline. It was awe inspiring and terrifying. She had a split second to remember about the missing grounding rods, when a stray arc of electricity blew through the window and rushed straight at her.

"Oh, my god!" she had time to whisper, before it struck her directly in the leg, blowing her backwards for the length of her room. She was knocked unconscious, immediately, as the raw force of nature surged through her body, racing to get to the ground. Blue arcs of electricity danced violently across her body, before withdrawing to the center of her exposed thigh. The tattoo pulsed brightly, a flashing blue, before finally settling into a scarlet and angry red. The color settled into the eyes of the skull, shining with an angry malevolence.

She felt like she had been unconscious for hours, but it was only for mere moments, before she came back to reality. Her body was a picture of aches and torment, every inch racked with pain. But, she barely noticed. Her mind was somewhere else.

"Oh, my," she whispered to herself. The world was different, everything that she saw, was different. Even though she had just been struck by lightning, she barely felt the pain. She should have been collapsed in writhing agony, or even dead. But, now, she was neither. She was able to get up, immediately, and walk around, completely absorbed in her new understanding of the universe.

Everywhere around her was color. She could see great waves of energy broiling and tumbling all around her, as the wind pushed through the broken window. "Wow!" she breathed. The wave of colors that rolled around her reminded her of the great vat of paint, after she had mixed multiple shades together, when she was a kid. She had used to stare at that rolling surface of color for hours, totally enthralled.

On impulse, she reached out with her finger and started tracing designs into the color, just like she once did as a child. "This is amazing!" she spoke, her mind pulled into the act so completely, that she had tuned out the rest of the world.

'A rose,' she thought. 'That would be perfect.' She had been drawing so many over the past couple of weeks that she knew it would be perfect. She could picture it perfectly, in her mind. Without a second thought, using her finger as a paintbrush, she drew one in the swirling mass of color.

She giggled as the shape grew, the dancing colors coalescing around her finger. It was almost as if it was drawn to her. In no time at all, she had a fully formed rose floating in the air, in front of her face. Jessica just wore a huge smile on her face, seeing her creation floating in front of her.

Suddenly, everything changed, in an instant, as her parents came running into the room. Jessica had thought that she had been playing with the color stream, as she was now thinking of it, for hours. But, in reality, it had only been less than a minute or two, since she had been struck by the errant strand of lighting that had come through the window. Her parents had heard, and had come running.

As soon as Jessica's parents came bursting in, her focus was lost, and the stream of colors disappeared in an instant. She blinked back to full awareness, not realizing that what she had been seeing was anything but a normal reality. She looked up at her parents, as they stared at her in fear. They were both looking at her, in shock.

"What in the hell happened here?" asked her father, with a wide eyed sense of amazement and puzzlement. He could see that his daughter was alright, so he wasn't as worried about her. He had been very worried about damage to their old house from the storms. It looked like his worry was well founded.

"Just the storm, dad," replied Jessica, almost dreamily. "Everything is okay. Well. The lighting strike did break the window, but that's it." Her mother said nothing, but did look at Jessica with some alarm, mostly due to how calm she was with the situation. But, she said nothing.

Her father had already moved on to the problem with the window. "Well, hon," he began. "I don't think you can sleep in here, tonight. We have to get that broken window boarded up and clean up this place. The wind still was whipping into the room, spraying rain everywhere. "I'll get some boards to cover up this window and we will take care of it tomorrow."

Jessica just shook her head, in the same dreamy way. "That sounds fine." Her dad just shook his head and walked out, intent on getting the wood and some tools. Her mom said something about getting a towel to clean up the mess, before leaving. Jessica just nodded.

When they left, she was still staring at an object that lay on the ground, in amazement. She had been shocked, but not terribly surprised, to realize that something had happened when she had been drawing with the colors that floated through her room. She smiled as she looked down on the ground. There lay a small red rose.......

When her parents came back into the room, five minutes later, Jessica was gone, no trace of her remaining.

Chapter 21

New Orleans

Voodoo shop

As Nicadimus had been walking back to the shop, he had been deep in thought, trying to figure out what was happening in his city and why. He had to track down the old man that had been drawing Voodoo power symbols and why. He had to be stopped. But, there were more pressing issues to deal with, first.

Nicadimus was sure that Kyle was as dangerous as he felt him to be. What he had witnessed at the shop was enough to convince him of the threat. If he hadn't been convinced, the raging thunderstorm, directly over his head, was more than enough evidence. Kyle was causing this, based on his moods, showing that he had the potential for astonishing powers, but he couldn't yet control them.

No, Kyle had to be stopped. Nicadimus was certain of that. That was why he had left him immobilized in the back room. Nicadimus was sure that Kyle had developed his powers to the point of being able to see the netherworld of energy, as he liked to call it, yet. No, he would be waiting for him, upon his return. Angry and hostile, yes, but still standing in the middle of the room like a stuffed mannequin.

Nicadimus would have smiled at the look of surprise on Kyle's face, when he was immobilized, if it hadn't been such a serious situation. Nicadimus could see that Kyle would soon be able to gain full access to his powers and would then, indeed, be a force to be reckoned with. He had to be taken care of, now.

Suddenly a massive crackle of lightning shot down from the sky to his left. The bolt of lightning slammed into the ground, arcs of white hot fire shooting off in every direction. It would have been a sight to see, if he hadn't had a brief but monstrous shock to his psyche. He suddenly felt an explosion of power rippling in the city, to his front, near his shop. "Oh, god," he whispered. "I'm too late...."

He started to move forward, but another bolt of psychic energy hit him from the side, near the lightning strike. He realized that there was another blooming of energy, coming from that direction, spreading out like the ripples of a bomb exploding. He had time to think, 'There's another.....', before that wave of pure power became visible to his practiced eye and shot across the street. It struck him with a blinding force and he was blown into an adjacent alley, crashing into the dumpsters and garbage cans. He slid on his stomach in a pile of garbage bags, completely unconscious before he stopped.

The following morning.......

"Come on buddy, wake up!" came a stern and commanding voice, bringing Nicadimus to near, but not quite full wakefulness. This voice was accompanied by a less than gentle kick to the foot.

"Whaaa?" began Nicadimus. "Come on," came voice, again, delivering a kick to Nicadimus's leg that woke him completely. "You can't sleep here, fella. Move along."

Nicadimus finally opened his eyes to find himself facing a beat cop with a very angry expression. Well, Nicadimus couldn't have cared less about the cop and his attitude. What he did care about was what had happened while he was unconscious. What had happened with Kyle? What had happened with the other source of energy?

He pulled himself painfully to his feet, marveling at the orgy of pain that his body was experiencing. He mentally tracked the arc he had to have flown, when he had been propelled across the street. What had happened? He had to find out.

The cop was giving him a menacing glare. Nicadimus figured that he probably did look like a mess, having just slept in garbage over the last night. But, he didn't really care. He had much more important things to deal with this morning, than some pushy cop. He pushed past him without comment, heading towards the street.

"Where do you think you are going?" questioned the cop, at his back. Nicadimus didn't bother replying, to him the cop wasn't even there anymore. At the end of the alleyway, he started running.

It had been at least eight hours since he had been in his shop, eight hours since he had left Kyle bound to the floor of his shop.

Nicadimus honestly didn't know what he would find. But, the activity last night wasn't very promising. In his heart, he knew that he was going to find something bad.

Within a few blocks, he was standing in front of his store, stunned, staring inside at the mess. "Oh, my god...." he whispered. First, the door was standing wide open, completely open to the elements. It had been heavily saturated with rain over the night, nearly flooding the interior. As he walked inside, he took in the mess, his store in near ruins and his stock lying cast about everywhere.

But, what really threw his mind into a panicked shamble, was the long wall, behind the register. Normally, it was covered completely by a long stretch of bookcase, filled with a large quantity of his ancient collection of Voodoo literature. Not anymore. The wall appeared to have blown out, from the inside, by a tremendous amount of force. The debris was spread across the entire length of the store.

Everything was coming together, he knew what had happened. What he had suspected was now verified. Walking through the hole in the wall, and into his inner sanctum, he saw that Kyle was nowhere to be seen. He had been left in the middle of the floor, safely connected to the wood through his spell. But, he was gone.

'What happened, here?' Nicadimus questioned, in his mind. But, he knew what had happened. Somehow, Kyle had crossed over, his powers elevating to unimaginable heights. Nicadimus figured that Kyle could now do everything he was able to do, if not more. Nicadimus knew the spells, Kyle could do it with his mind. He had just sealed his death warrant.

Nicadimus closed his eyes, breathing deeply, as he whispered some arcane words, under his breath. His speech was nearly unintelligible, a rapid recitation of words that were long and inarticulate. But, they worked.

When he opened his eyes, the world was changed. It was a swirling kaleidoscope of color that danced and sparkled across the room. He saw what he wanted, almost immediately. His eyes had been drawn to the center of the room that was now completely empty. Kyle was long gone.

But, the part that interested him the most was what had been left behind by the boy. Nicadimus could see the pile of blue shards that were scattered around the floor. He knew what they were, immediately. When he cast a spell of that nature, a binding spell, he manipulated the earth's energy and changed it to suit his needs.

In this case, he had turned the energy into blocks of ice that had frozen him to the ground. There was no way that he should have been able to get the spell broken, but it appeared that he had done just that. It looked, from the evidence that he could see, that Kyle had literally shattered the ice. How in god's name was that possible?

There was clearly a level of magic happening here that he had never known, a level that he didn't think was possible. Only a gatekeeper had the level of skills and knowledge to be able to manipulate the earth's energies. A regular person should not be able to develop these abilities so far, so fast.

Nicadimus stood up and moved right towards his old map. This needed to be finished, now.

After chanting the required spell, he slit a small cut in his hand, releasing several drops of blood onto the map. "Come on," he whispered. "Show me where you are, Kyle." He watched through hooded eyes, as the blood formed into a single droplet, seeming to float on the page. He continued to stare at it, as it revolved in circles around the page, bouncing from street to street, searching for his prey.

Then, suddenly, something strange happened, something Nicadimus had never before experienced. The drops had been focused, zeroing in upon their target location. They had been moving steadily south, towards the water, when they seemed to go crazy. The single bubble of blood burst apart into multiple smaller droplets. These went absolutely crazy. They moved and swirled in circles, racing across the map, before finally settling into multiple and obviously random locations.

It was at that moment that a piercing bolt of pain struck Nicadimus, directly in the skull. It seemed to have come out of nowhere. But, still staring at the Netherworld, he was able to see it, right as it struck him. He could see a bolt of energy, a dazzling blue in color, come flying through the ceiling of his shop, before barrelling into his skull, the force of which drove him to his knees.

"Agggghhhh!" he screamed. "Get out of my head, you bastard!" Nicadimus knew immediately what was happening, but was still shocked that Kyle was able to do it. Nicadimus was on the receiving end of a psychic attack. Only a very talented gatekeeper could perform such an attack. That Kyle could do something that Nicadimus had only just learned to do was terrifying.

Nicadimus was capable of manipulating the Netherworld's energy, but it took a lot out of him. He felt the enormous power and energy that was being delivered into this attack and felt real fear for the first time in a very long while.

'So, you think you can find me?' the voice said in his head, seeming to come from everywhere at once. *'I don't think you want that, anymore, old man. I suggest you stay away from me, before I decide to take care of you!'* The last words were delivered with such force, that Nicadimus fell to the ground, nearly sobbing.

"Oh, my god," he whispered, again.

"What has he become?" Nicadimus knew that Kyle had to be stopped, but he honestly wasn't sure, anymore, if he could. After a time, he was able to pull himself to his feet, realizing that the attack was over, leaving his head aching. The loss of confidence in his skills hurt worse than the pain, though.

"What am I going to do?" he asked himself, in shock. But, just as fast as he said it, he knew. He had to get a hold of that book.

Arthur had been overnighting the book to him. He had to get it and find the spell that he needed to increase his powers. That was the only way he could beat Kyle and even the balance of power.

With a new and steely sense of determination, Nicadimus grabbed several of his throwing knives from the wall and secreted them away throughout his clothing. He was going to war, and he wanted to be ready for anything, as he walked out the door. In the back of his mind, he realized that one of the spots on the map was directly over where he had seen the massive lightning strike from the night before that had caused the energy wave that had knocked him unconscious.

Chapter 22

New Orleans

Kyle had left the Voodoo shop in fine spirits, late the previous evening. His astronomical rise in powers had left him feeling positively giddy. The additional knowledge of the energy that circulated around him was an amazing experience. The fact that he could manipulate it was amazing! All he had to do was think about it, and it happened.

He had thought about being able to increase his abilities to push thoughts into his mind. He knew exactly how to do it, now. When he thought in the color world, he was able to see how he could push the colors, which seemed to be related to his feelings, over to someone else. What he wanted them to see or hear was piggybacked on top of that color. It was as simple as that.

He hadn't tried it yet, but he knew that was what would happen. He could see the thought waves coming from the 'thing' that had talked with him in the store. He could feel her manipulating his mind, as they talked. It was both eerie and intoxicating, as he had learned immediately what he had to do, in order to perfect that skill. He couldn't wait to try it out as soon as possible.

He also had discovered a new talent, one that he had not anticipated being able to do. He knew now, from his experiences in the shop, that he could manipulate the energy into interacting with the real world. That had to be how Nicadimus had trapped him. The moment that Kyle had seen the blue and icy boots that were encasing his legs, he knew that was what the crazy old man had done to him.

From there, it was quite simple to figure out how to get loose. All he had to do was think about it, as he waved his hand over his secured lower half. He had been able to watch as a stream of blue energy shot from his fingertips and interact with the ice. It had shattered on impact.

That moment had changed his life. He had felt the raw energy surge through his body at that moment. The power was incredible. The potential was beyond belief. But, he still wanted more. He felt the draw to the northwest. He knew, without a doubt, that the spirit, or something, that had spoken to him was that way. He didn't know where, but he knew he had to go.

'But, how?' Kyle asked himself. He knew enough of his geography to know that he couldn't get up that way, at least by his boat. But, how? He thought about using his skills, figuring that it would be much easier, this time. A car? Probably the best bet. He had thought about the boat, but knew that he could never get it up that way. There weren't any rivers. Besides, he still had the old ladies credit card.

Standing on the street, thinking about this all, he realized he felt another pull coming his way, this time much closer. He hadn't been outside, during the storm, so he didn't know that there had been a heavy lightning strike just off to the east. He hadn't seen it, but he was able to sense it. "Interesting...." he whispered, raising his nose into the air, almost as if he was smelling something.

Looking through his eyes at the color world, Kyle could see a sharp pulsing bar of color in the direction of the east. It was a wave of light that rolled and flowed in a deep shade of red. "What is this?" Kyle asked, his eyes wide. For some reason, he felt *very* excited by the light. He felt like it was calling to him. He had to go.

Kyle adjusted his sight to normal, just by thinking about it and it happened. He hurried along down the street, feeling the invisible pull that was calling to him. It was almost as if it was a part of his soul, he felt. He couldn't live without heading there.

The night was calm, now that the storm had settled. It was almost unnaturally calm. For anyone to have seen the raging storm, mere moments before, they would have been deeply unsettled at the level of quiet that had descended upon the city. It was if the heavens had been switched off by a benevolent and all powerful being. Kyle didn't know about benevolent, but he certainly felt all powerful.

The energy that flowed through him made him feel like he could do absolutely anything. Though he was no longer looking through the color spectrum of the world, his eyes were burning a deep and aqua blue. He started experimenting at what the limits were, as he walked, of this new power.

He looked at a pile of trash cans in a side alley. Several cats were busy nosing through them, looking for food. Kyle had never been much of a fan of cats, so he didn't mind in the least at what he was about to do. As he imagined it, it happened. What happened, though, happened so fast that even he was surprised.

All he did was imagine the cans being swatted down the alley like they were nothing heavier than tin cans, rather than the full and very weighted objects they were. He simply looked at them and waved his hand to the side. They instantly flew down the side alley, heavy dents in the side. Trash sprayed everywhere, as the cats leapt into the air, screeching in fright.

Kyle watched in amazement as his thoughts became real. He laughed aloud, delighted at what he was now able to do. The cats ran away, terrified. Kyle imaged a minitornado of trash chasing them down the alley and nearly doubled over in coughing fits from the merriment of it all. "This is great!" he roared. But, he quickly realized he wasn't alone.

Though it was terribly late, this was still New Orleans. It was truly a city that never sleeps. He looked to the side, realizing he could hear some thoughts invading his mind. There they were, a man and a woman, obviously just leaving a club, as they were slightly inebriated. He didn't need to see their walking. It was very obvious by the slurred state of their thoughts.

'Woow, didya see that?' said the man, in his thoughts. Kyle could tell that he had believed he had said it aloud and was surprised when his girlfriend hadn't said anything in reply. It wouldn't have been possible for her to form a coherent sentence, even if he had spoken aloud. She was beyond three sheets to the wind drunk. Kyle found that he was able to not only read her thoughts, but he was also able to see the most recent images from her mind.

"Acid....." he whispered, amused. "She had just dropped a massive tab of acid in the bar that she had been at. Her mind was gone! Briefly, Kyle realized he could even see what she was seeing and he nearly burst out laughing.

She stood in stock-still amazement, staring at him. She cocked her head to the side, slightly. He looked just like a giant Easter bunny! He had large swatches of color revolving around him, in just the area that he knew was wind pulsating around. "Trippy," he whispered.

Seeing that now would be an excellent time to mess with someone, he tried to send a 'push' over to her, trying to insert his own thoughts into her mind. He realized instantly that it was working, as the vision that he was seeing through the woman's eyes changed in an instant. When that happened, he was instantly thrown from her mind, as she lost it, screaming.

He knew instantly that the woman had seen what he had sent to her. He had made himself look like a demon, complete with a halo of fire wrapped around his body. The scene looked like something out of the lowest levels of hell. It was terrifying and caused her to nearly black out in fear.

Kyle laughed aloud in delight, seeing the terror in her eyes. She grabbed her boyfriend and literally dragged him up the street, pulling him along physically. "This is awesome!" he said. "I am the greatest!" He walked up the street, his walk much brisker, as he hurried along towards the power that drew him along.

If Nicadimus had seen him now, he would have attempted to kill him on the spot. But, such a thing was no longer certain, not a definite conclusion to a battle that was coming. Kyle glowed a deep and radiant blue, infused with an energy that spread all around him. It was almost a halo that encapsulated his entire body. Little tendrils snaked away from his mind, almost absently, dancing in every direction. It was clear that they were heading towards people.

It was happening without Kyle's conscious thought, now. They were touching briefly on the minds of people that he passed, almost sampling them like a fine wine, before coming back to the host. For that was what Kyle was evolving into, a host. He hadn't knowingly concluded this yet, but he was taking something from these people upon each 'touch'. Maybe a better description would have been a parasite. He was feeding off of these people.

Yes, he had discovered how to insert thoughts into people, 'push' them, if you will. He hadn't yet realized that he was gaining their energy, as he took their thoughts. His power was growing upon each transferral. But, he was discovering the limits of his power, seeing that there were not any, up to this point. He kept finding new things that he could do, delighting in the arcane and powerful skills that he now commanded in himself.

For a second, he thought about whether he was losing his humanity, but then decided it didn't matter. The Kyle that used to work in Japan was nothing, he was a mere cattle. The Kyle that was here, now, was a god. 'Am I a god?' Kyle asked himself, internally. 'No, I think I am better than a god. I am stronger and smarter.'

He switched his vision over to the color world, the Nether, and reveled in the radiant glow that circled him. He could see his mental probes, as they left in every direction. 'No, I am definitely better than God.' His smile was beautiful, almost angelic.

But, it was clear that there was not a shred of humanity left in him. That Kyle had been burned away, the blackened embers of his soul had peeled back, like a rotten piece of fruit, showing the raw and tempered insanity that now controlled him. He had become everything that Nicadimus and the Order of Gatekeepers had feared, an example of everything that they were sworn to protect the world from. Kyle had turned into a monster that was a predatory plague upon the world. His grin, as he walked, was chilling.

Ten minutes later, Kyle had exited the downtown area and had reached the outskirts of the urban stretch. In New Orleans' past, he supposed this was one of the enclaves of the very rich industrialists that built the city. It was a fashionable street, filled with very old and graceful homes that were aging like well-tended sentinels. He thought it interesting, maybe even lovely, this old street with towering Cypress and Oak trees lining the streets.

Maybe the old Kyle would have been awestruck, but the new Kyle, Kyle 2.0, as he was starting to think of himself, really didn't care. He only had eyes for the old plantation house up the street and on his left. That was the source of the power, the energy that had interrupted his thinking and drew him this far away from what he now knew as his true purpose.

He didn't really care about finding the tattoo ink anymore. He had realized that there could never be another being as supremely powerful as he. If someone, by chance, managed to be 'improved' by the ink, then there would be little they could do to impact

Kyle's abilities, or existence. He was too far along in his 'evolution' to be worried by mere mortals.

The house was gorgeous, save for one detail. Kyle could see that it had been recently struck by a bolt of lightning. 'I wonder if that was from my storm,' he questioned himself. He knew that this was where the energy was coming from. He knew!

His eyes were drawn to an upper story window. It had been blown apart, obviously smashed inward by an intense burst of raw energy. He was drawn to it, captivated by it.

That was when he saw her.

She was standing on the porch, simply staring at him in wonder. Kyle stopped his wild train of thought and stared back, equally transfixed. He knew her. He wasn't that far gone to not be able to recognize her. "Jessica...." he whispered. There was something about her that drew him.

'What is it about her?' he asked himself. She was beautiful, he knew. That much was obvious. But, there was something more about her. He didn't realize it, but now he had the same heightened senses that Nicadimus was possessed with, and had used to detect Kyle. He had used it to sense the power emanating from Jessica. It was awesome and it was powerful.

That was when he switched his vision over to see the color of the Netherworld. His eyes were drawn immediately to her. She was glowing! He saw that she was possessed with an eerie and radiant red glow that spilled subty from her eyes. It wasn't bright yet, but it was strong. Kyle sensed that she was immensely strong, perhaps even more powerful than him.

'Wait,' he thought. 'She isn't stronger than me. Yet.' He knew that she was going to be, though, someday. Oddly enough, he wasn't threatened by it. He was intrigued. He walked to her, a smile of pure happiness on his face.

Even though it was covered, he could still see the outline of the tattoo through her clothing. It was the same as his. But, the eyes were glowing a deep and penetrating crimson. He knew how she had changed and he was happy for it. He was thrilled to have someone else with the power, even better that it was her.

"Hello, Jessica," he said, "It's nice to see you again." She turned to him and smiled with a daydreaming look, while her hands drifted lazily in the air, in front of her.

Chapter 23

New Orleans

Nicadimus could feel how wrong his city was. "Why didn't I take care of him?" he cursed himself. "Why was I weak?" But, inwardly, he knew. It wasn't a weakness, it was a spark of humanity. He knew that the taking of a human life was not to be taken lightly. It had to be carefully thought out, planned for, all details covered to ensure he was right about the evil that he was eliminating. He couldn't live with himself if it turned out that he was wrong and had just killed an innocent soul.

But, he knew differently, now. It was obvious, painfully obvious, how wrong he was. The evil that was inside of Kyle was brimming over the surface, spilling out into the real world. The lightning storm from the previous night was evidence enough. The simple fact that Kyle was able to control the weather, but didn't seem to be aware of how to do it was enough. The moment that Kyle was able to control the weather, he could rain havoc upon the city. He would be able to harm so many people.

No, he had to be taken care of. The power that Nicadimus felt coming from Kyle was terrifying. He didn't even have to figure out where Kyle was in the city from looking on the map. Nicadimus was able to feel where he was at. He could look into the distance and literally see the washing of color coming from the distance, a physical wave of blue that broiled in the skies above the city like a thunderstorm. He could see it and felt like it was coming for him.

"What do I do?" Nicadimus asked himself. For the first time, he felt unsure of how to proceed. He felt like Kyle had grown passed him, suddenly having more power than him. Nicadimus wasn't sure if he would be able to stop him. The binding spell was one of his most powerful and Kyle broke it. That was before….what could he do now.

That was when the thought struck him. The solution wound its way up through his troubled mind. The book. It should be arriving today, he realized. Arthur would have finished his magic of translating and sent it. Nicadimus realized that it very well could be waiting for him, right now. He had to get to it.

Nicadimus headed right over to his box, opening it with a level of anticipation that was palpable, almost physical in its need. He was desperate to get the skills he needed to be able to fix this. If the imbalance increased any further, then he realized that the other gate keepers would be able to sense the issue. They would be coming for him. He couldn't have that. That was a battle that he knew he could never win. One, maybe two of the gatekeepers, he could conquer. But, all of them. Not a chance.

"Yes…." he breathed, as the light from the morning sun's rays illuminated the interior of the box and he saw a package that was postmarked from Massachusetts. It was the book. Eagerly, Nicadimus pulled it from his delivery box, rushing back into the ruins of his store, tearing the paper off as he was moving.

As the mottled and wrinkled leather binding came into view, its surface cracked and dried with age, Nicadimus finally found his heartbeat slowing. Just the act of holding this book, this well of knowledge and potential salvation for him, was immensely calming. He felt his center coming back, his abilities to manage the world around him. Even though the turmoil that Kyle and the 'other' that he sensed was still paramount in his mind, he felt, for the first time, that he was going to be able to make it. The answer was within this dry and dusty tome.....he knew it.

Normally, he would teleport himself back into his private quarters in the back of the store for something like this. But, that wasn't an option anymore, he reflected. No, the situation was too urgent. He dropped the book right onto the sales counter and tore the last of the wrapping off, fully exposing the book. Nicadimus felt his pulse start to race again, as he saw the hand written notes that Arthur had inserted into the book, numbered by pages.

'This was it,' he reflected. 'The answers were here!' Nicadimus continued, eagerly, pulling the papers from the book and starting to quickly scan the contents. "Wow!" he exclaimed immediately. He was reading what Arthur had sent him, and was immediately amazed.

The sorcerer, or sorceress, he thought, with a wry sense of amusement, as some of the best gatekeepers had been women that had owned the book had been powerful. He could see some of the initial enchantments that had been outlined and immediately realized that they were psychic dynamite. If someone, the wrong someone, ever got ahold of this book, then there would be hell to pay.

The first spell that Nicadimus read was one that reverses one's age, giving the user back their youth! "Wow!" Nicadimus exclaimed. That would be an amazing spell. It was literally the fountain of youth. He would be able to achieve what so many had sought after, for generations. It was worth a fortune. But, that was not anything that Nicadimus was interested in achieving for the money.

He smiled….it would be nice. But, the upside of the risks would be too great. He knew that almost immediately. 'The last time,' he thought. 'The last time I tried a spell of this magnitude, I lost a huge chunk of my life.' No, it wouldn't be worth it. He certainly didn't trust himself to be able to get that achieved. Not yet, at least.

He tabled that one for later, once he was able to gain more power. He thought he could do it, then, but certainly not now. It wasn't worth the risk. He continued on reading, seeing what else was in this text. "Ha!" he exclaimed, actually amused for the first time in days.

He could see that the magician that created this book had a bit of a sense of humor. The next couple of pages were 'self-help' sort of spells. It was funny to see that even back then, a couple of hundred years ago, people were interested in 'helping' themselves. 'I guess this is a sort of mail order catalogue,' he thought.

The next spell was related to making money. 'Nice, but not really something he needed,' he thought. That was when he found something worthwhile, when the reading got to something he had barely had an inkling of. He started reading about an ancient and parallel part of earth, called the Shadow World.

"The Shadow World," he reflected. As he read, he started to make some serious connections in his mind. Things started to come together and he began to see how much of his power originated from this place. The energy that came from this place was what allowed him to do what he could do. He was able to access this energy, due to his birthright, something that was passed down from his mother, on a genetic level.

But, he had barely touched upon these skills, he realized. He had some of the seeing.

He also could create things from nothing. There was so much more! He saw that he could use the energy to move things. He could use the energy to bind things, something that he already knew how to do. He could even use the energy to read minds! 'Kyle,' he realized, with a start.

The energy could be used to create the most powerful of physical and psychic attacks. He wasn't interested in hurting people, but he wanted to know how to do these things, in order to stop dangerous individuals, like Kyle. "But, how do I do it," he reflected. "How do I tap into this energy at a stronger level?"

That was when he saw it! There was a whole list of skills that he knew he would have to get, in order to be able to become stronger and more powerful than Kyle. Kyle was strong and only getting stronger. Nicadimus started reading. There was the seeing, a skill that would give him complete access to be able to view the Shadow World.

Then, there was the wave. He realized with that one, that he would be able to move objects with his mind. He could create energy waves and propel them across the Shadow World. Because that world was parallel to the real one, it interacted, thus he could literally throw and pull things, just by thinking about them.

He also found out about a very powerful skill called the flame. "Huh," he whispered. "Pyrokinesis." He would be able to make heat and fire from merely thinking about it. "I'm going to set you ablaze kiddo." He was thinking about Kyle, knowing that it would probably be the only thing he could do to make it fully over and save the world.

He kept reading and realized that there were so many more amazing and startling skills. He saw that one allowed for mind reading and mind control. One also allowed for him to control the weather and then water. 'This is horrifying,' he thought. He was, once again, thinking about this book getting into the wrong hands. He kept reading and saw so many more skills that he would have to learn. But, there wasn't time.

A part of his mind was also processing through how many of these skills were ones that Kyle could already do, for some reason. The book that Nicadimus held allowed for him to utilize ritual and prayers, as well specific potions to allow for the skills to be learned and gained. Kyle had bypassed all of that. He was able to grow at an exponential rate, picking up these skills without even working at it.

'No,' Nicadimus thought. 'This ends now.' He pulled out a pen and started marking off the skills that he thought he should be learning first. He had to fully see the Shadow World, not just the fragments that he could recognize, at this point. He needed full access.

After that, he picked up several of the power skills, for both attacks and defense.

He quickly gathered up the necessary materials that he needed for the potions and set them up on his altar. Grabbing one of his knives, he closed his eyes and calmly started lowering his breathing and heart rate, centering himself for the work that had to come and the inevitable change that he was about to wrought on himself.

He slowly opened his eyes, his vision showing a dark and placid black. He stared at the array of arcane tools, material, and ingredients that rested before him. A slow smile curved on his lips. He was ready.

Chapter 24

Leaving New Orleans.

Kyle couldn't believe his luck! The girl that he had felt drawn to, from the moment he had first seen her in the tattoo parlor, was sitting beside him in the car that he had 'encouraged' a passing motorist to donate to the cause. She was gorgeous, of that no one could question. But, the discovery of her being like him was nothing short of amazing. He couldn't even begin to relate to himself how important it turned out to him that someone else could do what he was able to do. How could he have fallen so short on his thinking before this?

When he had seen her on the porch, aimlessly drawing in the air, he had felt the electrical connection between them, immediately. She must have, as well, as she looked up at his approach and stared at him, fully focusing into the real world for the first time, since the event. She smiled at him, instantly feeling the connection, as well.

Kyle knew all about the event. He didn't even have to reach out to hear what she was thinking, as she was projecting on a massive scale. Switching over to his color vision, as he was thinking of it, he could see her eyes blazing with an unholy red fire. She had a halo of red that encircled her, showing what looked like a ring of fire around her head.

It was intoxicating. He was drawn to her, in a way that he never imagined possible. "Jessica," he whispered.

But, he hadn't whispered, he realized. He had said it in his mind. Nevertheless, she had also recognized it and responded. "Hello, Kyle...." she thought, instantly knowing everything about him. Kyle could see, and feel, the ruby tendrils of energy leaping from her and coming straight at him. He didn't flinch, never even blinked an eye.

He had to reflect that she intimidated him, as most girls did. But, he was trying hard to not back down and become the complacent and shy young man that he had always been. He was mesmerized, fully in her thrall. Even when the energy pierced his skull, burrowing deep into his brain, he was still staring at her intently. The intensity of the feelings he had circling in his mind belayed the mental pain that he should have been feeling, as her probes raced along neural pathways and instantly scanned millions of his memories. He was being invaded, a psychic assault on the mind. But, he was unperturbed. He gave himself fully to her, embracing her reach and allowing for her to see everything.

He, in turn, was able to see everything in her mind. At a glance, he replayed her memories in his head, as she did from his, seeing how she had tattooed the arcane voodoo symbol on to her leg. He realized it had been that, along with the ink that she had grabbed, that had drawn the lightning to her, energizing her with the power. He could see immediately that she was more powerful than he. It didn't bother him in the slightest.

"It was the tattoo that I got, wasn't it?" he asked her, marveling at the simplicity of it all. "That is the real source of the power."

Jessica was still working her way through the new emotions and skills that she had acquired. She was still lazily twirling her hands in the air, softly giggling to herself. "Yes," she replied, "It's the tattoo, but you know what is really doing it...."

"The ink," he said, flatly. "I knew it."

"Of course you did, Kyle," Jessica answered. "It was the start. But, the lightning is the boost. Isn't it cool?" She smiled in satisfaction. She slid her skirt up slightly, exposing the top end of her thigh and the fiery red outline of her recently created tattoo.

The ink glowed with an unholy red aura. He couldn't help but stare, before blushing and turning his head away, quickly. But, not before he could see her smile, a self-satisfying smirk that spoke volumes, though he didn't quite understand the meaning. He looked back up at the road, concentrating on his driving.

"So," she continued, "I can see that you got the same tattoo as me." She gestured at the icy blue Skull that was emblazoned on his hand. "How long did it take, before you realized what you could do?"

"I knew, almost immediately," Kyle responded. He hesitated, but then plunged ahead with wild abandon. I was able to read minds, almost as soon as I had an accident in

Japan."

"Really....?" Jessica asked, almost sardonically. She had already known that, as she had been able to read minds, almost from the beginning. When the color world had stopped flowing wildly around in front of her eyes, she had been able to feel the telltale whispers of her parents, as they ran towards her room. They had been terrified, that much had come through easily. She hadn't known what was happening then, but it had clarified soon after.

Now, though, nearly four hours later, she had felt her mind grow and grow. She didn't have to even think about feeling into Kyle's mind. She just looked at him, and his thoughts flowed over to her, without any conscious effort on her part. It was so easy, she knew. She also knew that it had taken Kyle a long time to develop his skills. She could see it. She was learning far faster than he was.

A thought struck her, a way to better understand what was happening to them. Yes, it was the ink, but he was right, it was also the tattoo. It was a combination between the two, both with helping and expanding upon each other. She pulled out her bag from behind the seat. When Kyle had convinced her to go with him, she had only stopped long enough to go back into the house and get her bag. Her parents had never even noticed, as she had already figured out how to move past reading minds, to influencing them.

She had nearly been a ghost, as she had drifted past them, unseen. They had been frantic with worry, as they had already discovered she was gone. But, their pleas had fallen on deaf ears. She no longer had felt anything towards them. She didn't even feel, in fact. She was so far removed from her old life, that she barely even noticed them.

Now, in the car, speeding north, she could only concern herself with increasing her power. She had no idea that she was mirroring Kyle's thoughts, almost exactly. He had only been worried about power, and how he could gain more. She had no concern for anything, but getting more power, herself. 'The book,' she thought.

She had no worries about Kyle hearing her in his mind. She had already learned how to block him away from that ability. It was only too easy, she had realized. After she had first allowed him to see into her mind, she had shut him out completely. Simply imagining a door was enough. She closed it and kept him at bay. There was nothing he could do to penetrate her thoughts. It was so easy, she realized, to keep him out, as well. It barely took any of her energy to do so.

This had prompted her to think about what else she could do. That had drawn her back to her tattooing book. 'Hmmm,' she thought, as she flipped through the old book of drawings. She already knew that the skull with the burning eyes was a picture of 'sight'. It gave the wearer the ability to read a person's most inner thoughts. When it was super powered, as she had come to think of it, it allowed you to control someone's thought, she thought, with a smile that would have chilled her mother.

The next page was of a wild wolf, coming out of the mountain side, followed by a horde of other powerful creatures. She thought for a moment, but then concluded it was something that gave you the ability to control animals. 'Interesting,' she thought, but not something she was immediately interested in doing.

"OOOOHHH," she whispered. The next page was interesting. It showed a priestess enveloped by flames. 'I bet that gives me the ability to control fire,' she thought. "I want it...." she squealed, just like a petulant child that had been denied a treat.

She continued flipping through the pages, learning about many more of the most arcane and powerful tattoos that they could get with the book and the combination of the ink. There was one that she determined was the ability to move things with her mind, but Kyle said he could already do that. She saw another that allowed them to move through walls. There was another that allowed them to teleport.

The last one……ooohhh…now that was interesting. She had to say that that would be a necessary one. Having grown up in New Orleans, she knew all too much about the history of the area and hauntings. This one would be interesting. She picked up her tattooing kit, leaning in towards Kyle. "Where do you want it?" she asked.

With a somewhat confused look on his face, Kyle could only respond with a "what?" He was more than a little taken aback by the changes in Jessica over the last couple of hours. When he had first seen her on the porch, he was drawn to her, yes, but not only physically, but as a protector. He had sensed an inherent vulnerability about her, at the time. She had just looked so lost and innocent, as she playfully drew in the color world. He had felt a need to keep her safe.

But, now, he had to admit, he was starting to get a little concerned and was more than a bit afraid of her. She had grown from that naive and sweet young woman into something different. The changes weren't immediately apparent, he could never have shown when it happened. It was just suddenly there.

Now, as he looked over at her, he felt like she had aged decades in a mere matter of hours, not physically, but emotionally and spiritually. She had an edge about her now, one that spoke volumes about what was happening inside her head. The moment he had tried to read her thoughts, again, he had truly become scared, because he had found the same doorway that the old black man, Nicadimus, had pushed at him. It told him that Jessica was suddenly becoming more powerful than him.

'How can that be?' he thought. In a matter of twenty minutes, she had been able to block him from her mind. 'Or, had she always been able to do that and she only let me see what she wanted?' The thought was very disquieting. It did nothing to help him quell his anxiety and, he was unnerved to admit, a growing sense of fear. His love and adoration of this girl that was sitting next to him, had gone to fear, in less than half an hour. 'What is happening, to me?' he worried. That was when she had leaned in with the tattooing gun and spoke. "What?" he had said. "I said," she repeated, "Where do you want it?" He realized that she was holding out the fully charged tattooing gun at him, obviously ready to give him another picture. His stare must have spoken volumes, as she continued. "Come on, you want more power, right? This is the way to do it?"

"What do you mean?" asked Kyle. He thought he knew, but found himself so unnerved by her impenetrable stare, that he couldn't think properly. Plus, he also had to reflect that her burning red eyes were also, frankly, terrifying.

'Is that what people thought of me?' he questioned. For a minute, he saw a ghost of a smile across her features, a micro-expression, at best, but he caught it. It was utterly devoid of emotion in her face, a predator that was staring at a prey.

She continued on, as if she hadn't done or said anything strange. "Every tattoo in this book gives an extra power to its user. You have several of these already, some you have told me, and others that I can see." Kyle just stared at her, out of the corner of his eyes. "I think we should get as many as I can do, in the time it takes us to get to this place you told me about. So, I ask again, where do you want it." Kyle submitted and she leaned in, starting to get to work. She was quick, working into the night, as Kyle continued to drive them north in their stolen car.

Chapter 25

New Orleans

Voodoo Shop

As the last of the sun disappeared behind the darkening storm cloud of yet another weather front that was moving into his city, Nicadimus awoke from the rubble filled floor of his shop. He had been working all day at mixing potions and muttering the arcane incantations that would allow him to seriously improve his skills. He had known that he was taking some serious risks with his personal health, by doing this, but he felt that he didn't have a choice. He had known that he was moving too fast, but had just gritted his teeth and hoped he was going to be able to do it right and make it through okay.

He couldn't help but think of the powerful spell that he had attempted, not that long ago. It had been a serious risk, and he had failed spectacularly, losing a portion of his time on earth, from an unnatural aging.

The day had moved quickly, as

Nicadimus had moved through the spells that he wanted. Too quickly, as it turned out. He had managed to get through eight of them: the Shadow world vision, thought control, flaming, and a few others, before he had felt a massive surge of energy in his head. For a second, he thought he had been dying from something like a massive brain hemorrhage. Then, everything went black.

Now, an uncounted amount of time later, he was awake, alive, but in serious pain. 'I did push too fast,' he thought. 'How bad is it?' As he sat up, he realized it was bad. He took one look at his body and realized that he had been ravaged. His hands now looked like an old man's skin. They were wrinkled and covered with age spots, nothing like the hands of the relatively young man that had woken up that morning in the alleyway.

"How much did I lose," he croaked, suddenly alarmed at his voice. It was the tone of an old man, dry and creased with age. He pulled himself to his feet, suddenly feeling the protesting of his joints. He groaned, as he was upright, moving to a large mirror in the other room.

"No......" he whispered. The face that looked back at him was old, easily in his sixties! He had aged nearly thirty years, in a day. "How can I fix this, now?" he groaned to himself. He couldn't beat Kyle in a mental fight, but now he certainly had no chance in a physical fight, either.

But, wait, he realized, that might not be necessarily true. Even though his once proud strength had been robbed from him, he had just realized his mind was stronger than ever, literally surging with energy and enhancement. His eyes widened, as he felt the power surge through him like a drug. "What can I do?" he asked himself.

He had already sensed the thoughts of other people around him, filtering in like moths on the wind. He had felt them there, but hadn't truly acknowledged them into his conscious thought. In fact, it was only right now that he had realized what was happening. Discovering that he could read thoughts was a wonder to him. Among all of his other skills, this would be helpful.

He had crafted the potions for control of the elements, as well as enhancements to what he could already. That made him wonder what was happening with his ability to see the

Shadow World. It hadn't taken any conscious effort to see Kyle's glowing aura. It had just been there. He wondered if this would be the same.

No sooner than he had thought it, then it was happening. HIs eyes just flipped over, and he was seeing the world as if he were looking through an infrared heat camera. The heat signatures swirled and eddied around him, moving on the volition of the wind. "Fascinating," he whispered. He could see the colder air on the outside of the building come into his shop. He could see the heat trickling out from the heating units.

He was very surprised to see that his face and hands were now covered in a multitude of mystical symbols and details. It hadn't been there before, but it certainly was now. He could see several of the skull-like symbols on his face, plus a multitude of many others. They glowed like white fire. They must have been a byproduct of the spells, he reckoned. It was scary looking, making him appear like a traditional Voodoo priest, readying himself for war. 'Oh well. Nobody can see them, but me.'

That brought him back to his original thought. "I wonder," he whispered to himself. What he was about to try, he doubted Kyle had considered. The kid just didn't have the wisdom of years, yet. Nicadimus knew full well that the heat around him was an enormous power source. Since he could see it, he reckoned he could use it. If that was the case, then he had just found a way to make himself a giant Duracell battery. 'This is where the energy comes from....' he determined. 'But, how to get it in me?'

Then, a thought struck him and he couldn't help but laugh. It was so easy that a child could have figured it out, when they started looking, that is. How else do you get energy into your body? Nicadimus just opened his mouth and started inhaling, the streams of red, orange, and blue, pouring into his mouth and rolling to the back of his throat. It absorbed instantly into his body and hit his blood, surging through him like molten lava.

"Oh....dear.....god!" he exclaimed, his body visibly shaking, in the quakes of the world's greatest muscle spasm. But, this was not in the least bit painful. He was experiencing the throes of a highly pleasurable experience. It was nearly orgasmic, for him, as he was heightened by the energy at every level of his being, from his vision and hearing, down to the smallest nucleotide in his brain.

"Wow....." Nicadimus breathed. He no longer felt like an old man. He was in his prime, again. His body might be old, but nothing else operated at that level. His mind was ready for war. He quickly learned that all he had to do was think it, and it happened. He visualized a great ball of energy flying across the room, and the next thing he knew, his already damaged shop was exploding in balls of yellow light.

That interested him greatly, as he had only seen specific colors come from one person, that of Kyle. His had been a brilliant blue. Nicadimus could only imagine what had happened to him. Apparently he was going to have to get used to eyes that looked like he was on kidney dialysis, he thought. Great.......

But, when he looked into the mirror, again, he was amused to see that his own eyes glowed with an amber-yellow resonance. He looked just like a great Puma, a wild Jungle Cat that was roaming this urban metropolis. He smiled, his grin only making the image that much more startling. Yes, he felt ready. His mind was in order and so were his abilities. Kyle wasn't going to know what hit him.

Heading into his back room, Nicadimus went to his map, no longer hurting and limping like the old man he now was. He walked with a swagger that bespoke a young man that was full of arrogant confidence. He noticed that he didn't even have to perform any rituals to his map, in order to get it to show what he wanted to know. It just lit up, the moment he walked towards it.

"Huh," he thought. It still showed multiple dots that were scattered throughout the city, as well as the countryside. It was a haphazard mess, he saw, showing that Kyle was still trying to block him from seeing. Nicadimus could sense him, just on the fringes of his mind. But, he was preoccupied.

Nicadimus had a flash of Kyle driving in an old car, which at a glance looked like a Porsche. He was momentarily distracted by the fact he had a passenger, a young woman with long hair. She looked up at him, in an instant, her eyes flashing a dangerous level of red. She released a hideous and very angry scowl, before she waved her hand violently in the air. His vision ceased, immediately, as a stabbing pain erupted in his eyes.

"Arrgggg.....!" he screamed. "What in the hell!" He was doubled over, in pain, clutching his eyes, as they throbbed mercilessly. "Who in the hell was that?!" He hadn't been able to get a strong look at her, merely a glance.

He couldn't believe what he had just seen. There were two of them? He knew that Kyle was dangerous, and growing stronger. But, the girl? She was like Mount Vesuvius ready to blow. The power that she had, wrapped up within her mind, was utterly terrifying. She was beyond dangerous. This mission had just taken on a horrifying and sinister level of urgency. Kyle could do damage and harm people. This girl could destroy whole cities.

There was no other reason to hold off any further. Nicadimus now had a sense of urgency that was beyond needful. He had to get out of here and on the road, now. He knew where they were headed. They wanted more power. It seemed like the way Kyle, and he guessed now, the girl, were able to become so powerful, was from a massive surge of energy. There was only one place that they could get that, up to the north of the city. He had to get up there, now.

Nicadimus grabbed his satchel and started putting a variety of things into it: his weapon harness, as many knives as he could find, and one special potion that he had crafted. It was Kyle's last chance, if it didn't work, then there was no other choice. As for the girl, there was already no other choice.

Nicadimus was out the door in a flash.

Twenty minutes later, he was entering Interstate 55, heading north in his old muscle car. He was going fast and accelerating. He wore a look of absolute determination on his face, though there was an edge of fear, as well. He feared he might already be too late.

Chapter 26

Myrtle's Plantation

Now well into his drive, Nicadimus was rapidly approaching his destination. It had been a race unlike any other that he had made to this location. Time was not on his side. He knew that if he did not get to the Plantation before Kyle and his mystery guest, things could become very bad. If he didn't get there first, then Nicadimus knew that the chances of Kyle passing him in power and thus being nearly unstoppable, were very high indeed.

The being that lived within the statue was immensely powerful, he knew. What she was, Nicadimus didn't know, but she was strong and able to grant immense abilities, if she wished. The skills that Kyle would get from the being would make his lightning strike look like a mere tickle, in comparison. He would be nigh unstoppable.

Nicadimus was driving at nearly ninety miles an hour up the interstate, his windows down, letting the wind into the car. Normally, he enjoyed this sensation, immensely. The smells of the Cypress trees, as well as the ever present tang of swamp decay that was in the air, always had a calming effect on him. But, now, he could smell nothing. He could detect nothing in the air, but an ominous undertone of evil.

"I'm going to be too late," he realized out loud. The evil that he sensed was a physical thing, hanging all around him, as real as the cloying mist that was rolling in from the bayou. It filled him with supernatural dread, a sensation that he didn't recall feeling since he was a young boy and his mother had initiated him into the order.

It was just then that he reached the last crest of the freeway. The turn-off to go to the plantation was just up on the left. He could look in the distance and almost see the first telltale signs of the old house. In a few seconds, the roof would be coming into view. That was when it happened.

Just past the horizon of the swamp, the whole entirety of the skyline erupted in a brilliant blue cascade of light. It was blinding in its intensity. Night became day, temporarily, leaving Nicadimus temporarily blinded.

"No!!!!!" Nicadimus croaked, seeing that he was too late. He involuntarily hit the brakes, causing his powerful car to go into a controlled slide. The flash of the light filled his vision, the glow making the last heat of the day shimmer across the pavement. He was heading right for the swamp.

But, he was never one to give in, never one that would give up, not until his last dying breath. Once the shock of what he was seeing had worn off, he automatically corrected himself and put the car back into the correct path, immediately accelerating. He left a track of black tire marks across the pavement for nearly ninety feet, as he headed towards what he knew would be the final showdown.

Mere minutes later, he took the turn into the Myrtles Plantation at a barely controlled slide. He hadn't even finished moving, before he was out and running to the back of the grounds, where he didn't know what he would find, but fully expecting the worst. He had already been working at completely charging his psychic battery, as he had come to think of it, on the way here.

He passed the old Porsche on the way, barely sparing it a glance. He knew that they were gone, without even having to look. The danger, and his knowledge of where it was truly at, propelled him towards the back gardens like a magnet. It was so powerful of a sensation and completely out of his control.

As he brushed past a large hedge of flowers and burst into the clearing beyond, he stopped dead in his tracks. He hadn't known what he was going to see, once he got here, but this was not it. He felt a momentary sense of confusion and let down when he got there. What he saw was absolutely nothing. The statue was sitting in a display niche, but that was it. It still held the weather beaten aura of age, covered with a light film of algae. The whereabouts of Kyle and his partner were unknown.

Then, a voice, barely a whisper, sounded from behind him. "Yoohooo...." it said. "Come and get me!" Nicadimus whirled, sensing a presence right behind him. He was ready for battle; this was it. But, again, there was nothing.

A little louder now, "Oh, you are going to have to be quicker than that, old man!" came the voice. It was clearly Kyle, Nicadimus could recognize now. He sounded in a jolly mood, full of mirth and a sardonic wit. It chilled Nicadimus, because he was no longer sure that Kyle sounded sane.

"Old man, indeed?" Kyle spoke from nowhere, and everywhere, all at once. "What happened to you, Nicadimus? You look like you have one foot in the grave, already!!!"

"Where are you, boy?" Nicadimus hollered, his voice still strong and powerful. "Come out, so we can finish this?!"

Kyle ignored him and continued,

"Knock, Knock, Knocking on Heaven's door!" he sang, laughing hysterically.

Nicadimus ignored the barbed comments, as he didn't get the reference, anyway. "I'm going to give you one chance, Kyle!" Nicadimus called out. He pulled out the vial from his satchel. "This vial will take away all of your powers. It neutralizes what has happened to you and you will be normal and human again." He held it up in the air, twirling in circles, so Kyle could see from wherever he was at.

"Now why would I want to do that!?" Kyle called out, his voice losing some of the good humor. There was a hard edge to him that Nicadimus recognized all too well. Kyle wasn't going to go down without one hell of a fight.

Nicadimus decided to lay it all out, right then. "Because, if you and your 'friend', don't do this, then I am going to have to kill you both," Nicadimus allowed. "You are both just too dangerous to leave alone. You are going to hurt or kill someone."

Kyle screamed back at him, in incoherent rage, "You just try it, old man," he screamed.

"I could squash you like a bug. *Your* friend, from the statue, you cannot believe what she was able to do for me, too me ....". His voice trailed off, into silence, but not before Kyle was able to hear the longing in his voice, almost like what he was given was a drug and he was continuing to crave it.

But, he was then interrupted by another voice, a silky smooth female voice. "Kyle, shut up..." it whispered, the voice rolling over the air like brittle and blowing leaves. He did, immediately, but not before Nicadimus could detect the fearful cracking of his voice, as he tried to respond. "You can try and stop us Nicadimus. But, I wouldn't recommend it. Kyle is much stronger, now. However, he has nothing near the power that I have...."

Nicadimus could sense, rather than hear, Kyle recoiling, almost as if he had been slapped. A yellow probe was sent out by Nicadimus, trying to ascertain whether or not this woman was nearby, and who she really was. He could physically feel it being slapped away, before it had even gotten more than a few feet from him.

"That isn't going to work with me...." the woman replied calmly. "You are not strong enough. Nicadimus suddenly felt real fear, not just the anxiety of earlier, but real fear. He knew that what this young woman was saying was true. He felt certain that he could best Kyle, in the end, but it would be a struggle. Trying to beat this young woman would be a battle unlike anything he had ever faced. She was so powerful, that her energy rolled away from her, tainting the countryside.

"Now that I have your attention, Nick," she began, "May I call you Nick? Never mind. Now that I have your attention, we are going to be leaving, now. When you see us, you are not to interfere. We are going to be leaving the house and heading towards our car. I repeat, you are not to interfere."

Nicadimus didn't even hesitate an instant, when she said this. He simply looked over at the vintage Porsche that he had passed, on his way to this grove of vegetation. He viewed the landscape through the

Shadow World, and thrust a massive ball of energy at the Porsche, impacting it at a high velocity. It was struck with brutal force, slamming into the side, crumpling it, before flinging it end over end across the parking lot. It came to rest at the beginning of the ancient family cemetery that backed up to the old estate.

The response, as he expected, was instantaneous. She screamed in righteous fury, reacting immediately. Nicadimus had seconds to react, himself, before he saw a gigantic red ball of absolutely the darkest energy come crashing down and out of the sky. It completely pulverized his car, collapsing the frame and body into a pancake of broken glass and twisted metal. It no longer looked like a car, but more like a black roll of dispensed tape.

He should have been furious, but he wasn't. It was the logical reaction to his opening salvo. It still hurt, but he figured he would be able to move past it, providing he was able to win today. There was no guarantee of that, though.

"Okay," he called out, "Very good. Now we are all on the same level. There is no leaving this place, so we might as well discover who is stronger, you two, or me!" He didn't wait for a response, as he walked back to the front of the house. He suspected he knew where they were, and was not about to give them a chance to get away on foot. There was too much at stake.

Within moments, he was at the front of the old mansion. The placard read, "Myrtles Plantation, built in 1796, by General William Bradford." The house was very, very old, representing one of the earliest existing residences in the entire state. During any other time, he would have been fascinated, but not today.

Reaching forward, Nicadimus grabbed the old door handle and pulled the lever open to its fullest. He pushed the door with a squeal that sounded like he was opening the vaults of an ancient crypt. When he was within the dark and shadowy interior, he continued on and to his destiny.

Chapter 27

Inside the Myrtles's Plantation

Nicadimus entered a dark and gloomy interior. He supposed it was probably a delightful place to visit, in the daylight. But, now, in the darkness of the early morning hours, it was disquieting, and disturbing. Walking into an old structure, built from long ago, was often an alien experience for most people. The size, shape, and structure of the interiors, were so foreign to most people, that they felt distinctly uncomfortable in places such as this.

Add to the fact that this place was supposed to be haunted, which he had already known, then you have a very creepy location. Most people would have said they felt that they had eyes staring at them, from the darkness, as if some other presence was in the place. Being highly sensitive, Nicadimus knew that for a fact. There were other people watching them, almost constantly.

The spirits of those departed were always around, always just out of sight for the normal. Nicadimus was not normal, by any standard. He not only could sense the ghosts of those around him, but he could, on occasion, see them. Apparently this was one of those occasions.

The moment that his eyes settled, and adjusted to the gloomy interior, he could see them. It wasn't Kyle and his friend, but a couple of small children. They were dressed in 18th century clothing and running madly across the middle of the room ahead of him. They were followed by a young and attractive black woman with her hair wrapped up in a white head piece. She looked very harried and overwhelmed by the energy of her charges. The young woman looked at him, for a second, with a broad smile. But, in an instant, they were gone.

Nicadimus rarely batted an eye at such apparitions, anymore. They weren't of interest to him and rarely even realized that he was there. He moved on, deeper into the room. The room was old and dusty, just like the furniture.

As he was looking that was when Kyle's voice erupted in the air, and in his mind. "Took you long enough, old man!" he taunted. "Little slow on the uptake!? Did you blow all of your steam off destroying my car? Have you got anything left, for me?"

"Oh, I've got plenty...." Nicadimus whispered. He was still seeing through the lens of the Shadow World and had noticed the heat left behind by Kyle and the other's footprints. They had left the main lobby, before continuing into what looked like a dining room. He had just started to follow in their path, when Kyle started whispering of all the obscenities that he was going to perform upon him, once he was dead.

Nicadimus didn't bother with a reply, knowing it would be pointless. Instead, he felt himself drawn to a large floor to ceiling sized mirror that divided the two rooms. It was a massive, gilded piece, decorated with filigree and glass, making it absolutely stunning. The actual mirror had a frosted surface that cast everything into a blurry sort of sheen. He found he couldn't look away from it.

His attention was interrupted, as he realized he could see something, a deep and dark reflection that was barely visible to the eye. Switching back to his normal world vision, he continued to stare deeply into the mirror, willing the tiny image to become clear, again. He had the distinct feeling that it was very important for him to be able to determine what it was that he was seeing.

He leaned in close, feeling as if it was a vision from the past. He could almost hear it talking to him. That was when the vision literally exploded in his sight. It barreled forward at tremendous speed, completely filling his range of sight, in an instant. It was Kyle!

Kyle erupted from the glass, his face a contorted mask of insane rage. Half of his body was hanging through the mirror, as tiny glass shards fell to the floor. He wrapped his powerful hands around Nicadimus's throat and squeezed, smiling menacingly, as he did.

From the corner of his eye, Nicadimus could see the shadowy figure of a young woman, before his sole and undivided attention was pulled back to Kyle. The face of the young man that hung before him was like nothing he had seen before, both hideous and terrifying.

The changes that Nicadimus had, when viewed through the Shadow World, were the results of the potions and spells that he had cast upon himself. He was tuning himself up in the natural order of the magic world. Kyle had just slapped a new coat of paint on himself and hooked up a bigger battery. Sure, it got the job done, but it would eventually crash and crash hard. Something would go seriously wrong.

Kyle had massive amounts of tattoos on his face and hands, as well as the exposed parts of his neck. They were a crazy conglomeration of skulls and symbols, as well as flames and wind that could be seen. He looked like an insane Maori warrior. There would be no reasoning with this young man, Nicadimus realized.

Even as he was being choked to death, he still fought to stay conscious and pulled out an extra vial from his pocket. He had planned ahead, figuring that redundancies were going to be crucial. He slammed the small glass cylinder into Kyle's mouth, crashing his jaws together. The sound of the glass shattering resonated from Kyle's mouth and into Nicadimus's skull. It was as if the world's volcanoes had all erupted at the same time.

"Aaaahhhh!!!" screamed Kyle, as he sprayed purple foam from his mouth in every direction. The sudden movement caused Nicadimus to fall backwards, pulling Kyle out and on top of him.

"What did you do to me?" he screamed. The boy was nearly incomprehensible in his rage. His mouth was quivering, as a flood of purple bile and then blue, cascaded from his screaming face. He stumbled away, in obvious pain.

Nicadimus knew that it had not been completely successful, as he had seen a tremendous amount of purple liquid come out of Kyle's mouth. That was the potion. The blue that he had seen, was obviously his power. But, from the way that his eyes still glowed, there was a lot left. Nicadimus followed, as the young man hit the back door at a run, crashing through it and into the back of the complex.

The young woman had been forgotten in this altercation, her skills and power not reckoned with by Nicadimus. He found this out, to his dismay. As he chased after Kyle, he felt a tremendous weight slam into his back, propelling him across the length of the floor, where he crashed into the old wood in a bundle of limbs. "Wha……?" he had time to get out, before impact. The wind was knocked from his lungs, temporarily incapacitating him.

He rolled over, just in time, to see the woman stalking in his direction. She looked furious, her eyes a blaze of red fire. He tried to get to his feet, still desperately gasping for breath. The young woman stalked forward, a demon on the warpath. She flipped both hands out, palms up, before they immediately filled with a ball of red-orange flame.

She threw them at Nicadimus, one after the other, screaming at the top of her lungs. "You, bastard!" He barely managed to roll away, before they smashed into the floor, digging deep furrows in the wood. It was chaos. He could barely react in time, before she was casting another attack upon him.

He had just crawled under a table, a vintage antique, when he caught a glimpse of her literally shooting flames from her fingertips. It blew apart into pieces, leaving him exposed to her wrath. She was nearly ablaze with fire, right now. Nicadimus could only gape at her, in awestruck wonder. How had she developed into this, so fast? He couldn't even begin to imagine. She looked like a hell spawn that had just crawled from the darkest depths of the pit.

Time seemed to slow, everything coming into focus around him, as he saw her raise her hands to strike, again. 'Well, old boy,' he thought. 'You better get a handle on this situation. Or, she is going to take you….." He mentally prepared a defense, seeing a giant wall form in front of him, drawing its energy from the room. Everything went blurry, as she fired her salvo of flames.

Coins for the Skull

There was a mighty explosion, then nothing. Nicadimus refocused his vision in time to see that he had managed to mentally pull a multitude of debris from around the room: tables, shelves, various bric-brac, causing it to form up into a giant and nearly impenetrable wall in between the two. The flames had crashed into the barrier, setting it partially on fire. Her attack blew a large hole in the nearly invaluable artifacts, but it missed him, entirely.

The fact that he was allowing for valuable antiques to be destroyed never crossed his mind as being of concern. He was just happy to have his head in one piece. "All right, little girl!" his voice boomed. "Now, I'm mad."

But, he barely had time to act, before she waved her hands in the air, in a somewhat dismissive wave. Nicadimus felt like he could actually see the wind spraying from her fingers, as a virtual hurricane was flung at him. The gale forces picked up everything in their path, crashing into him and knocking him into the wall on the other side of the room.

"Ohhhhh......" he groaned, pulling himself out of the mess and to his feet. Immediately, he could see where she was stalking towards him, readying herself for the kill. This time, it was fire. Her fingertips were dripping with flame, as she readied herself.

Nicadimus didn't even think, he just reacted. Pulling his hands from within his jacket, he flipped his large buck knives at the girl, one after the other. He had figured he should be able to get her with at least one. That would incapacitate her enough to be able to finish her, he hoped.

He needn't have tried, as she simply fired a burst of flame at each knife. It was a salvo of superheated air, melting each, on the spot.

Nicadimus simply stared at her, in shock. He could see how she was readying herself for the attack.

He stood up to face her, his mind pulling the energy around him into a psychic shield of yellowish haze, much like the restraints that had been formed around Kyle's legs to hold him to the floor.

Nicadimus's eyes burned with a yellow glow, his own energy elevating to insane proportions. Jessica didn't know it, but he was quickly inhaling as much of the heat energy from around the room, preparing for a battle unlike any he had ever attempted. She just looked at this man and the awful power he seemed to possess, and felt a trickle of fear. She knew that she should have been able to kill him with that first blast. But, she only saw his back smoldering, there had been no damage, nor holes in his body.

Still, she barreled on with no pause. She had to remove this threat, and do it now. Her own eyes blazed like the sun, as she lifted her hands and threw more balls of fiery energy at him. They struck with brutal force, but he only staggered, not going down, as she expected. What was even worse, was there did not look to be any damage to his body, again. "What?" she asked, confusion finally coming into her mind.

She didn't wait for him to respond, instead choosing to attack again. She waved her hand in the air, rapidly, in the manner that she had practiced for years on her art pad. Rapidly, the air around her filled with a wide collection of cannonball shots. They were a wide variety of sizes, but all horrifying looking in their intent. With a scream of pure evil, she thrust her hands forward, sending her deadly cascade slicing through the air and at Nicadimus.

The attacks erupted all over his body, spraying yellow and red flames across his body. It was a massive explosion, a sinister display of violence. But, when the smoke cleared, he remained standing. He looked slightly stunned, but he was unharmed. For the first time, Jessica looked a bit upset, unsure of herself. However, that moment passed and the gleam of darkness covered her eyes, as she readied herself, again.

"Sorry, child," Nicadimus replied. "You are not ready to play at this level." Nicadimus raised his hands and great beams of amber lightning shot forth, from every fingertip. The bolts of energy exploded across the room, striking her fully in the chest and propelling her backwards into the far wall. She collapsed to the floor in a smoking heap, unconscious, or dead, he didn't know.

She started to stand, almost immediately, pulling herself to her feet and grimacing at him, growling deeply in the back of her throat. "You're done!" she hissed, "Old man, you are done!" She stood up and held her hands high, her entire body becoming enveloped in a bubbling cascade of fire. "You…..are……done!"

He just shook his head silently, willing her to give up. "I don't have time for this, little girl." He waved his hands into the air, clenching his fists tightly.

"Aaaaaaahhhhhh!!!!!!" He ripped his hands down in a crash, bringing the entire second floor down upon her. She disappeared in a flood of wood and debris.

Nicadimus collapsed to the floor, nearly spent. His energy was almost out, his body battered and nearly broken. "Oh, god," he gasped. "I don't….know….if I can…do this." He was nearly in tears, gasping for air, but he struggled to keep going.

"Kyle!!!!" he struggled to get out, trying to use lungs that were nearly depleted. "I'm coming for you!!!!"

Chapter 27

Outside of the Myrtle's Plantation

After Nicadimus had gotten back up, he had staggered to the door that Kyle had left from, still calling for the boy to show himself. Nicadimus knew that he was almost done, so he quickly started to recharge himself, taking in great gulps of the Shadow World energy. He could feel his battered body start to knit back together, the power flowering back into his veins. He was starting to feel re-energized and ready for the next battle. He just needed a little more…..

But, that was not to be. He had barely managed to move away from the house, before Kyle began taunting him, pushing him to defend himself. He didn't have a chance to fully recharge, having to ready himself for what was coming next. "Hey, you old bastard!" called Kyle, with a real sense of malice in his voice. "You didn't finish me. I'm waiting….."

Nicadimus readied himself. He desperately tried to inhale some more energy, as he moved forward, determined to get as much as he could, before committing himself to this next battle. The one with the girl had been brutal, almost sapping him completely. He had felt as weak as a newborn kitten, when he had stumbled from the building. He still felt horrible, but he thought he would be able to continue.

Moving cautiously, Nicadimus slowly edged his way down the grassy path, heading past the multiple outbuildings and cottages on the property. He felt he knew where Kyle had headed and was moving there with haste, himself. There was really only one place that it could be, after all, for something like this, Nicadimus thought. As he rounded the path at the end, he took in the massive plot of the Myrtle's Plantation Family Cemetery.

It was a large and very Gothic influenced cemetery, filled with rows of tombstones and family Crypts that must have gone back generations. Everywhere that he looked, there were marble pillars and crouching gargoyles staring at him from high up on the creepy structures. Nicadimus was not easily rattled, but the gloomy appearance of this place, cast by the ethereal glow of the moonlight, and Kyle's near inhuman sounding cackling that resonated throughout the grounds, nearly shook him.

"Ahhh, haaa, haaa!" whispered Kyle, sounding like a demon. The voice came from everywhere and nowhere, at once. Nicadimus spun in all directions, intent upon finding the source of the noise, but seeing nothing. Upon the last turn, it happened. He saw him.

Kyle was standing at the end of a path, head down, his arms gently folded in front of him. He was just standing there calmly, as if he had been there for hours, rather than a mere second or two. Nicadimus was certain that he hadn't been there when he had last looked.

Kyle slowly raised his head, his eyes all but lost in the burning blue fire that consumed them. The multitude of tattoos that covered his face also glowed with an unholy light. Nicadimus was taken aback at the sight. Kyle looked absolutely evil.

"Welcome, Nicadimus…" Kyle spoke.

"I'm so happy you made it." Kyle's face was slightly burned at the mouth, obviously where Nicadimus had put the potion. There was a hole in the side of his cheek that allowed a horrific vision of his bloodied teeth as they gnashed together.

Nicadimus readied himself, prepared to defend against whatever onslaught that Kyle could now perform. He had no idea what Kyle was now capable of doing. Based on what the girl had done, he could only guess what he could do. It could be anything. As it turned out, Nicadimus was about to find out, and soon.

The air started to crackle, energy waves pulsing like fiery blue light in the surroundings. Nicadimus felt the hair on his head start to stand up, as space around him became super charged with power. He looked up at Kyle, realizing that sparks of electricity now danced between his eyes. A crack of thunder sounded in the distance, as a massive bolt of lightning slammed into the ground, inches from Nicadimus's feet, blowing him backwards.

"Haaaaaa!!!!!!" screamed Kyle. "Almost got you that time!" Nicadimus lay on the ground, stunned at what had just happened. He was already on the defensive, again. This was not looking good for him, he realized. These kids were just too powerful. He had barely managed to beat back the girl, but Kyle was still very, very strong. Despite the fact he had been robbed of some of his power, from the potion, he still was immensely more powerful than Nicadimus.

"Would you like another taste of that?!" called Kyle. "Or how about something different?" Nicadimus was in the middle of pulling himself painfully to his feet, when he saw something strange happening. There was a small pond off in the distance. It was rumbling and boiling violently. Before Nicadimus could say or do anything, the entirety of the water surged from the pool, rolling in a giant wave at him.

The water crashed into him with blinding force, driving him against the nearest mausoleum. He was crushed underwater for a lifetime, it felt, his body being thrown in every direction, as the liquid swirled and eddied. Finally, it drifted away, leaving Nicadimus gasping for air on the muddied ground. "Oh, god...." he groaned.

Kyle just cackled and laughed. "You like that!" he screamed, switching from humor to violence, in a second. "What else you want, old man? I've got more up my sleeves."

Nicadimus never would know how he did it, but he pulled himself to his feet, screaming on the inside of his mind. He wouldn't give Kyle the satisfaction of knowing how badly he was hurt. Nicadimus could feel the energy drifting through his body, trying to put things back together, the wounds healing slowly.

The fact that he was still standing seemed to momentarily unsettle Kyle. He had thrown some of his most powerful spells at Nicadimus, and they had not stopped him. He should have been absolutely crushed, but he wasn't. This momentary lapse was all that Nicadimus needed.

He mentally activated the powerful shell that he was capable of erecting around himself. Kyle saw it happen, knowing what the blue shell was all about. "Nooooo!!!!" he screamed. "You cannot stop me."

Kyle immediately raised his hands to his front and blue streaks of flame shot forth, streaming like pillars of napalm at Nicadimus. The force of the blast blew into him like a bomb erupting. It was like being in the mouth of a furnace. Fire spread in all directions, curving around the shield that had been placed. It was as if two powerful and opposing forces were crashing against one another, the energy displaced in all directions being massive and catastrophic.

The buildings around them started to melt, the marble structures flowing all around in a cascade of liquid. But, still, Nicadimus pressed on, moving against the onslaught of violence. He could barely see Kyle through the blaze, the shield glowing bright as it fought to hold back the immense power that was being inflicted.

"You.....are....not....going..to....win.....boy.....!" Nicadimus called out, angrily. "I can't let you." He still pushed forward with all of his might, fighting with every ounce of his being to get close enough to Kyle. As before, Nicadimus realized that the source of the young man's power seemed to be his eyes. They were always a brilliant shade of blue, but when he was emotionally charged, they flashed like heaven and hell unleashed. This was one of those times.

Suddenly, Nicadimus realized how he was going to finish this. He knew how it was going to have to happen. He knew it was going to have to be quick, as he was nearing the end of his psychic charge. There would be no opportunity to gain more, as Kyle was on the offensive and wouldn't quit, until one of them was dead. He readied himself, drawing everything he had left, knowing that he would probably only have one shot at this.

He had remembered the massive psychic shock wave that had blown him across the street. He didn't know if he would be able to do it, but it was the only shot that he felt he had left. Still holding the flames back, he pressed forward, closing his eyes and focusing his energy. "Mmmmmmmmm," he whispered, "Ahhhhhh!" He could feel the power surging up his body, bouncing from every synapse, as it coalesced in his brain. That was when he released.

The wave of power blew from his mind like an atomic bomb erupting, the shockwave repelling the flames back at Kyle, in an instant. They washed over him like a flamethrower, spraying him backwards and into the mausoleum wall, behind him. He was unconscious, in an instant.

Nicadimus collapsed to his knees, nearly spent. Every inch of his body was bruised and lacerated. Blood flowed freely from his ears, eyes, and nose, showing that something had ruptured in his brain. His breathing was labored, as he suddenly realized that he must have had several broken ribs.

Looking over at Kyle, Nicadimus thought that it was probably over; Kyle was finished. He was a broken and bloody mess. The entire front of his body was covered in blackened burn tissue. His hair and most of his clothing was gone. But, his eyes still blazed with an insane fury. "It's not over…." Nicadimus whispered. Painfully, he pulled himself to his feet and started over to him.

Chapter 28

Inside the Myrtles Plantation

Inside of the building, near the massive rubble pile of debris, a new person walked slowly. In the dark shadows, it would have been hard to tell if this person was a male, or a female. No one saw, or heard, this new person approach the property, or enter it. Nearing the mound of the second floor that Nicadimus had pulled down, the figure stooped low, waving a set of youthful looking hands at the mess.

Slowly, piece by piece, it levitated into the air and was cast aside. The figure grinned, obviously delighted by the abilities. This too, went unnoticed. It didn't take long before the bloody and unconscious form of Jessica was exposed. The hands pulled her free, gently picking her up with a surprising amount of strength and cradled her close.

"Okay, my dear," a deep and definitely male voice spoke. "It's okay, now." He walked her out of the building and carefully placed her into the passenger side of his car, before moving back towards the garden. He had someone else that he was dying to meet.

Outside, in the gardens, Nicadimus started moving slowly towards Kyle. He realized that the boy had figured out how to bring in the energy from the Shadow World. Kyle was rapidly breathing, the visible waves of energy going inside of him. Even from here,

Nicadimus could see where Kyle was starting to heal. Nicadimus knew that it was only a matter of time, before Kyle was fully healed and ready to attack again.

Standing over top of the body,

Nicadimus was able to see Kyle, as he desperately tried to fix himself, still not willing to give into the damage that he had suffered. He was defiant to the end, even though he was as helpless as a kitten, right now. "Don't you try it, old man....." Kyle hissed, malevolently.

Nicadimus looked down at the young man with a sense of pity. But, that wasn't his place to give a free pass. He had to take care of this. Nicadimus reached into his pocket and pulled something loose in each hand. Yes, he knew what had to happen, how to end this. Kneeling before Kyle, Nicadimus stared deeply into the young man's blazing eyes. "Please.....don't!" Kyle whispered, nearly crying. He, too, knew what was about to happen and it terrified him.

Nicadimus leaned forward, with his hands outstretched, looking ready to claw Kyle's eyes out with his fingers. He pressed forward, dropping two of his golden coins onto the brilliant blue and fiery eyes. Murmuring softly to himself, whispering in an arcane tongue, he pressed down hard, as yellow light flashed around Kyle's eyes.

Kyle screamed, insanely, the burning from his eyes spreading out from beyond the socket, scalding the skin. But, still, Nicadimus pressed, not being willing to give in, until things were completely finished. He watched as the blue light became softer and softer, the yellow flashing of the gold suppressing it completely. Then, it was gone.

Nicadimus pulled the coins away, seeing the destroyed and scarred remains of where Kyle's eyes used to be. The kid's eyes were gone, nothing remained but fused and blackened tissue. The skin around the eye sockets was also covered in third degree burns, all roughly in the circular shape of the coins.

Nicadimus could see where the boy was still alive, but there was not any sign of his power. The energy that Nicadimus was able to detect in dangerous people like Kyle, was nowhere to be seen. It was finally over. He fell backwards, with a sigh of relief, breathing freely for the first time in days.

Nicadimus stood and started stumbling away, unsure what he should do next. He felt like he could use about a week's worth of sleep to get over this ordeal. After that he had to figure out how to reverse the unnatural aging that had happened to him. He had a lot to think about, that was for sure. But, sleep first. That was when the voice sounded from the other end of the path. "Well done, Nicadimus" the newcomer said.

Nicadimus turned, feebly, unsure of what he was hearing. The voice was oddly familiar, but also alien to his understanding. He looked up and was shocked by what he saw. Standing there, was the last person he had ever expected to see. "Arthur……?" he questioned, in confusion.

Nicadimus was shocked, but he was, in fact, looking up at Arthur. His translator colleague was standing in front of him. But, it was not the Arthur that he had expected, far from it.

The Arthur that he knew was an old man, gray haired and wrinkled. He was a bit arrogant and difficult to deal with, but he was a brilliant man that was able to draw upon a lifetime of experience. The person that was standing in front of him, however, was a young man, barely into his twenties. His youthful appearance was nowhere near what Nicadimus expected. "Arthur?" he asked, again. "What happened?" "The book, Nicadimus," Arthur replied. "The book." Nicadimus only gave him a confused expression, unsure what he was getting at.

"You don't think I have only been translating all of this time, do you?" asked Arthur, with a condescending tone. "Oh, god," whispered Nicadimus. "You didn't." He finally realized what had happened, and was stunned.

Arthur just fired off a smile at him.

"That's right, old timer. I've been powering up, all this time. You wouldn't believe what I can do, now." "But, your age?" asked Nicadimus. "You did the spell to reduce your age? Don't you know how dangerous that is?"

Arthur just laughed. "Not sure what you are doing wrong," Arthur replied. "But, you really should see what I can do, now." He smiled broadly, showing the depths of his greed. "Well, just wanted to check in with you. Since you seemed to have taken care of this fellow, I guess I'll have to concentrate on getting the power from the girl." He pointed at the mewling and pitiful figure of Kyle that lay in the mud.

"I guess I'll be seeing you." Nicadimus nearly screamed with anger at the danger he realized he now faced. That was when Arthur simply snapped his fingers in the air, before everything went black for Nicadimus.

Sometime later.......

After Arthur had left, driving away in his own vehicle, with the unconscious form of Jessica strapped in at his side, the statue in the garden started to glow brightly. It flashed powerfully, before the being stepped away, walking down and into the cemetery. She walked past Nicadimus's unconscious form, without a glance. She only had eyes for Kyle.

"Wake up, worm," she commanded, kicking him slightly in the side. Kyle only groaned in pain.

"Help, me...." he whispered, painfully. His body was nearly destroyed, nothing left to put up a struggle.

"I give you the power, and you waste it," she hissed, showing real and violent anger. "I will show you what happens to losers....worm!" She grabbed Kyle by the foot and started dragging him away. He cried painfully, as she held him in complete control.

When they got to the statue, it glowed brightly, almost as if it was a doorway. The being walked into the light, dragging the sobbing Kyle into it, before the glow extinguished, leaving an empty alcove. There was no trace of Kyle, it was as if he had never existed.

An hour later, Nicadimus opened a cracked and bloodshot eye, glancing around the ruins of the cemetery. It all came crashing back to him, in a second. "Arthur!" he groaned, in an old man's voice, cracked and brittle with age. His power was nearly gone.

As he expected, Arthur was gone. He knew that the young girl, Jessica, would also be gone. So, it came as a horrible shock to see that

Kyle was also gone. "What????" he whispered. "How am I going to stop them, now?" Nicadimus rose shakily and moved back down the path. He had no idea what had happened and was still trying to puzzle it out, by the time he got to the parking lot and remembered his car. Shaking his head wearily, he started the long walk back to New Orleans.

Prologue

Somewhere in the Caribbean.

Jessica opened her eyes……."What happened?" she asked. "Who am I?" She looked around the room, scared beyond belief.

"You are quite safe, my dear," spoke Arthur from a darkened corner. "We have a lot to talk about." It was interesting that she did not ask where she was, but who she was. He sent a mental push to her, accessing her brain and releasing large amounts of natural sedatives, causing her to go back to sleep. He stayed in his corner, smiling about what the future held for him.

Author Chad Dingler lives in Tennessee with his wife and three daughters. In his free time from being a long time professional artist, he creates fictional adventures.

 Chaddingler83@gmail.com   C.Dingler_author

If you enjoyed this novel please leave a review

Book two coming soon!!!!!

Made in the USA
Columbia, SC
17 October 2020